monsoonbooks

THE DEVIL'S GARDEN

Nigel Barley was born south of London in 1947. After taking a degree in modern languages at Cambridge, he gained a doctorate in anthropology at Oxford. Barley originally trained as an anthropologist and worked in West Africa, spending time with the Dowayo people of North Cameroon. He survived to move to the Ethnography Department of the British Museum and it was in this connection that he first travelled to Southeast Asia. After forrays into Thailand, Malaysia, Singapore, Japan and Burma, Barley settled on Indonesia as his principal research interest and has worked on both the history and contemporary culture of that area.

After escaping from the museum, he is now a writer and broadcaster and divides his time between London and Indonesia.

THE DEVIL'S GARDEN

NIGEL BARLEY

monsoon

monsoonbooks

Published in 2011
by Monsoon Books Pte Ltd
71 Ayer Rajah Crescent #01-01
Singapore 139951
www.monsoonbooks.com.sg

First edition.

ISBN (paperback): 978-981-4358-42-2
ISBN (ebook): 978-981-4358-43-9

Cover design by OpalWorks.

National Library Board Singapore Cataloguing in Publication Data
Barley, Nigel.
The devil's garden / Nigel Barley. – Singapore : Monsoon Books, 2011.
p. cm.
ISBN : 978-981-4358-42-2 (pbk.)

1. Botanic Gardens (Singapore) – Fiction. 2. Changi POW Camp
(Changi, Singapore) – Fiction. 3. Singapore – History – Japanese
occupation, 1942-1945 – Fiction. I. Title.

PR6102
823.92 -- dc22   OCN742334469

Printed in Singapore
15 14 13 12 11   1 2 3 4 5

CONTENTS

INTRODUCTION

Between February 1942 and September 1945, Singapore suffered one of the cruellest occupations of the Second World War as the conquered Japanese territory of Syonanto. Local civilians were subject to arbitrary killing, dispossession, torture and deprivation of the essentials for life and lived in fear of informers and a ruthless secret police force. Some 130,000 Allied POWs were incarcerated in shocking conditions that brought many to their deaths and cost many more irreplaceable years stolen from what should have been the prime of their lives. Allied civilians were imprisoned in the Changi jail and ravaged by disease, malnutrition and neglect. The city itself was extensively looted and destroyed. Yet, in the midst of all this, the Botanic Gardens—linked to the famous Raffles Museum—remained, for some time, a haven of tranquillity and greenery where Westerners, Singaporeans and Japanese continued peaceful co-operation in the service of science and culture and hinted at the possibility of an alternative world. This was not without its tensions and would lead to bitter recriminations after the war but such a phenomenon contradicts some of the received orthodoxies and extreme stereotypes that are still fixed in the popular memory of the occupation. Motivations, loyalties and identities were far more complex and uncertain than those assumed by subsequent history.

The characters depicted here are partly inventions, though events are largely based on those recorded, publicly and privately, by witnesses and actors of the time. Professor Tanakadate, for example, is a genuine character—recalled fondly in a memoir somewhat hesitantly published by a member of staff after the war, at a time of still-strong anti-Japanese feeling—although he was subsequently replaced as a result of being seen, by the occupation authorities, as excessively pro-Western. He has been fused for reasons of literary economy with another real figure, the elegant and scholarly Marquis Yoshichika Tokugawa, who remained a powerful protector of the institution throughout the war years and was an important political and academic figure in post-war Japan after the Allied victory. The character of Alexander Hare, friend of Stamford Raffles, and referred to coyly in his wife's memoir as 'the eccentric Mr Hare' is painted very much from life and a member of staff of the museum and gardens, Carl Gibson-Hill, was indeed more than a little obsessed with research on both him and the natural history of Cocos-Keeling.

The situation of intercultural understanding is always fraught with difficulty and war is always rich in absurdity as well as suffering and heroism. It will come as no surprise that this story deals in all three and the only apparent contradiction between them, without apology. As has often been noted, one should not make predictions, especially about the future, and none could have guessed, even remotely, what that future held for Singapore after the war—which lends poignancy to the accounts and predictions written with such great confidence at that time. Being a place that was always referred back to another imagined homeland, different for each racial group, it was at a conceptual crossroads, having position but no single location on any political map. The creation of a distinctively Singaporean identity lay yet well in the future but there can be no doubt that the experiences of the war, even the rather unusual ones drawn on here, were an important part of the process by which that came about.

PART I

THE FRUITS
OF VICTORY

Lieutenant-General Tomoyuki 'Tiger' Yamashita poked distastefully in the dust of the Raffles Museum with the toe of his boot. The pose was like a 17th-century French aristocrat 'making a leg'. A staff field photographer—recognising his cue—darted forward, bowed, snapped, bowed, darted back. The General looked up at the hole in the dome, the satisfactory product of one of his own, non-photographic Canons—through the aperture you could see the edge of the Rising Sun flapping above—and then back down at the shattered display. 'The Singapore Stone' he read, scanning the information panel with one finger and moving lips. His English was not good but the Chinese calligraphy was just readable. One of many such ancient stones scattered over the whole archipelago. Possibly 12th century, possibly inscribed in Kawi script, possibly related to the legend of the strongman Badang who flung it there in a competition with a champion of the Rajah of Kling. But possibly none of these. A failed attempt at decipherment by Stamford Raffles. Blown up by the piqued and practical British in 1843 to build a lowly bungalow. Inscription on the surviving main fragment rubbed away by the illiterate backsides of sepoys who used it as a seat. Salvaged by the awed and romantic British as a poignant monument to the tooth of time. Sent to Calcutta. Sent back to Singapore. He bent over the lump of crumbly red sandstone and harumphed skeptically. It hardly seemed worth all the bother. Still no one even knew what the inscription meant. Anyway, it was no longer Singapore but now Syonanto, 'Light of the South'. History lay not in the past but in the future. The British empire lay in ruins and its monuments were soon to be consigned to museums or erased as if by careless Japanese backsides.

He stepped forward, commander of the 25th Army, lord of the Greater East Asia Co-Prosperity Sphere, planted his boot squarely atop the stone, cocked his arm on his waist and ran his hand over his cropped skull and walnut-shell of a face as if smoothing them for the world. The reporter darted forward again, bowed over his instrument, crouched, flashed, bowed and scuttled away. The picture would look good back in Tokyo and with all the political enemies he had there—those toadies of Tojo's—he could use all the public support he could get. He liked to feel on top of things and if you put your foot on a rock, people assumed you had climbed a mountain. It was like the way Chinese made offerings of the snout and tail of a pig and their stupid ancestors simply assumed they had got all the rest in between. As he stepped back, Tiger looked down at his boot and irritation flicked at the corner of his mouth. Dust had stuck to the immaculate toecap. He had complained to his servant about this before. The man had sighed, cringed respectfully, hands clasped to head in expectation of merited blows, and blamed the Australians. Until proper supplies of boot polish from Dai Nippon could be arranged, it seemed the man was forced to use an inferior Australian brand called Vegemite.

Tiger put both hands behind his back and spun on his heel, scattering the officers and municipal officials around him. Across the vestibule stood the bronze statue of Stamford Raffles, his true enemy, now removed from his previous and unacceptable stance, gazing out to sea with visionary eyes from the front of the Victoria Theatre. That Victoria Theatre where the Lautrequish posters, now torn down, had advertised a performance of the scandalous insult to Japanese dignity that was Gilbert and Sullivan's 'Mikado'. Perhaps it had served him well. The absurd figures of the Mikado had encouraged false British arrogance, now richly repaid. He had ordered the actors shot in a final retrospective review.

Raffles had been facing the wrong way as it turned out, for Tiger had come not from the sea but from the north and no one in the audience had shouted 'Behind you!'. He walked across to fix Raffles in the eye, like a sergeant he was about to humiliate. Awkwardly, because the statue was mounted on a plinth, he had to look up. He had joined the army principally because it allowed short men like himself to shout and sneer at tall ones. And now that had become the whole of Japanese foreign policy. He noted the bad posture, the severe underdevelopment of the calves and snorted skeptically. An army reject. In Penang, they had manhandled fat-bummed Francis Light off his podium and snapped his sword. Here, the treatment had been more gentle, perhaps misguidedly so. Tiger turned to the museum staff and rapped out instructions. A wooden box was rushed up and set beside Raffles so that the general could climb up, now a wobbly good three inches taller than the statue. The museum staff were nervous. They held their breath. The last encounter between the two sides had ended badly.

The Japanese had seized the obvious photo opportunity of the removal of the statue, under the supervision of a young lieutenant, with staff officers and joyful populace looking on, all hoping for a treat. Accordingly, a band of Western prisoners and Tamil workmen had been whipped up. They had slung a rope round the disgraced imperialist's neck to hoist Raffles off his base with block and tackle and swing him across to the waiting truck as the dignitaries stood around laughing like good ol' boys at a Southern lynchin'. But Raffles had been parsimoniously cast hollow and, being severely wounded in the upper body by Japanese shrapnel

17

during the assault on the city, the fissures had allowed rain to seep into the central cavity. As the men heaved and strained, he had initially swooped angelically enough overhead, then suddenly tipped and sprayed the Japanese staff officers with urine-hued water. It was the sort of pratfall that an Asian audience savours and a British commander—resigned since birth to being thought a silly-arse by foreigners—would have laughed it off, perhaps even played it up for the crowd, stamped and brushed himself down, cheerfully offered to lend the old man a penny, 'Lucky he tipped forwards not backwards, eh? All things considered, what?' There came a roar of unrestrained hysteria, followed by a terrible silence as it became clear the Japanese were not laughing, then screams as the soldiers unslung their rifles and began beating and stabbing at the crowd, trapped in the narrow space. Several had been killed. All the photographs had been confiscated and destroyed. Officially, it had never happened.

Tiger tottered momentarily atop his box and the onlookers gasped at the prospect of a—to them—lethal pratfall before he steadied himself. He toyed for a second with the idea of drawing his sword, holding it to Raffles's neck in mockery of chortling execution but something told him that would simply not do. Instead he posed, embraced the previous, deluded imperialism in comradely fashion, arm about neck, smiled benevolently as the photographer snapped and flashed below. Looking down, on the top of the plinth, he was surprised to see an outline map of the Straits area. Raffles's foot was stamping on British Malaya.

'The British pride themselves on their sense of humour,' he smiled at the cameramen. 'So let me tell you a joke. There was a company of British troops at the Battle of Singapore.' He looked around. They were all listening, pencils poised. 'They saw a solitary Japanese infantryman shooting at them from behind a rock.' He crouched and pointed, dropped his voice. 'The British commander sent the whole company to skirt round behind him and waited. There came shots, explosions, screams, then silence. Finally, one of his soldiers crawled back, badly wounded. "Oh my God!" cried the commander. "What happened?" With his dying breath, the soldier replied, "It was an ambush. There were TWO of them!".' He laughed and stamped his feet on Raffles's. A ripple of laughter ran round the room, a spattering of applause, the loudest from his dutiful ADC, Captain Yoshi Oishi. Tiger bent down to descend, placing his arm on the young man's shoulder and brought his mouth close to his ear.

'Have him melted down for scrap,' he hissed through his smile. Captain Oishi made a brisk military note.

Then Tiger frowned and pouted. There was a flash of gold over there in a glass case. He walked over and peered through the glass. Gold jewellery from Sumba or Sumbawa or somewhere—he was too vain to wear his glasses—the names now irrelevant anyway. They would all soon be changed to Japanese names, all swept away with the rest. Tiger was partial to gold. In a cave in the Philippines, he had several tons of it, looted from various local conquests, melted down and turned into trim little ingots, together with a gold Buddha figure that residual superstition prevented him from pulping. When transport became more assured, it should be sent back to Tokyo—well most of it. The gold Buddha he would certainly keep for himself—possibly more, depending on which way the political wind was blowing. The prisoners who had buried it had all been discreetly disposed of. Perhaps it might be safer here, in Syonanto, where he could keep his eye on it. In the interim, his ADC would call round tomorrow to pick up those trinkets that had found pleasure in his sight.

But wait. There were white faces back there, surely British faces. What were they doing in *his* museum?

* * *

'It's not just the books, Major,' corrected James Pilchard. 'The books are fully formed. They can stand on their own two feet. They will survive somehow. There's the matter of a large metal trunk that's missing. It's my ethnographic and ornithological notes—fragile, unborn, full of unmade choices. If they get mishandled, they could be lost for ever.' He wondered why he was making all this fuss but there were some things you just had to hold on to even while the world was collapsing around your ears—*because* the world was collapsing around your ears. He could see that Spratt was one of those people who had learned to enjoy the misfortunes of others. The war must have come as a great comfort to him.

Major Spratt looked out through the hut window and across the burning parade ground, as he had looked out over so many parade grounds in the East, and sighed. He had reached the age where a man's nose begins to collapse into formlessness and, with the little moustache underneath, it looked as if he had a mouse hanging down the middle of his face. He drew on his empty pipe and conjured up ghostly memories of the taste of real tobacco and the smell of his leatherette-upholstered Ford Prefect back in Aldershot. He did not like James Pilchard. He did not like his attitude. He even made 'sir' sound like a sneer. A stuck up, arrogantly dishevelled young man with a terrible lack of team spirit and no awareness of military priorities. He had a beard dammit. A reddish, curly beard, untrained, untrimmed. He had not so much grown a beard as just stopped shaving. Spratt recognised the control of hair as the clearest mark of the control of body and spirit. And Pilchard was public school and only in his mid-thirties. He looked at you with that superior leer they all had, imagining the rules did not apply to them. Spratt was a grammar school boy, an insider on sufferance only. Good enough for the colonial army but not—it had always been made clear—Sandhurst material. It would not be the worst loss of the war that Pilchard's bird notes should go astray. He probed the pipe bowl with the blunt end of a pencil, then remembered that it was empty.

'Ornithology? No need to get in such a flap. Not, strictly speaking, my pigeon, old boy.' He smirked and savoured the joke. 'From every perspective a civilian matter. Feel free to have a word with General Yamashita if you want.' He stifled a grin. The Japanese did not allow contact between POWs and civilian internees. If they even knew Pilchard was here in the camp, outside Changi prison proper, they'd have kittens, turn nasty like as not, dish him out a good beating. He might even end up in Outram Road. People tended not to come back from Outram Road. Still, at least he wasn't collaborating with the Japs like the rest of that shower from the museum and the water and electric wallahs.

In the hot Singapore sun of the square, two sweating men—one scraggy and bare-chested, the other pot-bellied and bear-chested—were flinging armfuls of books from the back of a Public Works Department truck into an improvised handcart. They tossed them deliberately high—windmilling in the air—to land with the sound of softly cracking spines and tearing paper. Spratt resumed smoothly.

'I can assure you, the museum's library will be treated with the greatest possible respect. Normally, of course, it would have been proper form to contact you first, you being senior museum officer, but these are not normal times. Colonel Saito was keen for us to get our university going, the Kempeitei secret police wanted the books out to make room for the possible overflow of their own files from next door. You should consider yourself lucky. The College got taken over entirely. And the Stamford Road YMCA is no longer big enough what with ...' his voice fell and he blushed, ran his hand nervously over his own fresh-barbered chin, '... their sorting out of the Chinese. It was important to strike while the iron was hot. I have thousands of men sitting around with their hands in their pockets. It's a matter of keeping them busy, not letting them brood and get slack, a matter of the utmost military importance. You can't expect to waltz in here and go on about a load of blasted notes about tweetie-birds.' He paused and puffed himself up. Pilchard winced. He knew what was coming. It came with tooth-grinding inevitability. He watched Spratt turn it into a sequenced military exercise as he paused, stiffened and thrust out his jaw in Churchillian bulldog parody. 'Don't you know there's a war on?'

All over the globe, the question was being used to justify acts of cultural vandalism. The fine china of civilisation was everywhere being smashed in military target practice or debased for the slopping out of army latrines, its embroideries ripped up to provide bandages and canteen dishcloths, its museums converted into military offices where daily orders were tacked up on the Georgian furniture.

'It's the Australians, of course, who are the main problem—well enough in a scrap, I grant you, but not sound like your English Tommy. Basically, they're a bunch of bolshie bastards.' Pilchard looked at the men unloading the books. Tommies they might be but they were enjoying the sacrilege of it, smirking with deliberate malice as they lobbed the odd bigger volumes overarm like grenades. There could be no going back now. It would not be the same world after the war and there would be bolshie bastards to spare everywhere. He studied Spratt curiously, like a specimen, saw the confused class hostility in his eyes and was amused to know himself a class impostor. If Spratt had known that Pilchard was a scholarship boy, from a home poorer than his own, he would not have disliked him any the less, for it. The British would turn on each other all right after the war but little men like Spratt would not be the ones left to tell the world to get its hair cut. It would be mob rule. He tried a different tack.

'The index cards, the lists of what was in the library, surely you brought those? The books were arranged by subject and carefully sub-categorised alphabetically ...'

'Just books,' said the major truculently and turned away. It was impossible of course but, at some level, he always feared that Pilchard *knew*. Spratt had seen his moment of triumph in quartermastering. Then he had met his Waterloo. For two glorious years he had been Officer Commanding (Butter) in Aldershot, towering over pyramids of bright yellow tins and then his world had fallen apart. The British Army was a global operation whose tendrils stretched to embrace the icy wastes of Arctic and Antarctic as readily as they gripped the globe's equatorial paunch. And all army posts required butter on their toast. Tinned butter that soothed British palates in such climatic extremes required careful formulation, developed over years of slow experimentation. A special Arctic blend ensured spreadability at -40°C while a tropical version still held solid at 40°C above. And then, in a still inexplicable moment of distraction, he had confused the consignments. In Arctic Baffinland, for three months, they had received butter that could only be worked with power tools while, in Kuala Lumpur, it sloshed from the tin as a greasy liquid that only the Indians enjoyed. The humiliation, the joy of his enemies, especially the Officer Commanding (Jam and Condiments Various), still woke him red-faced and heart pounding in the middle of the night. There had been an enquiry, harsh words in his file and they had laughed and posted him out east to learn what climate and quartermastering could do to each other, expiation through perspiration. To him, it was still a greater shame than the fall of Singapore for, at least, when he handed over three years of military supplies—lock, stock and oil barrels, all intact—to the Japanese, they had been in apple-pie order. He was sure they respected him for that.

'The orders just said books.'

* * *

As a child, James Pilchard had been greatly impressed by imperial pomp and circumstance, as known chiefly from the church parades of the Boy Scouts. His collecting had begun with the postage stamps of empire, a rare blaze of colour in a Birmingham childhood composed otherwise of muted greys. Most, of course, bore the stuffy, decollated profiles of King George and Queen Mary, like china dogs on the mantlepiece, but there was enough background variation—plants, animals and exotic vistas—from around the empire to stimulate the interest of a bookish boy with no brothers and sisters. The stamps had fired in him the urge to travel and he liked to think that this had refuted the old adage that 'philately will get you nowhere'. Collecting had continued to relieve the dullness of a medical degree, a vocation which, in his family, seemed the epitome of learning and respectability. But he had been cruelly disabused by his time in Singapore, first by the obsessive mediocrity of colonial life with its tin trumpets and tin gods and then by his service in the Volunteer Force, lasting two appalling weeks during which the stammer that had afflicted him most of his life completely disappeared. Much of it had been spent lying flat on the ground as, above him, bombs tumbled, like shiny black rat droppings, from the backsides of invulnerable aircraft. He had seen selfless heroism of course but sadly misapplied, as men laid down their lives to protect the strategic installations that their comrades, the following day, would be ordered to lay down their own lives to destroy. In the middle came a very awkward and unacknowledged period of 'realignment of the front' where both sides suddenly realised that something must be wrong because they were now both trying to blow up the same targets. That 130,000 Allied troops had surrendered to 30,000 Japanese that they could have simply kicked to death, argued that something was badly amiss at staff college and Spratt was a good example of his kind— pompous and resolutely stupid, an ocean-going buffoon—fit to be impaled on a pin and set in a glass exhibition case of military idiocy as the specimen type. The old description of the army as 'lions led by donkeys' popped up in his brain from somewhere. He was sure the British commander had contemplated the total cock-up with something like 'I blame myself for all this, chaps. But you, of course, will be the ones paying for it.' The very best specimens, the highest-ranking officers with the fancy plumage, had been shipped off by the Japs months ago. No one knew where. Perhaps they had been shot. The men all rather hoped they had.

He was back in Bukit Timah. They were hot and filthy, tired after a night sleeping fitfully under trees, being eaten alive by mosquitoes. It was not clear which of them was supposed to be in charge. In the Volunteers, pulling rank was considered bad form so decisions sort of just happened by default. At dawn they had broken open tins of bully beef and eaten flakes of stale meat enrobed in fat and salt, so that now they were thirsty. There was a noise down there by the road and suddenly Japanese were running along the tarmac, crouching low, trundling two heavy machine guns between the ruins of a light-engineering works. He had never actually seen Japanese before and he tried to fix them in his mind. They could have opened fire with their old WWI rifles, killed a couple of them maybe, before the machine guns found them with the inevitable outcome they had been watching for days. As good as dead. As bad as dead. They kept quiet. The soldier out front seemed to hear a noise, turned, shading his eyes

with one hand, then smiled slowly. There was a little Chinese boy,
quite naked, standing half-hidden in the ruins watching him. The
soldier laughed, bent down and made clicking tongue noises as
you might to a nervous cat and beckoned with his fingers. The
little boy looked at him, eyes wide with fear and then his face
broke into a broad smile and he stepped out unsteadily into the
sunlight. The soldier raised his rifle and shot him dead with a
single round through the forehead.

Pilchard blinked and wandered out over the square. He could feel a tremor running through his arms and hands. From afar, he spotted Sergeant Fukui, a thoroughly nasty ex-greengrocer from Osaka, who loved to make trouble. He was doing his rounds, hitting people, kicking things over just for the fun of it, a couple of beefy Korean conscripts, acting as a sort of mute bodyguard, dogging his steps. He had passed Pilchard in the prison proper earlier, pausing to receive the obligatory bow, when he had dropped by to torment an unfortunate prisoner named Churchill, and might just remember him. Pilchard ducked behind a shed until he had passed, looked at the sun to judge the time. He had to be back in jail for the midday meal and he had a couple of calls to make along the way. Strictly speaking, he was probably still in the military as a Volunteer, should have saluted Spratt, stamped his feet, all that other nonsense like in the OTC. Too bad. A while ago, the Japanese had ordered all officers to remove insignia of rank and it had created a pleasing anonymity, almost invisibility, like a big city in a blackout as if everything henceforth was off the record. Pilchard had retained khaki without badges, like a defrocked scoutmaster. But you could still tell who was who. Authority brought a walk, a look, a tone of the voice even when opposing the authority of others. He, himself—he knew—had it whether he liked it or not.

The area was less a single camp than an assembly of old British barracks, mostly wooden-built, split and rotten, eked out with tents and informal shelters of bamboo and thatch that clustered round the walls of the old prison. When they had marched in—all the men had cried as the women and children followed singing 'There'll always be an England'—it had been virtually an empty shell but barter, theft and ingenuity had worked wonders and now there were at least basic comforts such as beds, water and zitheringly erratic electricity. Pilchard's collector's heart was gladdened by the rich variety of humanity gathered together: black, brown, yellow, white, Christians, Hindus, Jews, Muslims, British, Australian, New Zealand, Dutch, Malay, Javanese, Moluccan, Indian. In Changi, of course, Indians came in two varieties that crosscut all other regional and caste labels—the loyal and the Indian National Army who had thrown their lot in with the Japanese in return for freedom and a vague promise of Indian independence. The former might be smiled at, the latter's stare must be avoided at all costs since they had adopted an almost hysterical brutality as the mark of their bond with Japan. And they specialised not just in beatings but rapes, the sort not done in the hot lubricity of lust but the cold, congealed determination to humiliate and completed by urinating all over the victim.

They had caught Manson alone in his cell in Changi proper and he had been slow to get to his feet. That had been excuse enough. One stood outside in the doorway, smacking a thick bamboo pole in the palm of his hand as the other two taught Manson to respect them. The screams electrified the very air. All other sound died as the prisoners listened but looked the other way. Then the shame, Manson's and their own, as they were unable to meet anyone else's eyes in case they saw themselves for what they were. The Indians had emerged, laughing and swaggering and all three had sauntered off, running their clubs along the stair rails like innocent, little boys playing on railings on the way to school.

As the thrumming died away, the sound of Manson's sobs became louder, the very heartbeat of the prison.

'Clang! Clang!' There were half a dozen young men, crouching listlessly on the ground under the front of the shelter. Javanese. Asians felt the lack of furniture less than the Westerners. They should have been smoking but cigarettes were an impossible luxury in the camp so their hands rested limp and empty like their eyes. Since his time as resident medic on the Cocos-Keeling Islands, Pilchard had had a special fondness for the Javanese that lived there. In Changi, they were sited beside the Dutch, recalling the way that the Hunnish army had always advanced across the land as a living map of its provinces. Theirs was naturally the worst accommodation, an old workshop where generations of tinkering mechanics had left a miasma of engine grease and rust. As always, he drifted towards it.

It was the privilege of East Indies colonial troops to be issued with high, leather boots that set them off from, and above, local inhabitants. Normally an object of pride, polished and cosseted, they had become a burden among the boot-admiring Japanese whose own feet, it was swiftly discovered, also fitted into them very nicely. The first few months had seen a terrifying series of confiscations, with beatings for thanks, and searches of their quarters that made impossible the normal illegal activities necessary for life. So now the prisoners were forced to roam barefoot, on feet now grown tender from footwear, while the treasured boots lay hidden away and slowly succumbed to rats and mildew. More military idiocy.

At the centre, an older, very dark figure, wearing only a flowery sarong, was the sole moving element. He was hitting a piece of metal with a solid wooden hammer, timing the blows so that they fell rhythmically and humming as he worked, like some Wagnerian dwarf. Pilchard knew Sergeant Dewa was a gong-player as well as an engineer. He circled the men from the rear, greeted, shook hands. None of them bothered to stand, simply reaching up apathetically to limply touch his hand. Finally he moved to the centre.

'Mas Dewa. What are you making?'

'Dokter. Toko's arm needs some work.' He indicated one of the men and bashed anew. 'One of the work parties found a crashed Kawasaki bomber. It didn't need its wing but Toko needs an arm. He lost it in an air raid.'

Toko smiled and held up his limb, now ending just below the elbow. 'Maybe it's the same machine that took my arm. Now it's giving it back.' He laughed. The artificial arm was a hollow aluminium tube, articulated but lockable at the wrist. On the end was a hand, carved out of wood, very lifelike, but with an extraordinarily exaggerated, erect thumb. Pilchard raised a quizzical eyebrow. Toko shrugged. 'For the wife,' he explained and everyone laughed again. 'Better than Nature.'

'When she sees it,' volunteered his friend, 'she'll think it's a pity they didn't shoot your dick off too.' Pilchard bent and examined the stump. As a qualified general practitioner, he knew nothing of amputations but it looked neat, a good flap of flesh to cushion the end.

'Nice work. Who did it?'

'Some white man.' To him they would all be the same. 'I never saw him. In those days we had gas.' Now it was a swig of rice toddy, or if you got really lucky, a scanty perfume sprinkling of precious chloroform, hardly enough to make you dizzy. Dewa laid down the hammer.

'I've got your stuff.' He spoke quietly and pulled an old Player's tin off the shelf over the workbench, took off the lid, fished inside. The two men looked around and shook hands. A small package wrapped in banana leaves, swiftly pocketed, moved one way. A smaller one moved the other. They stepped apart quickly. Finished. All over.

* * *

Dr Catchpole sighed and ran a tired hand over his sweaty face, taking care not to jostle his wig. He had always hated museum visits by imperial worthies. At least, in the old days, they could only give you a bad report or cut off your funding. They were unlikely to cut off your head. Now they might well do just that. The two Japanese, Professor Tanakadate and tiny Dr Hanada, put their shoulders behind his and shuffled him forward towards the General, like a children's toy. His colleague, Dr Post, lurked treacherously in the background, looking anxious. They bowed. Catchpole bowed a second too late, bowed shallowly, fearful of wig loss, spoiled the effect and got flustered. Around his neck hung a large bakelite hearing aid receiver that amplified speech to the headphone draped over one ear. To improve reception, he pointed it at people, like a box camera, but with overtones of an entomologist staring at bugs through a magnifying glass.

Prof Tanakadate stepped forward smoothly.

'General. I should like to present my assistant, Dr Hanada, and our partner, Dr Catchpole, the eminent ichthyologist.'

Tiger scowled, he tucked his thumbs into his waistbelt and his voice dipped down into his military growl, a sound like gravel under jackboots. 'Itchy? What is itchy?' He stared shamelessly at the wig. It looked like a mass of shredded horseradish. That must be itchy. 'And why are there *gaijin* in the museum? Who are you? What is all this?'

The Professor smiled unruffled and bowed again. 'The General has perhaps forgotten his old schoolmate. Time has been kinder to him than to me. Tanakadate.' He bowed again, grey, unmilitary hair flopping over his forehead.

'Eh? Tanakadate? You?' His eyes popped. 'Forgive me. So many people. So busy. And nowadays everyone where you don't expect them to be.'

'We are honoured that the General has made time to visit us. Had we known in advance, we might have arranged something more worthy of him.'

'Why these *gaijin*?' Catchpole, pale expert on tropical fish, had retreated into a still alcove and was to be seen floundering awkwardly back there, in disreputable alpaca, between two refracting glass cases. 'Why are they not in Changi? Are they German?' He was doubtful about Germans, having fought them in Shantung in the last war but drunk with them while serving as military attaché, in Berlin, before this one.

'It seems there was an agreement with the ... er ... outgoing governor that some staff might stay on to help our takeover. Dr Catchpole arranged the whole matter.' He nodded at the chubby figure treading water and peering at them timorously through glass. 'It is an arrangement that has been greatly to the advantage of Dai Nippon, rather than having them in prison.'

'So they are collaborators. And Changi is not a prison. It is a processing centre for aliens.' It was a mere administrative reflex, displacing another. He embarked on a swift ill-natured tour, stumping along the wooden corridors, hands clasped behind his back He peered into the library.

'Books,' he said.

'There is some disorder while we are moving some of the less academic volumes to the prisoners in Changi.'

'There are no prisoners in Changi. They are detainees only.'

'Quite so.'

Tiger grunted and set off again, the floorboards resonating loudly and untigerishly under his boots. Through the ethnography gallery that traced the Malays' endless birdlike ingenuity in teasing twigs and vegetable fibre into human culture.

'Jungle stuff,' he snorted. Through fish, monkeys and insects to arrive, finally at … 'Birds,' he nodded and half turned, then frowned and turned back. It was a display of brightly coloured finches or some such, stuffed and spaliered like a Kyoto cherry blossom into a sort of family tree against a backboard. He read aloud. 'Birds of Cocos-Keeling. Collected by J. Pilchard 1940.' Cocos-Keeling was a place of interest, the new front line, as yet still held by the British, a communications centre, the only place from which the Allies might now attack the Asian mainland by air. A hundred miles closer, on Christmas Island, sat a division of Japanese troops, sharpening their bayonets, just waiting for the order to advance before sweeping on to Australia and final victory. He tapped at the glass. 'Where is …' he leaned back to see the name '… Pilchard?' He looked up. 'Which one is Pilchard?'

'Not here,' said Tanakadate hastily. 'Gone.'

'In Changi!' sniggered Catchpole from afar, a practised hatdoffer, the class sneak.

'In Changi or not in Changi?' echoed Tiger sweetly. Tanakadate squirmed and glared at Catchpole.

'Oh yes. In Changi. I forgot.' Tiger's voice dropped back into military growl. Addressing his ADC, Captain Oishi.

'Find him. Fetch him. Send him to the Kempeitei next door. Let them ask him some questions about Cocos-Keeling but not about birds. I wish to have everything on this Cocos-Keeling.' He bowed, turned on his heel and stamped out swiftly, hands behind his back, bent forward, the museum staff flocking after like geese. As he passed Raffles he sniffed contemptuously, then dived into the back of the fat, leather-smelling Daimler that was now his. He adored it, shiny and solid as if carved from black marble. Its bench seats made *him* feel well upholstered. 'Back to HQ!' He settled into his seat. 'Raffles College!' he added happily, as if they did not know where it was and young Captain Oishi leapt to his place in front and slammed the door in one smooth drill movement. The driver, knowing what the General liked, floored the accelerator and they tipped back into the softened red oxhide and sped off with a gratifying spray of gravel and a cloud of wasteful, blue smoke.

* * *

Over by the prison wall, Corporal Higgins was snipping away industriously inside a sort of frayed canvas lean-to that looked like a giant's trenchcoat, trimming neatly around the irregular ears of a gnarled Aussie commando, perched on a soap box. Muscularity was a sort of disease that had invaded the man's entire body. He even had clenched, muscular hair.

'Always hang on to the tools of your trade, lad,' me Dad used to say—not that he meant it in quite *that* way you understand—and it's advice that's stood me in good stead over the years.' He was a tiny, impish wisp of a man, willowy and deft, like a tickbird on a buffalo. The commando was not listening, they never did. It made no difference. Chatter and snip came together even if it went right over their heads. 'A little more off the top dear?' The commando grunted and groped at his own head with blunt fingers, then shook it. There were no large mirrors in this 'salon', just a fragment hanging on a string from the doorframe that required a face to be viewed in parts and mentally recombined. The customer stood up, a long way up, reached in his top pocket and took out a single crumpled cigarette, considered briefly but weightily and broke it in half, giving one part to eye-rolling Private Higgins and replacing the other, then lumbered off on splayed feet.

'Thank you, dear. I'll put it in the vault.' He leaned round the edge of the shelter and called after. 'Anything for the wife?' The next customer moved forward and slumped on the box, looking around with studied insouciance. Higgins poked fussily into the nest of red hair with scissors and comb. 'I really am going to have to take my clippers to you dear. You can't keep passing through here and coming out looking like the cat's furball. Even the Japanese are going to notice. Let me at least trim the beard.' Pilchard sat resentfully for several minutes as the scissors teased and snipped, squirming like a little boy suffering the wipe of a mother's spitty handkerchief. Higgins sighed.

'Oh go on, then.'

Pilchard rose and slipped nichodemously behind the sheet at the far end. On the other side stood the mildewed, stucco wall of the prison, surrounded by a fly-buzzing drainage ditch. He clambered down into the depression and approached the entrance to a big concrete pipe that led through into the storm-drain. It was barred by a grille of iron bars but two were rusted and removable. He lifted and climbed through, set them back in place and twisted their smooth faces outwards to match the rest. The drains were only flushed twice a day to save water so he removed his careworn sandals and splashed barefoot through unpleasant ankle-deep sewage and up, beneath the double outer wall, to emerge behind the latrine sheds in the area known whimsically as Crouch End or Lower Tooting, back into the jail itself. No one was on the lookout for someone breaking *into* a jail and Pilchard knew that security was brutally but only capriciously enforced so that the greatest risk was from a Japanese soldier grabbing a sly cigarette here out of sight. A bucket of water stood ready and he sloshed it, grimacing, over his feet and made his way, heavy-footed, up into the men's section, hauling himself up the stairs by the hot and crumbly iron handrails.

Changi was an ugly, fairly new confection of iron, brick and concrete, perennially dank and—with only the sea-facing cells able to catch even a breath of wind—as steamy as a pressure-cooker. The contractor had enjoyed a cosy and mutually profitable relationship with the Public Works Department so that rising damp, penetrating moisture and leaks from the roof now met and pooled resources on the second floor. It had been built for 600 inmates and presently held five times that number, including—with poetic irony—several of the civil servants who had cut corners on its construction. The one extravagance, the expensive steel doors, imported from England, that had once been a matter of pride, with fine Bramah locks and a series of sliding panels and peepholes that would have been the envy of a Chinese conjuror, now stood useless, open flat against the wall, a mere, hard-boned nuisance.

The women and children were segregated off in a separate wing, but, in the male block, each cell had been built for two with the modern marvel of a crouchhole toilet. Most were now shared by five inmates, so three had no bunk but since this was only a slab of concrete anyway, the difference was less than might be imagined. The actual occupancy of any particular cell was in constant rearrangement as overcrowding and boredom bred feuds, fights or the furtive physical affections that could be even worse. At night, inmates stretched out on the steel mesh that denied the use of the central well to would-be suicides or crept out into the courtyards and offered themselves a living sacrifice to the mosquitoes rather than the heat. Apart from the tormented dentist called Churchill—that even the Japanese found funny—the most luckless prisoner was a pale and peaceful Czech embezzler, known inappropriately as 'the bouncing Czech', who had seen his rapist, murderous and bestial companions liberated by victorious General Yamashita and sent back slavering into the community while he was retained as a dangerous enemy alien. At least, as sitting tenant, he had been able to take the best cell in the house.

Endless discord had been brilliantly sown by the Japanese when, at the last moment, they drove in two hundred mixed Jews and Armenians, mostly money-changers from what the Europeans called Change Alley and everyone else knew as Chincharlie. The Jews were persecuted by Germans, therefore clearly *not* Allies, therefore enemies of the Japanese, but the British were horrified that the Japanese viewed them as white without further qualification. They had been anyway none too happy about the olive complexions of some of the Mediterranean French and a disquietingly dusky Spaniard in the wine trade. A petition had been sent to the nonplussed commandant suggesting they be reclassified as 'Eurasian' and removed at once to the Sime Road camp. Then the Jews further hardened the hearts of oak against them by not knowing their place. It was discovered that they even referred to the lavatories not by some patriotic and affectionate term of whimsy, derived from the Motherland, but openly called them 'The Wailing Wall'. The other internees, shocked, had fussed and fumed like an outraged residents' association. Now they sent another petition to Colonel Saito who puzzled wearily over the alien classifications involved. Finally, the interpreter threw up his hands. 'British say Jews are Korean,' he extemporised, and the British case was won. The Jews were accorded separate quarters in the old rice store—immediately dubbed 'Aldgate'—and their womenfolk designated as cleaners and washerwomen in the women's section.

Even within the British themselves, the rubbing along of different classes caused constant friction. The public school men fared best. After all, they had been raised in a system of arbitrary authority and violence with only scant food and distant dreams of ultimate liberation to sustain them. They knew from experience the dangers of such hothouse environments and the importance of battening down the hatches in order to retain their sanity and just face life day by day. Outrageous behaviour was dismissed with a sighed 'It takes all sorts …', Japanese-imposed indignities accepted with 'We mustn't make a fuss for the sake of the women …' And women. They could live without them as they could do without tablecloths and napkins. Pilchard was an old Malvern College man. He had survived there by collecting beetles. Here, he had his Cocos-Keeling fieldwork to remember, to revise, to reinvent. He panted into the cell.

'Good Lord, old man, what happened to you? Was it the Nips? The INA?' O'Toole was a craggy rugger player in his fifties with a well-macerated face, his nose spread sideways to make a physiognomy that could have modelled for Picasso. Beside him was a housewifely stack of threadbare shorts and vests. He had been killing time, as he sewed, by trying to recreate games played in the past, attacking holes in his clothes with great swooping stitches such as a fisherman might use to mend his nets. It was hopeless. Like his washing, memories were all one grey blur punctuated by varied injuries. Occasionally, he had done a little banking to fill in between the matches and the rugger suppers that were yet another blur.

'One darn thing after another, eh, O'Toole? Mmm? What happened? Oh, I see. You mean the beard.' Pilchard tugged at a few random red strands of hair. 'Higgins insisted on having a go at it just to keep his cover.' It was thanks to the beard and the hair that he was no longer at liberty. The occupiers had been glad enough, initially, to retain the academic staff of the museum to keep looters at bay and give a token nod and a wink towards their own cultural pretensions, but shaven-headed Japanese could not cope with the sheer physical indiscipline of Pilchard's body. The Professor, a suitably eruptive Tokyo vulcanologist appointed Director, had wandered in through the door on his first day and found him, shod feet up on the desk, digging in his ear with one finger while swigging from a mug of tea. Pilchard saw himself as paid to think. So he had been working hard, thinking about rearranging the display of Malay birds—the pose being one conducive to thought. For newly conscripted Tokyo professors, to point one's feet at a superior was a grave insult in itself. To do so wearing extremely baggy shorts and no underwear, with an insouciant smirk on his face and a finger in his ear, had nearly cost Pilchard his life. But, even in his better days, Pilchard had never 'dressed'. Rather, he had simply 'worn clothes'. The Professor had been taken aback and asked to be introduced. Then he had inquired, in his most official, stocktaking voice, 'Tell me. How many people actually work in the Gardens, Dr Pilchard?'

'Oh … about half of them,' he had replied with another casual grin. Of course, the joke had been unwise but also irresistible and he had been somewhat surprised when the Professor hauled a huge old Webley revolver from the sagging side pocket of his suit, ripping it in the process with the front sight, pointed it at him and screamed spittle-spraying words that he did not understand, Japanese words that flew past like shrapnel. An hour later, the soldiers had come for him and dumped him in Changi. Intercultural humour was always a difficult thing to judge. From this, he had learned that respect was not something you had to *feel* to make the Japanese happy. You only had to ritually *show* it and, in fact, the more clear it was that you showed it while feeling the very opposite, the better they liked it. Perhaps his present life, the whole war, could have been avoided if he and the Allies had understood that earlier. Anyway, he *had* offered the old fool a cup of tea.

'Where's Manson?'

O'Toole shrugged. Manson was their talisman, the reason they only had three to the cell. He was a former engineer on the Malay Railways but had never been the same since the attack by the Sikhs. For long periods, he now thought he was one of the steam engines that he had lovingly maintained and he ran around the stairs and landings chuffing and working his arms like pistons and with a beatific expression on his tooting face that was the envy of other inmates. Harmless but irritating, he had repelled several tentative boarders with his whistling and fidgeting and the constant shameless jiggling with his emergency pressure release valve. 'He's out shunting—running round somewhere with that stupid smile on his face. Daft as a Christian—as usual. Today, he's started operating his wet season timetable.'

'But it's still the dry season.'

O'Toole mimed astonishment. 'You don't say. Could this be a sign Manson is going round the bend, do you think?'

Pilchard grinned ruefully. Even in peacetime, his medicine was helpless before afflictions of the brain, the mind, perhaps both. 'I take your point but lunatics are usually the most ruthlessly logical of people. That's why they are lunatics.' He took out the banana-leaf package and laid it carefully on the bed, a slight gloating in his face.

O'Toole looked over. 'You got it then? Not from the Javanese, I hope. You know how dangerous that is. They're all bloody informers.'

Pilchard nodded. 'They're all right.' He unfolded both ends carefully, unwrapped and peeled back the flaps of green leaf to reveal the treasure inside, held it up to the light, sniffed it. It was smooth and translucent, a relic of a higher civilisation now fallen. 'Looks good quality. Not even second hand.' Jeyes, onion-skin, medicated, interleafed for box dispenser—sheets of toilet paper blessed with the holy cross of Izal. Worth its weight in gold. He went over to the crouchhole toilet. This convenience had so impressed local inmates that they had nicknamed the prison 'King Georgie Hoteli' but, under British occupation, it had been unanimously decided at a meeting, that crouchholes should not be used for the purpose designed. "Point of ordure, Mr Chairman!" Pilchard had quipped at a sea of stonily uncomprehending and disapproving faces. Pilchrd flicked up the grill and reached inside. Another Player's tin. He stowed the paper inside, carefully keeping back one sheet, replaced the lid and slid it back into concealment under the rim.

'How much did you pay?'

Pilchard smiled. 'I didn't pay. I traded. A bulb from the headlight of Spratt's truck.'

'How the hell did you manage that?' Grudging admiration showed.

'I didn't. His driver did. A Korean. I gave *him* Gracie Fields for it.'

O' Toole sat up, all ears. 'A Korean? You're bloody mad. And your postcard? The one with her in a headscarf? The one outside Rochdale town hall?'

Pilchard nodded.

'What the devil did a Korean want that for?' He lay back again, frowning.

'Maybe she reminded him of his mother? No. He just wants it to trade with. Some homesick Yorkshire lad, like as not, would give his eye teeth for it and eye teeth are worth a fortune in here.'

O'Toole shook his head.

Like most Western males, Pilchard cared nothing for matters of hygiene, whereas some of the women next door were almost incapable of doing without toilet paper and literally wept daily with humiliation over its absence. The Javanese, who had sold him the paper, would naturally have nothing to do with it. They washed carefully, with left hands, after defecation. Western practice was to them shocking, scandalously filthy, but they had experimented with using the paper for rolling cigarettes, the disinfectant flavour being the welcome revenant of the cloves they normally worked in with their tobacco. For Pilchard, it was the paper's literary potential that attracted. The Japanese were obsessively opposed to the keeping of records and diaries and Pilchard simply accepted this as one of the irrational obsessions to which armies were prey. In a while, they would probably forget all about it in favour of some new idiocy, the possession of combs or torches. Toilet paper was easily hidden, might even pass disdainfully unexamined, could be disposed of without arousing suspicion. Occasional searches were made and anyone caught with informational contraband could expect to be dragged away to Kempeitei headquarters and tortured hysterically. At the museum, they regularly heard the results of such searches, the screams of their neighbours in the former YMCA, often followed by an abrupt silence even more terrifying. It was clear from those screams that the Kempeitei did not favour exquisite subtlety in their interrogations. No slow dripping of oil on the head, in steady rhythm and darkness, over the course of a month. Their methods were a matter of ripping boots and fists, ropes and barrels of water.

He and O'Toole exchanged conspiratorial grins. 'From faeces to thesis,' quipped Pilchard, twinkling a pencil out from behind one ear and propping himself up against the hard surface of the bunk to begin rewriting his Cocos-Keeling fieldnotes—weeks, months of research distilled down to a few lines of what he himself recognised as a slightly lunatic hand—as O'Toole closed his eyes, chased images of Gracie Fields away and settled back to skeptically re-examine a referee's decision about a touchdown that now lay some three years in the past. Soon it would be time for lunch.

* * *

41

'Where the hell's my pencil?' Spratt let his eye roam over the rickety table, the floor. He checked his pockets. It was gone. Someone had nicked it. Men were always nicking stuff these days. It was a disease. He balefully eyed the men working on the truck. If this were Aldershot, he'd have the lot on jankers but, for the moment, he was too weary to enjoy his rage, make a proper theatrical production of it. Pencils were hard to come by. Now he would need to nick one from someone else. He wandered irritably out and over to the books piled in the handcart and saw several periodicals on the birds of Malaya, the sort with numbers instead of pictures on the cover, so you knew they were serious and full of Latin. There might be something by Pilchard in there. With a snarled 'Carry on' to the men, he bent and seized one and walked with purposeful buttocks over to the latrines, tearing at the pages as he went. It was hard, shiny, unabsorbent paper that gave off a chemical smell. It would just about do but you had to be careful. Crumple it thoroughly before you wiped. Cut yourself if not. Bible paper was better but he retained a superstitious fear of sacrilege. With the Japs against you, you didn't need to risk upsetting God as well by wiping yourself on one of the abominations of Leviticus. Anyway, Bible paper was too good, absolutely the best there was for a roll-up. He closed the door of rough planks, twisted the bent nail that served as a bolt, tensing against the sudden heat, and settled over the hole, trying to ignore the hot miasma that rose with the buzz of flies and a sound like sizzling fat. The drains weren't flushed out continuously any more. Prison bred a schoolboy obsession with entrances and exits, boundaries and barriers, control of the body, the ever-present threat of lethal dysentery. Contrary views existed cosily, side by side. When someone died of disease in here, the medics spoke of the invasion of the body by the hostile outside, while the chaplain of liberation and blessed release from the body and its confinement.

He scanned the wall. Occasionally, important news from the hidden radios would be pencilled in the darker corners to escape Japanese eyes—'latrinogrammes' they were called—and had proved, on the whole, less confusing than the news whispered at roll call. There, 'Rations are increased' had become 'Russians are in Greece' which had led to wild and misplaced rejoicing among the Armenians—though the latrinogramme 'French push bottles up 5,000 Germans' had caused great puzzlement among the Asians. Today, there was only the standard wittily scrawled 'For the war effort' with appropriate arrow. He grunted and settled back and spread out a crumpled study of the mating patterns of the Brahminy kite. A hundred feet down the same pipe that led from scribbling Pilchard's cell, scholarship was being returned to the soil of Asia.

* * *

The canteen was already packed, though it would be at least another ten minutes until the food was late. Pilchard settled in a corner with his back to the wall, clutching tin mug and spoon like a child at a Salvation Army bun fight and observed dispassionately. As at school, food was the internal clock around which all other activities revolved. Even though it was always the same, watery rice porridge, *bubur*, and tea without milk or sugar, a form of pointless expertise had developed around it. The rice mixture was brought in in buckets, crusted thicker on top and watery at the bottom and doled out into prisoners' mugs. There were three schools of thought about this. The first held that there was most solid nourishment in the viscous, top layer so it paid to come early. The second held that all the mystical 'goodness' was leached out and lay only in the watery bottom layer so the trick lay in ensuring you got to the front of the queue towards the end of one bucket but before they started on the next. The servers knew this and some would deliberately switch buckets before they were quite empty just for the leering sense of power it gave them. The Bishop of Singapore, on his watch, had almost provoked a riot by stirring up the depths to the top with a muscular egalitarianism that had earned him a reputation for communist leanings. The third school held that it all depended on the amount of gritty lime the Japanese had added to the rice as an insecticide, which varied from day to day and so it was a lottery. The result was that the queue became a caricature of hypocrisy with an alternation of shoving and dithering punctuated with smooth 'After you!'s or sharp little 'Excuse me. I think it is my turn!'s as people tried to shorten the odds in favour of their own view of the world. Rarely, there was dried, salt fish or meat to add relish to the porridge but mostly it was a diet of tasteless or slightly mouldy wallpaper paste. In his pocket, Pilchard had his secret boy-scout ingredient—earthworms of the phylum *Annelida*, captured in the gardens and sundried on the window sill to little salty wisps of pseudo-bacon. As always when they lugged in the *bubur*, he smiled and thought of the Malay proverb 'the rice has already become porridge' something like 'no point in crying over spilt milk'. No point indeed.

Today, it was pompous, suspiciously chubby Arthur Truefitt, from the water board, on duty at the rice table, wielding his ladle of authority like an alderman's mace as the rice buckets were dragged in and the crowd fell hungrily silent and watchful. Changi was a very paradise for frustrated colonial bureaucrats with constant elections for camp commandant to deal with the Japanese, a representative to supervise each floor, endless specialist committees on matters as diverse as religious services and latrines and a complex system of rotating chores that ensured a constantly elevated sense of social injustice. Its administration required a greater density of officialdom than the Chinese empire. Pilchard rose to his feet and used his youth and height to drift with passive, genteel violence to the front.

By deft manipulation of his implement, allowing porridge to slop down the side of the mug and back into the bucket or not, he reckoned that the officiating ladler could adjust the amount dispensed by at least fifteen percent in either direction. Today, Pilchard knew, it should be all right. After all, he and Truefitt were on the Christmas planning committee together and in staunch alliance against those extremists who wanted to ban carols of German origin from the festivities. But they were also on the education sub-committee and there bitterly divided on the topic of whether geography and history should be taught to the children in secret defiance of Nip orders to the contrary, for Pilchard remembered his own childhood and knew that both were essential supplements to the thin gruel of reality from which they would otherwise build their worlds. Truefitt looked him in the eye and hesitated, then scooped the ladle around the bucket, not waiting for the level to adjust back down, and quickly plonked the ration squarely in the mug without further droolage. The Christmas committee meeting, after all, came before the education sub-committee meeting.

* * *

There was no shortage of doctors on the wing. In fact there were more than they knew what to do with, given the almost total absence of drugs and their helplessness without them. The hospital wing was known, with deliberate whimsy, as 'Cripplegate' and Pilchard was on the afternoon rota. It would be busy since people regarded medical consultations as a form of social therapy, comforting, validating, good in themselves. Miller, an Australian mine engineer with a swollen belly like a separate fitment hobbled in and sat down heavily, wincing.

'It's me Niagaras, Doc.'

'Niagaras?'

Miller chewed at the air in frustration. He had a face like a collapsed lung. 'Yeah, Niagaras. Oh Jeez. You know … Niagara Falls, balls. They aches something cruel. Wakes me up at night when I'm in bed. A while back one of the lads give me a bit of melon and I thought it was that upset me guts. Like I was melancholic.'

'Have you suffered any recent injury in that area?'

'In bed, Doc? Nah. That's one place I keeps out of trouble.'

Pilchard sighed. He was *not* going to examine him. He recoiled powerfully from the notion. In peacetime, bodies might be variously erotic or medical. Years of training prevented their being both at the same time. Here they were simply universally repellent.

'You're sure it's not rice balls?' It was the local term for a common prison complaint. 'Erosion of the skin of the scrotal sack with attendant inflammation and infection? The result of vitamin deficiency.' The man shook his head. Pilchard looked him in the eye, man-to-man, no-names-no-packdrill. 'Look. When did you last have an orgasm, Mr Miller?'

Miller rolled his head and blushed like a schoolgirl tickled under the chin. 'Aw Doc. There ain't no sheilas in here and I've had other things on me mind, what with the malaria and dysentery. Cripes, I hardly *knows* me cellmates.'

Pilchard grunted. His wife flashed across his mind. His other half. Perhaps less a half than a sixteenth as it turned out. Margaret had fled to Australia on one of the first evacuation ships. Not that he had had much time for the pleasures and duties of marriage. He refused to go down that gloomy path.

'Not since your last bout of malaria then? Well, that may well be the trouble. The elevated temperature and so on. Hard on the genitals which function at their best at a lower temperature than the rest of the body. Hence their dependant siting. Find some way to drain away ... er ... try the usual form of release. You know what I mean.' Miller blushed again and looked fixedly down into the corner of the room. There was a cockroach there, eavesdropping without shame, waving its antennae.

'You mean crack one off, Doc?' His voice was high and incredulous.

'If that's what you call it. At least once a day. For a few days. See if that clears it up.'

Miller shook his head in shocked disbelief. 'First time a quack's told me to do that. When I was a kiddie lots told me not to. Make you blind. Make hair grow on the palms of yer 'ands. Priests too—though there was some of 'em at school only too keen to give a lad a hand. I grew up poor and I was lucky to be born a lad otherwise I'd have had nothing at all to play with. Here, it seems like a waste of good porridge. Still ...' He lumbered to his feet, all bony arms and legs, the chair scraping back and rubbed his hand over his grinning jaw. The cockroach ran for cover. 'Can you give me a prescription for that, Doc?'

* * *

'Singapore is a colony but it has its own colonies. It is an island become a prison and within that prison is this special place where women are further imprisoned. But we are not alone in this. There have been other places just the same. Imagine Australia on the map,' said Pilchard drawing in thin air. His audience sighed wistfully. He had attracted a mere thirty-odd of them, mostly squatting on the floor, with chairs awarded to a few on grounds of infirmity or eminence—categories that were nearly identical in the women's prison. Only thirty but then 'Some Little-Known Facts about the Cocos-Keeling Islands' was not a title to pack them in. Before the war, the room had been some sort of a warders' common room and dismembered remains of lurid pictures, random bosoms and necks—mostly Western—torn from newspapers, were stuck to the brickwork. The odd Islamic pinup—swathed from head to toe, all the provocation crammed into the face—peered and pouted between. Lady Pendleberry, in a chair in the front row, cleared her throat manfully and one woman sobbed and was shushed. 'Now move your eye northwest to Java. Between the two, nothing but thousands and thousands of miles of empty ocean, punctuated by two tiny eruptions of land, Christmas Island and the archipelago of Cocos-Keeling.' He made it dramatic, waved his arm again, pointed on the non-existent wall map to the invisible islands conjured from the dust motes dancing in the air. Outside, the POWs had their 'university', drawing on the prodigious and absurd mix of submerged expertise that the military normally ignored. Out there, they were learning everything from poultry-keeping to philosophy with one or two hiccoughs. 'Introduction to the Japanese language' had not proved a popular course but a pale clerk from the Pay Corps triumphed with a bloodthirsty history of the Byzantine Empire, interspersing tales of horror and voluptuousness with lyrical passages of art appreciation. Then an embittered Australian ranker had stirred them with a demotic examination of the heresies of the mediaeval Christian Church. 'Jansenism? It means most of you are poor buggers, totally buggered from the start and there's bugger all you can do about it.' Then there had been trouble over geometric forms scraped in the dust, the guards taking a proof of Pythagoras's theorem for an escape plan, while two Kiwi commandos had had a nasty fist fight over the pathetic fallacy in the work of Wordsworth.

The occupants of the female wing of Changi, known unflatteringly as the 'bitches' barracks', had set their own sights somewhat lower. Despite malnutrition and deprivation, their lives were a whirlwind of colonial gentility—bridge and needlework, concerts and poetry contests that denied the reality of the occupation. They were yellow and papery-skinned, even the natural exuberance of the children dimmed by hunger and they all smelled seedy and unwashed, the armpits of their faded frocks rotted through by sweat. From somewhere Pilchard remembered that starving bodies give off acetone. Acetone removes nail varnish. But none of them were wearing nail varnish—from malnutrition many had no nails—and no unruly male desire stirred at the sight of them. Even the Japanese guards no longer made a point of coming round at shower time. The women were still scratching from delousing. The best way of dealing with lice infestation was to drape clothes and mattresses over an anthill in the yard. The ants rushed out and stung the lice to death, even digging their eggs out of hidden seams but then you had to drive away the ants by smoking the clothes which made everyone smell like kippers for a week. Unfortunately, they hadn't had time to do that properly before the talk.

For now, edifying lectures were to be added to social life and special permission had been unexpectedly granted by the Japanese for male visitors to deliver them. Normally, mixing of sexes was not encouraged. In an act of petty spite, families were deliberately broken up and isolated from each other but love, as always, had found a way. One man per week was permitted, under guard, to take over the female dustbins delivered into the yard of the women's quarters by one of them, empty the bins on the male side and bring them back. A stringent secret rota, organised on toilet paper pushed through a slit in the brick wall, ensured that married couples should be paired and briefly coincide over the

49

reeking garbage. Hands might fleetingly touch, screwed up notes be dropped, damp-eyed, reassuring smiles be silently exchanged amidst the buzzing flies and the stink of decay. For these precious moments, wardrobes were ransacked, precious dresses borrowed, even a priceless dab of scent behind the ears might contend with the sickly-sweet stench. The Japanese never seemed to wonder why the only occasion when prisoners dressed up was to move dustbins and why the experience invariably seemed to move them to tears. For them foreigners were just crazy.

'Christmas Island may be characterised as a large heap of guano populated by swarms of coconut-eating crabs and is currently otherwise under only Japanese occupation. On the other hand, I spent some time on Cocos-Keeling and it remains—thus far—held by our own forces ...' Lady Pendleberry, dressed in a vest under a ratty *peignoir*, like some impoverished *aristo* after the French revolution, rapped her stick loudly against her chair.

'Dr Pilchard! I'm sure if my husband, the Governor, were here, he would wish me to remind you that you should beware of saying anything that might be of the slightest use to our hosts. Even here they have ears.' She turned and glared at Miko, one of four inoffensive and unfortunate Japanese women, ears modestly covered by their hair, married to British husbands, who had ended up here in a sort of limbo of administrative disapproval. Japanese, but not Japanese enough for the Japanese.

He smiled ingratiatingly, 'I am afraid, Lady Pendleberry, that any such information I may once have possessed has long since been seized by the Nips. My notes at the museum ...'

'I should have thought that any such dangerous material would have been destroyed in good order. And this is no time for defeatist talk or running down our allies. Don't you know, young man, that there's a war on?'

'Oh, do wrap up Betty. Leave the poor lamb alone.' This from the figure beside her, a stout lady with swollen and bandaged ankles and tired, mottled arms and dressed in an extraordinary patchwork dress. The Japanese normally left the prisoners much to their own devices, mounting the occasional search for illicit radios, contraband or simply objects they might want to steal. Yet, at unpredictable intervals, like a capricious wealthy relative, they gave unexpected and ill-judged presents. Recently, out of the blue, they had delivered two large crates of female underwear of a design so bizarre—capacious and flounced, some in loud, thick tartans—that they seemed to hail from an eighteenth-century brothel specialising in Scottish-themed perversities and had provoked real fears among the women that they were all to be shipped off to become 'comfort women' elsewhere in the archipelago. Possibly the INLA would be involved. Indians, after all, were known for their ragged and unruly bagpipes. Nothing of the kind had materialised, however, and gradually the huge knickers and vests had been reduced to reason, snipped up and stitched into a hundred more serviceable garments, the offcuts—too valuable to waste—being made into patchwork dresses and skirts. Pilchard recognised the wearer as Dr Voss, the elected women's commandant. Doctors seemed to gravitate towards positions of authority—except for him of course. He smiled wan thanks.

'Like so much else,' he intoned. 'Cocos-Keeling all began with Stamford Raffles, or rather with his friend, Alexander Hare, a trader who ran a company called the House of Hare and registered in the city of London. He was known amongst the British as "the eccentric Mr Hare". We shall see why in a minute. Between 1811 and 1816, the British ruled Java, having seized it from the Dutch to prevent the French making use of it who, in turn ...' Lady Pendleberry cleared her throat and impaled him on her glare. '... Anyway, he came to an agreement with Raffles who sent him off to combat piracy in Borneo and there he wheedled a large estate out of the sultan and chopped down the trees to build ships. The labour was supplied by Raffles from among his Javanese convicts and Hare both charged for their board and lodging and then sold the ships back to the East India Company for yet more money. He was doing very nicely. And then, of course, the British withdrew and the Dutch came back and ran Hare out of town as a British stooge.'

Lady Pendleberry harumphed.

'That is ... our gallant Dutch allies came back and drove Hare out at bayonet point. And so he embarked his followers on his ship and set out on an odyssey around the archipelago. You see, he had become a collector and, like all true collectors, that passion had taken over his life—an omnivorous, all-consuming passion that devoured everything in its path—until he neglected everything else, his job, his friends, his family—everything. In fact, he became the outcast of the islands. By the time he finished, the eccentric Mr Hare would have over a hundred of the finest examples of their kind and could never resist buying more—to the point that it became difficult to move the collection about.'

'Then why on earth did he keep moving?' interrupted Dr Voss.

'Well ... once the Dutch found out about the collection they always ran him out of town.'

'But you haven't told us what he collected.'

'Oh. Didn't I mention? It was ladies. He collected ladies.' There was a stunned silence. Two Japanese women began whispering and looking puzzled. The word 'ladies' echoed around interrogatively. 'An ethnographic seraglio, a harem. Female slaves, like one of the old rajahs. He wanted one of each tribe of the Indies and aimed for exhaustive coverage.'

Lady Pendleberry snorted and made to say something but

Dr Voss put a restraining hand on her arm and threw back her own head and laughed. 'How gloriously stupid! How appalling! A hundred women? Would any man think that would make him happy? A harem of the local races? The poor booby must have got more than he bargained for. It's like a doctor deciding a drug was good for you so a hundred times the dose would be a hundred times better. How did he justify having so many?'

Pilchard smiled.

'Well. It's like a museum. In a museum, when you write a proposal to make an acquisition, it only ever comes in two forms. The first is "We already have ninety-nine of these so we must have another to complete our collection". Or "We have ninety-nine of those but none of these so we must get at least one to correct the imbalance in our holdings". I imagine Hare's logic was much the same, one or the other, depending on circumstances.'

'But presumably he did not limit his activities to arranging them in glass cases and just dusting them off from time to time as in some living museum?'

'Apparently not. The male offspring, he formed into a brass band. Apparently they were quite accomplished and in great demand for social occasions.'

'And the females?'

Pilchard blushed. The abraded saucy pictures on the walls zoomed into focus.

'Er ... well ... It's not entirely clear. His enemies, of course, claimed that he ... er ... ploughed them back in.' Lady Pendleberry transferred her stick to the 'present arms' position and rose like a black storm cloud over the sun.

'Enough! When we came here this afternoon, we did not expect smut and innuendo.' She breathed through flared nostrils. 'A little geography and geology would have been quite in order, even a modicum of natural history might have passed without comment, though it is always dangerously physical. We did not expect the documentation of depravity. Dr Pilchard, as a public servant, you should be ashamed of yourself.'

'Oh put a sock in it Betty. Thank god this is more interesting than last week's "Punctuation in Shakespearean English". I want to know more.' Other women murmured assent. 'You go if you want to. Nothing wrong with a bit of historical "how's yer father". You weren't such a prude when we were at school together.' Pilchard thought he heard a threat of inconvenient disclosure there. 'Carry on Dr Pritchard.'

'Very well then.' It is hard to stalk out haughtily when dressed in pink tule with holes in it through which show chicken-wing legs, but Lady Pendleberry made a worthy attempt.

'Now,' Dr Voss smiled, settling roundly in her chair. 'Let's get back to the dry bones of history and, please, for God's sake, Dr Pilchard, try to put a little warm flesh on them.'

Part II

The Garden in the Wilderness

Pilchard looked back the way he had come. From afar, the whiteness of Changi prison gleamed like a jewel in a setting of base metal, the streaks of lichen and decay invisible at this distance. It was possible to imagine it as a sort of enchanted medieval palace. Clustered around it were the carbuncles of barracks— Selarang for the Australians, Roberts for the Brits and the Dutch and a strip of no man's land in between to keep them apart. But the perimeter leaked like a sieve. Goods could be traded in and out on a flourishing black market fuelled by the work parties who stripped their worksites bare. Charged with clearing a warehouse, they would steal not only from the cargo but virtually demolish the building. Some were from London dockers' families and had generations of traditional skills in low thievery. Beams and hinges would be magicked into thin air. Doorlocks would evaporate, nails from the walls, pipes and taps would suddenly dissolve into nothing. Give us the job and we'll finish the tools.

From the tarmac road, radiated a network of dirt tracks linking up the little Malay villages and their emerald fields. Here, the locals dwelt in insanitary ease, replacing the lost income of fishing—prohibited by the Japanese—by a windfall of commerce. Chinese middlemen had moved in, relations of sponsorship and clientship had blossomed, trading circles spontaneously formed themselves. In less than three days, the same distributor-head of a looted Morris might be stolen by POWs on the docks, smuggled into the camp, smuggled back out to the Chinese, exchanged in half a dozen trades and sold back to its owner as a replacement through an established store. Life reasserted itself.

They had come for Pilchard before breakfast, Sergeant Fukui, a rat-faced Korean, and worried-looking Truefitt, floor supervisor with his clipboard, and kicked him listlessly awake.

'You come! Speedo! Speedo!' He had struggled unwillingly to consciousness. In Changi oblivion was a precious state, almost holy, that had to be respected by others.

'What? Who? Why?' Giggling Fukui mimed exaggerated cutting of throats and kicked again. O'Toole watched impassively.

'Shitbags,' he observed quietly and dispassionately, to no one in particular, as if identifying a particular species of insect. Manson woke up and let out an experimental hiss of steam, boilers not yet up to pressure. Truefitt sweated copiously.

'They've got a chit. From Yamashita's own office.' Droplets began to gather at his temples. 'I hope you've not been up to anything that will get the rest of us into trouble, Pilchard.'

'Oh for God's sake stop kicking me. There's no point.' He struggled for sandals only to have them kicked away again.

'Speedo! Speedo! Japan number one. Britain number ten.' Fukui all teeth and spit. Why did he smell of garlic? It was the French who were supposed to smell of the stinking rose.

'Yes. Whenever I do number one's I think of Japan.' Pilchard struggled to his feet. 'If I don't come back O'Toole gets my kit.' Spoken with the force and clarity of a deathbed declaration.

The battered face crumpled into softness. 'That's very decent of you, old man.' He leant up on one elbow. 'But don't you go worrying about that. It's probably just some admin thing. You'll be back in a jiffy. Seen it happen loads of times.'

'Speedo! Speedo!' Jostling and shoving. The droplets at Truefitt's temples gathered and flowed. Manson let out a whistle and juddered his pistons threateningly. As they marched him away down the gloomy pre-dawn corridor, Pilchard could hear the whispered news of his removal already rustling through the prison like a swarm of cockroaches and felt a sudden puzzled numbness, as of a man reading a newspaper and coming abruptly upon his own obituary, written by a normally authoritative source.

He did not wonder what it was that he had done. We are all overdrawn at the moral bank and, anyway, the old rules no longer held. All pretence of living in a just or even comprehensible world had long disappeared. But he did worry slightly over which of his offences they had discovered. That could shape his end. Was he to be swiftly executed or merely to suffer endless, unspeakable pain and mutilation? Or would one come before the other? Would it be the march onto the parade ground in the hot sun before ranks of horrified troops, the forced kneeling, all the time making the decision whether or not to beg and grovel wretchedly for mercy? You knew it would be pointless but it seemed stupid to toddle off into oblivion without even playing your last card. After all, for one who had no faith in an afterlife what did the dignified manner of your going matter one way or the other? At the hospital, if you were the doctor on duty, they always wanted you to say that so-and-so popped off laughing and joking, saluting and singing the national anthem. In reality, most went screaming and cursing if they had the strength or whimpering if they didn't. They had already reached the administrative block, a series of tired, brick huts faced by an open corridor. He was already being pushed and shoved into an office, already bowing at someone he had not bothered to identify through the mist of fear and confusion. It was one of those irreversible moments in life, a climacteric, that governs everything that is yet to come, the opening of a buff envelope that held the key to one's future, the saying of 'I do', the signature on the army application form. There was an officer's voice coming at him. He tried to concentrate, blinked the sweat

61

out of his eyes.

'The paper says you will report at once to Stamford Road. The order is straight from headquarters. You will carry this pass and wear this armband on your right arm.' The uniform pushed over a piece of cloth bearing a red sun and a snarl of characters. Pilchard was dazed. He was to go back to the museum? Someone had pulled some strings. He was not going to die after all. He immediately began to regret his missed breakfast. And then they had taken him to the gate and just pushed him out. No transport. Nothing. An orphan. Barely a penny in his pockets. Gesturing with their rifles that he should walk, no longer the master race. 'Japan number one. Britain number ten!' It sounded like the house chants of his prep school. On such childish principles are great empires based. Fair enough. The morning sun was still gentle on his face. He felt like a bigger schoolboy getting a sudden, extraordinary day off while everyone else was still swotting at their lessons and set out, hesitantly at first, then—like Felix—kept on walking, kept on walking, even humming to himself and possessed of a curious lightness of being.

* * *

'Hong Kong' Fong settled back in the great rosewood chair that was the over-literal mark of his office, Chairman of the Chinese Traders' Association. His hand dropped casually to find the comforting chip in the antique mother-of-pearl inlay of the armrest and he explored it with a canny fingernail, experiencing the same guilty pleasure he had got as a boy from picking at the scabs on his knees, finding the fault lines in them, easing them up, enjoying the rush of blood as they came away and their sticky chewiness on his tongue. He had been smacked by his mother for that. He was too young for this job, too insignificant, too small, a child again. They all knew it. With his taste for linen suits of skimpy, modern cut, he contrasted with these old patriarchs, from established trading houses, sitting round the table in their motheaten silk tunics and embroidered slippers. Most of them were barely out of pigtails. He spoke the wrong language too, the Cantonese of his Hong Kong parents, not their Baba Hokkien mix of mainland language and Malay. He was not King's Chinese. He was his own man. HK. Above his head, a poster from the Propaganda Department made the point. It showed an elderly Chinese merchant in despair over his boarded-up shophouse with its Union Jack while next door, a young, laughing Chinese, looking very much like HK, was chubbily beating off the customers clamouring for his Japanese products. A slogan read 'Make Fortune By Cooperating With Japan'. It was the Japanese who had chosen HK over the heads of his elders and he felt the resentment that radiated from these old men so used to deference and submission from wives and children, employees and colleagues, even from salaried government officials. They made absolutely sure he felt it.

'We are required to submit figures on the degree to which the campaign to replace British goods at home with Japanese goods is progressing.' They looked at him sourly and said nothing. Everyone knew there were virtually no Japanese goods to replace the British goods with, that the whole thing was empty words. They were expected to survive indefinitely like camels living off their humps yet, among them, HK was the only one with no hump. The others had long prepared for war in depth, had hidden stores in hidden locations to which no one person held a map. True, thanks to informers, the Japanese had tracked down some reserves of the second rank and broken them open, forcing staples out onto the markets but mountains of rice, rivers of soy sauce and lakes of oil formed a whole secret landscape as yet unrevealed. Meanwhile, in the world the public saw, nothing at all was being delivered to their empty warehouses while the whole island was being ruthlessly stripped bare of goods and even scrap to keep Japan going, for the Japanese recognised no basic human needs, in their conquests, that could not be met simply with more submission and flags. Flags had, of course, arrived in large quantities. They all had them outside their shops and, inside, an amuletic photograph of the pinch-faced, weedy Emperor. There was the same one there on the wall, squinting down on them where once Chiang Kai-Sheck had hung from the same rusty nail. Being slightly smaller, it was framed by a rectangle of greasy dirt. HK coaxed.

'The figures, of course, do not have to be entirely accurate. The marking of a general trend will be sufficient to satisfy the Japanese.' They stared impassively back. Blank defiance. The Japanese had come to him. It was, surely, his personal problem. Not theirs. Everyone knew that the merchants' written records had always been imaginative works of fiction, spun from nothing, conjured up for the tax authorities. The real figures were in their heads. HK began to sweat. 'Some sort of a gesture is required. That is all.' His voice had taken on a pleading tone and he hated it. One or two of them had picked up on it and begun to smirk at his discomfort. A few years back, when the Japanese had attacked Manchuria, they had held meetings like this—actually in this very room—about the enforcement of the boycott on Japanese goods declared by the firm-fisted patriots of the China Relief Fund. 'Help Britain and you help China' had been the slogan pushed at them then. But at that time, HK had sat at the bottom of the table and held his tongue. Tongue. His mind wandered. He thought wistfully of the things he had done with Lily last night in a little shophouse in Geylang. At least he could still keep it up, unlike these old men, for all their ground rhino horn.

Loh Ching laid the long nail of an index finger gently on the tabletop like a householder testing the surface for dirt. It had the same effect as if one of the others had rapped on it loudly with a hammer and silence fell immediately. The senior trader. His face was as sere as one of the seven sages, head of the house that the legendary Whampoa CMG—richest man on earth at the time— had founded a century before. He spoke softly, making everyone bow their heads and strain to pick up his words. Serenity was a mark of rank that Loh Ching used to float above the merely material world.

'We are simple men of business, not of politics. Singapore is not our home. Let us not talk of home. Singapore is nobody's home. We have no roots here. People simply live here to do business. As a young man, Mr Fong embraces ... current realities ... without the attachment some of us feel to our ... older, loyal customers.' HK gushed sweat into his singlet. It was damned hot up here on the first floor of the shophouse. And this was dangerous talk. Anyone here could be an informer. God knows, he was half an informer himself. 'I have a simple suggestion to make that should render all parties content.' He looked slowly around at the row of bowed heads and respectfully downcast eyes. A suggestion from Loh Ching was as good as an order. 'I suggest that we should concentrate on selling Japanese goods to the British.' There was a silence in which the street noises became suddenly very obvious, a honking horn, a shouting child.

HK thought desperately. What the hell did he mean? 'The British?' he said. 'The British are all sitting with empty pockets in Changi. How can we sell to the British? *What* can we sell to the British?'

Loh Ching smiled patiently and sighed at the obtuseness of others. 'Perhaps you have not heard what has happened.' Happened? Had something happened? Apart, that is, from the invasion of Singapore—sorry Syonanto—the killing, the terror, the collapse of their whole world. 'There has been a sign from Heaven.'

'From Heaven?'

Loh Ching nodded. 'It was outside the Victoria Theatre several days ago. Stamford Raffles pissed on General Yamashita.' They giggled like schoolboys. He had said 'pissed' just like that, right out loud. 'Many people saw it. They say that as the Japanese were attacking his statue, it suddenly came to life, stood up and peed on them to show its contempt. The Japanese were very frightened and tried to shoot Raffles but, of course, the bullets just bounced off and he laughed at them. A man of iron! So they shot many of our people instead, then crept back later and dragged him away to the museum, like mice round a dead cat. It is a clear sign for us that they do not hold the mandate of Heaven, that they will not be here for long, that the British will surely return. As leaders of the community, we must look up to the heavens, not just down at our own feet. We must be ready when they do return.'

Oh God. It was old man's talk. Tea-leaves, omens, looking at clouds. Loh Ching was sitting there chuckling, just like his grandmother would have done over her I-Ching reading, pretending they were still in China—a China most of them had never actually visited. In the old days, there had hung a great, ironwood panel along the side wall, carved with the curlicued ideogram for 'long life', picked out in gold with the Seven Sages in jade, scattered the length of its sinuousities like pilgrims along a cosmic trail. During the bombardment, it had fallen from the wall and killed a sleeping watchman, lying, in apparent security, beneath it. *Then*, Loh Ching had argued that this had signified the futility of further resistance following lack of foresight. The lesson of his childhood was that there was no point in confronting their credulity. That would make them angry. He must respectfully undermine the old fool from behind. He put a radiant smile of grateful enlightenment on his face, nodded enthusiastically, cringing forward.

'But the British have no money and we have no goods. How may this be?'

Loh Ching sighed again—a dog barks, the caravan moves on—and smiled like a man finally allowed to lay down his trump card.

'We shall extend each other credit. It is to be a matter of trust between us, us and the British.'

HK's head was swimming at the pointless stupidity and sentimentality of it all. The blood suffused his face as he raged internally with the urge to shout and bang on the table and make these dozing idiots feel the bite of reality. Then his breathing settled and his eyes cleared. It was like the tune coming through all the background elaborations on one of the jazz records he collected. The elements began to fall neatly into place like the pieces of a jigsaw. There was a scheme here that could work and then, in a flash, he saw it all. The British prisoners had a central fund into which the wealthy had been allowed to pay money. Such small wages and allowances as came from the Japanese were also paid into it. The merchants would supply goods against IOU's guaranteed by the central fund. Colonel Saito, the camp commandant, he knew, would permit it if a sufficient percentage were paid into his own account. Prices could be pitched high and Saito would make sure just enough stuff got through to the prisoners to keep the system going and all sorts of neat little scams could be bolted on along the way. It would increase the sales of Japanese goods in the short term. If the Japanese prevailed, losses would be small and the merchants would be seen as having co-operated in the promotion of their exports and they would still be in business. If the British returned, they would be patriots and receive payment not in the downward-spiralling cherry blossom that was Japanese banana money but aromatically convertible Straits dollars. He inclined his head.

'As always, Loh Ching sees further than us all.'

* * *

There was no sign, of course, of the little, single-decker bus that used to run from outside the gates, its patient terminal, so that climbing aboard conveyed the sense of using a taxi. Pilchard adjusted his armband, making sure it was visible to all and kept boldly to the very middle of the road, not wanting some rifle-wielding, sharp-shooting guard in a distant watchtower to suddenly spot him from afar and detect in him an escaping prisoner. His scuffing and insecure sandals gave him an old man's shuffling and apologetic gait—a fitting target for any bored sentry—and his heels pained him, the skin cracked and ridged like cheese graters. At the beginning of all this, the CO of the Volunteer Force had addressed them all and told with medical certainty that they had nothing to fear from Japanese infantry. He had listened with incredulity as it was explained, with complete seriousness, that Japanese were all bandy and physically unable to climb out of a trench so that they would perish, in their thousands, in the roadside ditches, like wasps caught and drowned in an old jamjar. They were short-sighted and with eyes so slitty they could not see at all in the dark or in rain. Good Aryans—no wait that was the other lot—good Britons had nothing to fear from them. That had proved to be untrue. They had pursued the retreating British with admirable agility, both in and out of ditches, and their snipers had acquired a fearful reputation for patience and accuracy in both rain and darkness.

Beneath the coconut trees on either side of the road, ramshackle Malay houses had sprouted and dirty, nostril-probing, naked children gathered to watch him walk past with the hungry eyes of tiger cubs not yet grown big enough to eat him. Pilchard felt horribly alone. Among such Muslim folk, there were no barking dogs, naturally, but even cats had become scarce so close to the wire, transformed readily by the camp chefs into rank 'catsoulet', 'catserole', 'purrgedel' and spicy but gamey 'tom yumm'. The grubby children were strangely mute. At the capitulation, it was the sudden silence of the Chinese—a people who normally lived life at full volume—that had been the really terrifying thing while, elsewhere in Malaya, loudly jeering Malays and Indians—in that first exuberance of 'Asia for the Asians'—had spat and thrown stones at the Allied troops as they marched past into captivity and danced with delight in the streets, while villagers had hastened to denounce any Allied forces hiding out in the jungle. It was clear local goodwill could not be taken for granted. Now, they were at the uncomfortable stage of a man waking up from the bleary pleasures of the night to face the intrusion and threat of an alien presence. Yesterday, a boy near the camp had been shot dead for flying a kite. The Japanese, to whom kites were traditional weapons of war, had assumed he must be signalling to someone. Now all children expected to be shot at and childhood was suspended for the hostilities.

The camp around the prison proper covered a vast area, being in fact several army camps collapsed together and penned behind barbed wire. Around the outer fence, left lazily uncleared of brush, was a maze of ditches and crawl-spaces used by the black-marketeers in their nocturnal comings and goings. It was tempting, but too dangerous, to take a short cut through all that tangled *Apama corymbosa*. Yet already, from this distance, he could hear the dull thud of the waves beneath the red cliffs of Tanah Merah, like an artillery salute, calling him down to the southern shore, while the siren rustling of the palm fronds above him spoke of sea and a fresh wind and a distant horizon and he found his steps taking a fork and heading in that direction, eyes suddenly wet with tears at memories of seaside holidays that crowded in unbidden. It took him a good hour to scramble down to the sea, on legs unused now to walking, to a little bay where, he remembered, the sand was purest gold and lapped by gentle waves that faded to a dimpled green. As he stepped out onto the beach and felt the wind that smacked the water, there was a fleeting impression of space and the salt taste of liberty on his lips. That sea there was the same one they looked at in Australia where they were free and there was no real fear—just the petty suburban worries that he would never consider again. Sand, eggtimers, tide, waves—a beach stopped the normal flow of everything, converted the straight line of time's arrow into zigzag back and forth or to circle. It seemed impossible that he could not, by some mere act of will, shift perspective and transport himself across that ocean.

He focused again. The beach had changed. Everywhere were coils of barbed wire rusting on great wooden posts. It was not clear which side had done it. He stopped near the edge of the sand. There could be mines too and any Japanese soldier who saw him here would open fire at once. And then the wind shifted and there came, not the smell of the fresh, open sea but a terrible stench. Pilchard had smelt death often enough in Changi to recognise its clinging, rosaceous scent. Bloated bodies were entangled at the feet of the trestles that held up the wire, dozens, maybe hundreds, half in, half out of the sea, bobbing jauntily in the little waves. The wind carried a castanetting noise, like the busy typing pool of an insurance office at full stretch, that he could not at first identify. Then he realised with horror that each corpse was swarming with a hundred feasting crabs, possibly *Carcinscorpius rotundicauda*, clicking away in frenzy with claws like manic chopsticks. So the rumours had been correct then. The Japanese had taken a terrible revenge for the succour the Singapore Chinese had given their cousins on the Chinese mainland, rounded up anyone on the lists of support organisations, anyone with Triad tattoos, in the end any young men at all who just happened to fall into their hands and brought them to lonely spots like this and Pulau Belakang Mati to be bloodily bayoneted, clubbed to death, machine-gunned along with the Sikhs who had refused to join the INA and the Malays who had so bloodied their noses. He swigged calming water hastily from his bottle, emptying it, and swallowed hard and a trifle unsteadily.

In early accounts of Singapore, this was where the Sea Gypsies had lived and the beaches had been littered with the skulls of those brought here in acts of piracy to be slaughtered. He had written a professionally dry paper about some of their more picturesque customs for the *Journal of the Royal Asiatic Society*. The British had had the bones cleaned up and flung in the sea by the sackload since there had been no invention of physical anthropology as yet to cry out against the waste of specimens. Now the skulls were back and there would be plenty of work for the anthropologists after this lot. As his vision cleared, two khaki-clad Japanese figures appeared, waddling up the beach a few hundred yards away, through a sort of sand mist whipped up by the breeze, gripping probing rifles, boots slung around their necks and bare feet slipping in the powdery sand. They pushed each other playfully, like schoolboys and giggled, the sound of their laughter cut through by the buffeting wind. This south shore was too dangerous, would be too heavily patrolled—asking for trouble. He must choose another way. He ducked back into the long grass and waited until their happy, chattering voices had passed and faded on the wind, then headed back inland through the tall, swishing stems that he identified provisionally as being of the genus *Imperata*.

* * *

In sick bay, Lady Pendleberry shifted her weight in the splintered cane chair. Both she and the chair had seen better days. She fanned herself tiredly, feeling no relief from the hot draught and thought of similar missions of mercy in the Norfolk village of her youth. Then, it had been baskets of coal and turnips for the old and sick, propped on the front of her bicycle, as she did the rounds of the bleak farm cottages. Cold had been the enemy then. These days it was heat and the remedy now was water and coconuts but it was all the same and just as pointless. Others would see the habit of charity as the mark of her simplicity and generosity but it was more that, when simply everyone was so far below you, their own petty social hierarchies faded to nothing and they all deserved sympathy equally. She ought to be knitting as she sat but she was just too tired. A Japanese pullover had been stolen the day before, already unpicked and mated with other old wool. Now it would have to be reknitted into new goods to sell back in town and it was her turn to effect the reincarnation. Mrs Grimes was panting wearily on the thin, stained mattress, her eyes closed against the weak light from outside. No sheet. No blankets. Just the formless cotton shift of the ward that would serve as her shroud when the time came—which would be soon. The bed was not best placed to catch any breeze but could not be moved. It was a heavy, wooden bed that stood out from the chipped enamel bedsteads of the rest of the ward and the reason was that a crystal set was hidden in the leg, that doctors listened to furtively through their stethoscopes during ward rounds. She was not supposed to know but then she had spent her life knowing things she was not supposed to know. Occasionally, it hummed and gave the game away and had to be surreptitiously kicked. Darkness gathered in the corners and she watched it advancing down the ward as night fell. It was supposed to be malaria but all they had to offer was boiled bitter papaya leaves, a cruel parody of quinine that was hardly likely to cheer Mrs Grimes up or break the fever. Everyone thought it tasted like quinine so maybe it did some good but no one knew for sure. But you could see that it went deeper than that and that it was as much despair as anything else. The old woman had just had enough of it all and had decided to go. For tuppence she would go with her, just lie down and feel the sweetness of turf rolling over her. Mrs Grimes drifted back to consciousness and reached out to grasp her hand. The touch was of sandpaper left out in the sun. She would want water which meant the long trek to the far end of the ward and the only jug. But she did not want water.

'It's George I miss,' she whispered through cracked lips. Lady Pendleberry patted and smiled comfortingly. George was the husband, killed in the bombing just before the surrender, some sort of lowly clerk at the waterworks, shabbily chubby—his rank in the scheme of things being fixed by his work cubicle without hatstand and piece of carpet, no telephone, second-hand Morris Minor parked outside—no driver of course. In the colonies you had to get used to people being out of place, usually rather above themselves, often beyond themselves. It was not just that they were not quite top drawer. Many had no drawers at all. And now even such authority and order as there once was had been swept away—except her own position of course, a rock above the flood.

'Do you think I'll see him again, your Ladyship?' She panted. 'In Heaven, I mean?'

'I'm sure you will dear, when you finally get there. But don't you go worrying about that now. Perhaps you would like some water?' The war had affected religious faith in different ways. Some of the women had embraced it with a simple fervour that had them on their knees at all hours, night and day, since only divine intervention could bring an end to all this. But faith could not hide the fact that the chaplain was forever wriggling on the contradiction between an all-powerful and all-knowing, benevolent god and one who let things like this war happen in the first place. Sometimes, according to the chaplain, their present plight was to be seen as a test of that faith, on other days as a punishment for pride. Lady Pendleberry could not see why an all-knowing god could not know the state of her faith just as well as anything else and surely it was viciously cruel to have set up this war as a sort of extended moral driving test? And since god and imperial destiny had parted company, she found that she had rather less time for god than before.

'George was wonderful. I'd never find another like him. In bed. You know. Just wonderful.'

Lady Pendleberry blanched and withdrew the hand that flew to her throat and felt for the absent string of pearls that had always hung there. This was the sort of intimate confidence that made her uncomfortable. Then duty reasserted itself and the hand went back.

'There, there, Mrs Grimes.' She patted again with a little more stiff superiority in her voice. 'Hush now. Don't upset yourself, dear. Just lie quietly and rest. Perhaps I should get you that water.'

'Sex,' said Mrs Grimes with unexpected volume and sitting up. Lady Pendleberry looked around anxiously at the forms in the other beds, mostly sleeping, though some were twitching and kicking in involuntary dance steps. It was vitamin deficiency. They called it 'happy feet'. They tap-danced silently on air for hours. She was aware of the horrible prominence of feet, horny, yellow.

Mrs Grimes sniggered. '... just wonderful.' She was going to make a scene, more intimate revelations, descriptions of beer-fuelled, brutish lust consummated up against the edge of the kitchen table in some artisan's dwelling, not at all the thing.

The lower classes occasionally showed themselves up like that at the end, as was only to be expected but, on the whole, one was surprised by how well some of them behaved. 'Sex,' she said again, loudly, shrilly, almost a shout, half a boast. 'He was wonderful with the sex.' Lady Pendleberry's hand was raised to her own mouth, wanting to hold it over Mrs Grimes's, to stop the cloacal flow of smut. 'Wonderful. I was so lucky in that department. Blessed. A woman couldn't find better. He was special, my George. He wasn't like other men.' Lady Pendleberry squeaked in horror, throat and face glowing with embarrassment and looked wildly at the ranged beds to see if anyone else was listening to this madwoman. Mrs Grimes smiled queenly at her then gulped and spoke with great weight as if fighting to pass on some final distillate of wisdom to the world. 'You see, your Ladyship, in all the years we were married ... he ... never ... once ... *bothered* me. Lovely.' She fell back, head to one side, a gargle in her throat and the pressure from her grasp abruptly ceased. A hand fell on Lady Pendleberry's shoulder and she jumped.

'Has she gone, Betty?' It was Dr Voss standing behind her, the other hand in the pocket of her white coat, stethoscope dangling, cropped hair, comfortingly mannish. Despite herself, a faint smile had crept onto Lady Pendleberry's lips. Hurriedly, she wiped it off.

'She went peacefully. A blessed release. She said she had a good life. At the end she spoke fondly of her husband.' Not exactly a lie. The chair creaked and sagged sceptically beneath her. Dr Voss sighed.

'If only she had hung on a little longer. She really should have, shouldn't have popped off like that.' She made it sound like a failure of etiquette. She leaned forward to ear level and whispered excitedly. 'We've got drugs coming, Betty. Anti-malarial, painkillers!' Her mind swam with pictures of crisp white

75

boxes, shiny phials. 'Imagine! From the Chinese merchants of all things. They're giving us credit. Who would have thought after some of the things we've said about them? If they had heard! There are times you just stop believing in the goodness of people and then something like this happens, so kind, so selfless.' She pulled Mrs Grimes's smock down with a reflex gesture of modesty and walked away to make the funeral arrangements, her step a little lighter but with tears in her eyes and her fists clenched on her damp hankie at the rediscovered generosity of mankind.

* * *

Pilchard found the devastation in the town astonishing. In the heat of actual conflict, it was not surprising that windows had been broken and even people killed but it was as if nothing whatever had been done since to even tidy up the mess, as if people themselves had been broken. Everywhere were gutted houses, looking as though their roofs had been knocked open with a giant spoon and their contents just scooped out. Blasted cars littered the roads and blocked the drainage ditches and unburied remains lay everywhere, pretty much where they had fallen, a prey to demented, slavering dogs who had clearly not coped very well with the undomestication so suddenly forced upon them. On one corner a richly red Chinese temple seemed to be doing a roaring trade, belching out clouds of clove-scented joss smoke. Chinese had not only selves and family to feed but also hungry ghosts. Yet, after the over-gleaned and desertic surroundings of the camp, everything here was still richly wasteful. One or two houses still held furniture and private possessions, possibly even food. He paused in front of a shoddy, jerry-built bungalow, Public Works Department, no porch, lower clerks for the use of. At the side was a space to park a car and a tap. It was dripping beguilingly.

There must be water from a rain tank on the roof somewhere. He turned in and crunched across weed-dappled gravel and into the welcome, stencilled shade of a scarlet bougainvillea. The tap gargled hoarsely then delivered up warm, brackish water, not exactly fresh but a roof source should be safe enough. He ducked his head under the flow, gasping gratefully, then carefully refilled and stoppered the bottle. Having come so far, it would be foolish not to have a quick look round. He scuffed up the steps and pushed on the door. Locked. A good sign, like an archaeologist finding the seal on an Egyptian tomb still intact. Round the back were French windows. He took a rock from the edge of the flower bed and paused in front of the glass, puzzled by his own reluctance to break it and so cross a line that would redefine the world of cultural regression and his place in it. It shattered under a single blow and he reached in and found it had been unlocked all along. In like Flynn, as the Australians said. So, now he was no longer a Roman citizen but one of the unwashed barbarians after the Fall, a hunter-gatherer, lighting a campfire on the mosaic floor of their banqueting hall and eating torn flesh with his bare hands before relieving himself, grunting, belching and scratching, in a corner. It had come to that.

Inside was a living room that said 'poor-but-honest'—neat but careworn in a way that showed too much washing and cleaning of cheap material and a space too small to ever be cool. The air bore the lingering kerosene undertones of Flit. On the sideboard, picture frames displayed white faces of women with big noses and bad teeth. A tobacco jar—empty—displaying the arms of Morecambe-on-Sea. On the lino, the pattern had gone but the surface was still polished—clearly had a good servant—while a runner merely accentuated rather than concealed the baldness, like a bad wig, and led him through a door into a passageway and down to the kitchen that glowed behind lowered blinds. He glanced into the seedy bathroom whose air was sweet with the caramel of mildew. It showed the usual sad housedruff that reveals the seamy underside of all our lives. A tin of prickly heat powder lay spilled onto the floor. A towel, clean but shredding at one end and two socks, whole but unmatched, abandoned orphans. On the edge of the bath, surviving slivers of old bars of soap had been parsimoniously pressed into a new lump, like an uprooted tumour, still bearing great pennypinching thumbprints and in one corner of the ceiling, a growth of mould had benefited from human absence to stage a great breakthrough and was now moving down the side wall in an unopposed advance. A poor white man in the East had no purpose, like an honest one in government. An image of the appalling Erica Rosenkrantz flashed into his mind, at the club, irritably cigarette-stubbing and snapping. 'People should not be allowed to be poor. It makes them such a ghastly bore.' The kitchen breathed old meat curries and onions but, compared to the prison, it was a glittering treasurehouse of cutlery and pans. Flies were still optimistically buzzing round a meat safe where something had decayed to a diarrhoeal smear on a plate. An unexpected sophistication was the long-snouted EverReady electric gas-lighter on the tabletop. He knew where to look. In the kitchen cabinet, lined with old newspapers, were a tin of baked beans and one of rice pudding—the 'Chinese wedding cake' of his childhood. In the drawer a tin-opener. The beans he set carefully to one side. The rice pudding he attacked, ripping open the lid, whimpering, sitting on the floor—barbarian that he now was—and sucking it down like warm and lumpy catarrh straight from the tin, cutting his nose on the lid but not caring. He wiped out the inside with a finger and sucked it. He had cut the finger too. With satiety came the urge to sleep, just like Goldilocks in the house of the Three Bears. He could not read the Japanese chit, taken from his pocket that he was bleeding onto. It looked like a waterfall of beautiful spiders. Was he given a time limit to get to the Museum? He had no idea. Anyway, watches were the first things the Nips had taken so that, under the sleeves of their uniforms, some wore several up their arms, like the spivs in cartoons. But that was another problem for another time. It must be about noon. Too hot to walk anyway. He picked up his tin and—fingersucking—made for one of the bedrooms, a real double bed, sheets, comforting softness, muted heat, ear-damping silence and lay down on his habitual side, leaving unacknowledged space for an absent other. Sleep.

He awoke in terror and the knowledge that he was no longer alone in the house. Motes of dust twirled in the sunlit air leaking through the blinds but the silence had a deliberate premeditated sound. The Three Bears had returned. He no longer remembered the sugary ending of the fairy tale of his childhood but it was a good bet that, according to the original version of the aptly-named Brothers Grimm, he was about to be consumed by them. Surreptitious noises are always much more audible than blatant ones. The skulking menace crept softly along on the other side of the bedroom wall, the length of the tight and creaking corridor, and entered the kitchen. There was a soft tinkle as the cutlery drawer was pulled open. He could picture whoever was out there looking down on the gutted rice pudding tin and observing its freshness. Who's been eating my porridge? There came a click that he recognised unmistakably as the sound of a rifle being cocked, then soft shuffling coming closer and he stared in horror at the slow clockwise turn of the doorknob. It was flung open and a screaming Japanese soldier leaped in, rifle raised to fire. Pilchard had his tin of baked beans still clutched in his hand and—unthinkingly—flung it like a grenade in full-force cricket delivery. The soldier just had time to look briefly surprised and fire his rifle into the pink glass ceiling light as it struck him straight between the eyes and he shimmied to the floor—knocked for six—beaned—in a parody of a stage swoon. Pilchard was out of bed in a flash, looking down on the sprawled figure. As a soldier, he should—he knew—now make sure, seize the rifle and stick the bayonet, snarling, into his victim's chest with applied body weight, twist and withdraw as they taught you in the OTC but it was somehow different doing it to a prone man rather than a sack of sawdust. As a doctor, he should ascertain whether he was still alive and offer succour. But there could be no talking his way out of this. The line between assault and murder was irrelevant to the Japanese so he must act like a museum curator and just put as much distance between himself and the scene of a crime as possible. He stepped over the still-prostrate form and set off towards the back door, hesitated, hand on doorknob, and came back. The tin of beans was dented but unbroached. He retrieved it.

Outside, a Raleigh bicycle was leant against the wall in dowager shades of British Racing Green. He noted the pared saddle and Sturmey Archer gears with approval, another dream of childhood. Clearly this was loot to be taken back and, anyway, according to the new morality, anything not in actual use was unwanted by its owner. On the rear pannier was a steel helmet, a tinkling symbol that he flung into the bushes, then cocked a bold leg over the crossbar and pedalled away, hell for leather, towards the concealing city.

* * *

On the whole, Captain Oishi disliked the military. Raised modestly by a hushed and widowed mother in Kyoto, surrounded by priests and cherry blossom and ancient temples, he was at heart a gentle soul and he struggled to keep the distaste he felt for the General off his face. The army had taught him the conformities of swearing and gambling and visiting prostitutes with publicly feigned enjoyment but brought few deeper changes or accomplishments to set beside his university studies in calligraphy. And he was instinctively kind. Occasionally he had ended up comforting the comfort women who sobbed on his slim shoulder as the meter of fleshly pleasure ran unheeded. He had been puzzled to find himself sleeping with the Austrian female, Erica. They had all been at the Raffles Hotel, she with a group of his fellow officers all loud with drink, worrying at bowls of peanuts with unwashed fingers. As a young man trained to be solicitous of the needs of older people, he had been sent to find her a tonic water. Rank was never totally ignored, even on such informal occasions, and youthfulness was always punished ruthlessly by messmates. She sipped it and made a sour face. But then it was a sour drink.

'Young man, when I ask for a tonic water, I expect it to come with gin in it. When I ask for a gin and tonic, I expect it to come with *two* gins in it. Also there is no ice. Instruct that short barman to fill a tall glass with ice and pour it in.'

He had approached the protesting barman, an ensoured Chinese, and coaxed gin, glass and supplementary ice cubes from him as he railed against wasteful Western ways. 'Ice. Ice. White people. Always they ask for ice. Japanese do not ask for ice. I have no more ice. At least, I have ice but not frozen yet. Do not tell others to come to me for ice'—and given them to her.

'This is special,' he had explained earnestly. 'Asian peoples do not take ice. They only have ice for you.' At which she had screeched with laughter, pinched his cheeks and begun singing some silly song about the stars being out tonight and telling if it was cloudy or bright and that had been it. It had been most interesting to see blonde pubic hair, though he pushed away the thought that, in that dim, curtained light, it might just have been grey.

The General was away supervising some tunnelling work down by the docks. The General was keen on tunnelling and preferred always to do it alone. Captain Oishi liked orchids and reading. Their interests did not greatly intersect, but, as in any successful marriage, that was quietly accepted.

A great, grey trunk had been delivered from Professor Tanakadate at the Museum, labelled 'Cocos-Keeling' and set by the door. He had been resisting it all morning, eyeing it shyly through lowered lashes, like a boy eyes a girl across the floor at a school dance, as he busied himself with tedious paperwork. He finally dumped it all in his wire out-tray. Now he deserved a little treat. He went over and looked down on the exotic box with a little tickle of nervousness. A box was exciting. You never knew what could be inside.

The tin trunk, of Birmingham manufacture, bore the stencilled name of RA Pilchard. He approached as you might an unexploded bomb, examining it carefully from all sides before he undid the straps riveted to the lid, unclicked the hasp, opened it slowly. The interior was painted in swirly, fake woodgrain of an almost ginger colour. Gummed on the inside lid was a list of folders, each tied with beige tape. They seemed to have been roughly rummaged through by someone in search of valuables—that would be the Kempeitei—papers were scattered everywhere and out of order. Checked against the list on the lid, some folders were missing entirely. The only unmolested one was labelled *Raffles*. He took it out and laid it gently on the desk and pulled one end of the tape so that the bow unloosed and the flap popped enticingly open like—he thought—a tightly unlaced bosom in an American film. He spread out the fan of loose sheets, settled neatly in his chair and began to read.

* * *

Pilchard could feel the muscles in the small of his back going into seizure, unused to such exercise. His body was beginning that slow process of betrayal called ageing. He tried to keep his mind busy. In younger days he had been an excellent cyclist and in the blank year after graduation, he had sold encyclopedias door-to-door from the back of his bike—a sort of encycled encyclopedia—reading the books in the long breaks between sales, sucking in yet more pointless information. The war seemed to have wiped all such knowledge away. He knew nothing. He was an empty vessel. He had no idea how to survive. Everywhere on the houses, fluttered little Japanese flags, squares of white with a red blob in the centre like used Elastoplasts. As he pedalled through the fishing village of Bedok, there were gradually more people on the streets, more signs of life struggling to resume, also more Japanese resisting that normalisation. He knew he was required to bow deeply, with alleged respect, to all of them, a requirement which was difficult to satisfy on a bicycle with a crossbar. Differences in interpretation would obviously exist and, sooner or later, one of them would object to his wobbled, sketchy nod of the head and step out into the road, with hand raised, to stop him for routine humiliation, violence and confiscation. He was too noticeable, anyway, on a fine bike like this that would invite envy and risk being remembered. In Katong, he passed the big, fake-Elizabethan mansions—some with rampaging rhododendrons but most razored to the orders of snake-fearing mems—facing out to sea and all looking incongruously like Surrey golf clubhouses, favoured by the wealthy, but all now with their Japanese staff cars parked shinily outside, chauffeurs polishing and posing. Finally, he halted in front of one of the big *peranakan* houses, doubtless the fancy seaside villa of some Chinese merchant, climbed stiffly off and leant his machine, with deep regret, against a wall that swarmed with bright ceramic tiles of chipped dragons and cracked bats. It shut off a large private garden shaded by various varieties of *Banksia*—what optimists termed 'trees of Heaven' and pessimists 'turd trees' from their elongated flower spikes. The bicycle would not stay there long. Within hours it would be broken down—frame, saddle, tyres and resold all over the island. Flat inner tubes at inflated prices. Already, a teenage boy in Oxford bags was eyeing it with blatant interest, from between the parted shutters of the first floor. Then a big American saloon screeched to a halt beside him and a young Chinese in a skimpy suit climbed out, reached back for a briefcase, glared at him and flounced into the house with shouting and gesticulation. Everyone lived with their old resentments. Pilchard shrugged and clutched his tin of beans and started walking again, while civilians dodged around him with downcast eyes as if he were excrement left embarrassingly on the pavement.

At this hour of the afternoon, the brothel-dwellers of Geylang had barely got out of bed to rest. By some odd numerical convention, only the hotels in even-numbered lanes were for whoring, odd numbers being reserved for perfectly respectable small businesses. A headache nested with insidious softness behind his eyes. Girls of all shapes and sizes were staggering about in various stages of careless undress, spitting and coughing over cigarettes, rubbing at eyes made sore by too much makeup and bar fug, groaning and snarling, scratching themselves between the legs. Later they would slurp down noodles outside the stews.

It was a relatively muted area at the moment, off duty, though later the dregs of the army would sink down here, as always, to be debauched and cheated in a token manner. Geylang had been servicing lascars and rolling sailors—all at sea on land—for a hundred years. At this hour, it was not to be expected that they would look after the passer-by with casual lust or even commercial appraisal and, as Pilchard passed by on his lonely Odyssey, the residents could not be bothered to make even a fleeting show of desire or desirability and, for his part, he felt no more attraction than he would at the zoo. He remembered vaguely that, in the best Japanese brothels, even those around Middle Street, normal practice, at the turn of the century, had actually been to exhibit the girls in cages so that they might be closely examined by the rising sons among their clientele who would then select one by lighting his pipe and passing it to her. A consenting puff sealed the deal and the pipe was passed back politely and silently to its owner. Sex would then be conducted in a series of mute thrusts into an appropriate orifice, even through the bars, without the exchange of a single word, since that would constitute excessive familiarity. How to suck seed in business. He realised, with sudden insight, that men do not pay prostitutes for having sex with them, they pay them for going away quietly afterwards without making a fuss about it, which was why non-communication was an honoured tradition here. Now all those highly reputed houses of ill repute had gone, swept away after the First World War as the Japanese became obsessed with their nation's image in the world. He felt a sudden weary urge to just sit and eat his beans but knew that the rice-pudding was more than enough, swinging, as it was, in his shrunken belly like a cricket ball in a sock. Anyway, later he might be really hungry for who knew when he would eat again? How would he buy food? For his medical services in the camp, he had received a stipend of 10 cents a month. In his pocket, nested a princely thirty cents. He realised that imprisonment, with its guarantee of one bad meal a day, had been freedom of a sort. Now he was turned loose and become immediately the slave to his own needs.

In front of him lay a major bridge over the Kallang river—

at this season a thick, malodorous trickle—with troops clustered around the checkpoint like flies on a dead dog. He sighed. This would mean trouble but trouble that could not be avoided, since, if he headed upstream, the river divided into two which would mean two checkpoints not one and each less busy so with fewer distractions for the sentries. A bullock cart lumbered up with a load of pineapples, blocking passage and halting all traffic as the soldiers helped themselves to fruit despite the wailing protestations of the Indian driver. He slipped the beans inside his shirt, took a deep breath and marched towards them all in the blank heat. Close up, the river smelt really bad, worse than he had ever known. The breakdown in sanitation affected the whole city then, not just Changi.

In an odd little Geylang dance, more a hokey-cokey really—left leg in, left leg out—he bowed deeply, shimmied his armband at them and fished out his chit from left breast pocket, presenting it bowed and two-handed. The soldier, a dumpy little man with a damp, worried look and a pineapple, fretted over it, pushed him roughly to one side. 'Speedo! Speedo!' and began shouting.

'Don't know your pass from your elbow?' muttered smiling Pilchard, visually all teeth and subservience.

A thin-lipped officer stopped looking over the edge, came across and studied the pass, gripping the balustrade all the way like a man suffering from vertigo. 'Stamforod Road?'

Pilchard bobbed enthusiastically and grinned like a madman. 'Hai, hai. Stamforod Road. Museum.' What the hell was it called now? 'Syonan Hakubutsu Kan.' The officer's face lit up. He giggled.

'Stamforod Road. I think you mean Kempeitei HQ!' He laughed and slapped playfully. 'I think you no like Kempeitei HQ!' Pilchard laughed back, then they both realised they were laughing and being friendly and stopped doing it. 'Syonan Hakubutsu

Kan.' The officer muttered and looked formally irritated as he squiggled some more spiders on the chit and pushed the paper back into Pilchard's hand. Then he took the guard's pineapple, slapped him with casual violence round the face and waved Pilchard dismissively away and went back to looking over the edge, as if deciding whether or not he wanted to jump.

As he hobbled along, stiff-backed, penguin-like, Pilchard was suddenly aware of other smiling faces. He was barely conscious, unfeeling, could take nothing in but the heat bouncing back from the road. All around, on the railing supports and at shoulder height, were impaled other heads, neatly sliced and trimmed at the neck like fresh-picked pineapples, mouths set in Mona Lisa rictus, skins a variety of shades of chocolate, sepia and yellow—Asian faces of all kinds at varying levels of decay but all tending towards uniform blue-black—death the great leveller. Beneath each was slung a sign in a variety of tongues. The English version read, 'I was a looter.' A European head would round out the collection nicely, he thought absently. Pilchard clutched his beans, that now seemed to burn in his hand, fixed his eyes on the road ahead and hurried on towards Lavender. Killing, then looting—two capital offences in a single afternoon—was not a bad score, if he lived to see the end of it.

A hot wind was gusting along the streets and he was horribly thirsty but Lavender was another place that specialised in the purely professional slaking of thirsts, for the low ramshackle houses had once been the favourite low resort of sexually rampant Australian troops—boys of an age where the male body is simply a noisy device for converting food and drink into lust and semen—now all penned back up in sober Changi chastity. It was clear that the Japanese had not yet taken up the slack but the ethnographer in him wondered whether the girls really even noticed the difference, so crushing was the weight of the military upon Singapore even in peace. In his early days here, like all newcomers, he had come to taste the local wine, excited by the heady eroticism of smooth Asian skin—its pores saturated with spice and coconut oil—the flowing, black hair and had sat, worshipping, before golden calves For two dizzy months they had all been beautiful and then familiarity had set in with its power to sap and drain enthusiasm. He had not come since.

Many of the bars were shut, seemingly for ever. Passers-by avoided him, afraid of being seen around a European leper, but he felt that, had they known of the thirty cents weighing down his pocket, they would have been on him like a pack of wolves. Most of the buildings here had been blasted by mortar and artillery fire and people were living under sheets in the ruins, taking water from standpipes in the middle of the street and hanging washing out to dry on the shattered roof beams. The markets that had flourished in the streets had withered into parody. A beggar sat smiling in the street and indicated a bloodied kneestump to all comers with the open-handed gesture of one who had just pulled off a difficult conjuring trick while, behind him, a corner stall that had once sold cigarettes now sold cigarette ends for reuse as if this were a totally normally activity. Yet, despite the deprivations, when the wind blew across, Little India still managed to reek of curried mutton and hot fat. He dodged around Bugis Street with its volatile, patrolling transvestites and headed towards Beach Road where shading trees tempered glittering views of the sea. There stood the arrogant Raffles Hotel, now renamed the *Syonan Ryokan*, still off-limits to other ranks—but Japanese other ranks now—and still striking attitudes behind its luxuriant *Ravenala madagascariensis*, Traveller's Palm—though not, of course, a true palm but related to the banana—its undaunted leaves shuffled by a hot but pleasant wind that buffeted in from the ocean and perhaps reminded it of home. Rickshaws with specially scrubbed pullers were ranged outside—the acceptable face of the East—as large cars purred up under the glass awning, disgorging sleek Japanese of both military and civilian stamp. On the ground floor, the bars and restaurants still hummed with cheerfully non-partisan profit and, in the upstairs rooms with their white telephones and soft furnishings—as was common knowledge—Korean 'comfort women' were deferentially available to officers around the clock beneath pink lightbulbs It occurred to him that the entire British Empire was really nothing more than the biggest whorehouse in the whole of Asia—one enormous ethnographic seraglio—where the very idea of 'a good time' was a sad but powerful delusion. And right on cue, the doors flew open and Erica Rosenkranz came clumping down the steps with a young Japanese officer on her arm making that characteristic grimace that, for her, replaced a smile, an opening wide of the mouth with simultaneous peevish crinkling.

As the wife of the erstwhile Austrian ambassador, Erica had officially progressed, in the course of the war, from 'neutral' to 'enemy alien', following the *Anschluss*. But the British had dealt kindly with both her and her husband, regarding them as sinned against rather than sinners, arguably innocent victims of a hostile invasion, thereby still allies of a sort, so that her enthusiastic embracing of 'friendly belligerent' status under the Japanese now smacked of ingratitude. After the Fall, her husband had answered the summons and returned circuitously home to what was now Nazi Germany's new Ostmark province but, since doubts remained over their reception there, they had chosen that Erica should stay just where she was. In age too she had long sought to remain exactly where she was, dressed too young, wore too much makeup, dyed her hair too optimistic a shade. All this went hand-in-hand with a wardrobe of gestures and mannerisms that someone had unwisely told her—at the age of twelve—

were winsome. As she approached her fiftieth birthday like an unexploded mine, they were no longer so.

At first, she had filled her dowager time with ladylike shopping and gardening, the delicate sécateur-wielding-in-white-gloves type that fiddled and fussed, more hairdressing than horticulture. Then she had conceived a fancy for botanical drawings, the cultivation of *Nepenthes* pitcher plants, the collection of botanical ephemera and gardening hats. Then she had started coming to the museum and gardens at all hours, seeking out Pilchard and demanding the identification of whatever bunch of leaves she happened to be clutching in her liver-spotted hands. In vain, the resident botanists told her, without conscious irony, that only her fruiting parts were diagnostic. Dr Post quailed before her aggressive femininity and before long, by a series of outflanking manoeuvres, she had wormed her way into becoming a patron of both museum and gardens. Within any public institution, a patron is a 'friendly belligerent' of the most feared kind for all learned institutions fear the public, as the staff inevitably come to run them exclusively for their own convenience. From there, she had moved triumphantly into occupation of the chair of the Gardening Club and finally the Orchid Club had fallen to her. She now paused on the bottom stair of the Raffles Hotel and shouted across the forecourt, unwilling to step out into sunshine.

'Dr Pilchard! Come here!' She waved her bag. 'At once! I have been trying to contact you. My monkey cups have sprung a leak—some disease I think. My urgent calls have gone unanswered for several months.' Pilchard paused and considered. If everyone felt ill all the time, as he did now, the world would be a very different place. Perhaps saints were just men with a good digestion. He might just walk on and ignore her and her monkey cups or pitcher plants. Or there was no reason, now that the world had ended, not to tell the old cow to just get thoroughly and joyfully stuffed. The occupation could yet prove liberating. No reason except a lifelong experience of being taught to seek to please. No reason except that unpredictable Japanese companion who was sucking the debris of terrible English fruit cake out of his teeth, had that haunted look that men often had around Erica and might well want to let out his rage and frustration in slaps and kicks. He sighed and crossed the forecourt, bowed low to him in appeasement though she would think it was to her.

'I'm so sorry, Mrs Rosenkrantz. I'm afraid I was quite literally detained.'

She pouted. and looked at his legs, devoid of the long white kneesocks that alone made men's legs decent. He was gripped by a momentary fear that she might be admiring them but that, after Changi diet, was mercifully impossible.

'Oh please don't explain', she crowed. 'Nowadays it seems everyone has excuses. Excuses are always so boring.' She flapped her sequined bag like a fan, chasing excuses away as you might an irritating wasp. 'I am sure someone might have given you a message. It is scarcely providing a proper service to the public to just wander off and abandon your post.'

'I expect you have been overwatering them—your pitcher plants, monkey cups.' It was the catch-all answer to all public enquiries about plants, undeniable since 'over' was meaningless. *Nepenthes* were amongst the most inept of Nature's plants, given to rot and dehydration, endless trouble to cultivators in their unceasing demands. It was only appropriate that Erica had conceived a predatory empathy for them, enticing victims with their sticky secretions and then devouring their dead flesh. If rumour was to be believed, the presence of an absent husband or, rather, the absence of a present one did nothing to deny Erica a vigorous sexual life. She had scandalously acquired much younger Chinese dance-partners that she had taken openly to the Germania club, there to foxtrot interracially. Such astonishing behaviour had been made comprehensible to the expats by the rumour that she was really from the Italian end of Austria and Neopolitans—as all British and Austrians knew—were scarcely European at all. Her Japanese companion, tired of being ignored in a foreign language, clicked his heels and inclined his head cautiously.

'Oishi, Captain.'

'Pilchard, Lieutenant, but different army.'

Erica raised her index finger to her mouth then held it up like a sailor testing the wind and did one of her puckish little-girl-having-sudden-idea expressions. 'I think, Dr Pilchard, given the inconvenience the Captain has been put to, it would be the least you could do to offer him a personal tour of the museum. My car is just here.'

They were sated with cake and tea, maybe they even had a stimulating cocktail or two under their belts, cooled and rested. Pilchard was hungry, weary, hot and not very well. As the sun beat down with swimming heat on his bare head, the world began to lurch and spin with craziness and the effort of holding things steady was abruptly just too much. Perspiration that he could not spare suddenly douched his back and the air lay heavy and immovable in his lungs. By the time the mist cleared, he found himself already in the car, in the front seat, heading down Stamford Road with the boys' school on the right. His legs were shaking. Voices came from the bottom of a deep well and the nearby sea roared in his ears as in a nautilus shell. He struggled back to the surface and now there were soldiers everywhere, a barrier across the road, some sort of a checkpoint. Over them, towered the authority of the YMCA, an architectural absurdity of half-tudoring—in a country that was innocent of Tudors—turrets and balconies and bay windows and an irrelevant *porte cochère* stuck on the facade like a clown's red nose. On the little green at the front, a crowd of young Chinese men were standing, silent with fear in the hot sun, hands behind their backs—possibly bound—with soldiers strutting up and down. And there, shuffling down the line, was a figure of horror, all in black, hooded—the Grim Reaper. Occasionally, it would pause, stretch out a gloved hand and touch someone silently on the shoulder, claiming a victim for death. The chosen one would be led away and stowed on the back of a truck.

'Informer,' said Captain Oishi, standing up in the car and beaming with satisfaction. 'You see the Chinese are keen to work with us to root out antisocial elements. Those criminals will be shot.'

Those, Pilchard suddenly realised, leaning wanly against the hot metal, were not army uniforms the soldiers were wearing but Kempeitei. The secret police. Even the Japs were afraid of them. He plunged deep once more into resigned turbulent dizziness then was swimming up to booming consciousness again. His eyes jerked open. Now there were schoolboys everywhere in thin white shirts and trousers—one, in glasses, painfully lanky, great dark eyes, Chinese hair spikily resisting the imposition of a Western haircut.

'If I'm staying a few days …' he was saying smoothly to Captain Oishi, speaking with the same excessive plausibility with which—at home—schoolboys presented forged letters excusing themselves from games, '… I'll go home first—just over there—and get my things.'

The boy set off with light, determined steps, firmly not looking back. Oishi dithered, seemed to feel an unwilling pang of sympathy, perhaps saw himself ten years ago and hesitated then, clearly anxious not to lose face in front of Erica and this other southern barbarian by shouting, waved to the sentries to let him go.

'One schoolboy more or less,' he shrugged, laughing, dismissing duty and embarrassment with a casual smile. 'What difference does that make to the world? What's your name?' he called.

The boy threw a smile back over his shoulder but did not stop. 'Lee. Harry Lee.'

Pilchard's world dissolved and disappeared again as if sucked down a vast clockwise plughole. Then he felt tiles, cool and solid under his cheek and cold on his bare legs. He was shivering. Looking up, there was the Singapore stone, its Indic script winking ruby red in the last rays of the setting sun that shone through the hole in the roof, still proclaiming its enigmatic message to an uncomprehending world. He was back in the museum. In his hand was a can of beans.

'Shut?' Erica was saying to someone he could not see in the echoing void. 'Shut? Well, I really think it's just not good enough. What sort of a place is this? Look at the state of Dr Pilchard, drunk as a lord—*as a lord*—and it's barely mid-afternoon. Make no mistake. I shall be writing to the General about it.' She stamped a little, slingbacked heel right in front of Pilchard's face. 'The Captain was quite looking forward to a tour. You have disappointed him. He also likes orchids and would love to the see the Gardens. I really think you people might all make a bit more effort. It's so selfish of you. Don't you know there's a war on?'

* * *

Professor Tanakadate's conscience had been troubling him over the matter of Dr Pilchard. He had behaved like an American cowboy—absurdly—waving that gun around that he had found on the grass outside. It was not even loaded. When he had ordered him shipped off to prison, he had lost control and given way to pique, to a momentary anger before barbarian behaviour, without realising the power he now held over other lives. It was as if, in his sleep, he had been connected to some mighty, amplifying machine that converted him into a weather god, turned his least tweak of displeasure into vast thunderstorms that might flash and roar and wash away whole villages. That was not the way a scholar should behave, especially towards a respected colleague. For a vulcanologist, the war had been a profound disappointment. He had hoped that Japanese expansion might bring him his very own volcano, even if only a small one. Just across the sea from here were some of the best, most active volcanoes in the world but they had all been assigned to lesser men, much less senior than himself, while he had been ordered to look after a museum and a dormant botanical garden. It was a situation that burned with injustice. Yet he could see that Pilchard had suffered in Changi and the considerable time that the man had spent there had given him time to appreciate the standard of his work from traces left within the museum. It had been the initial misfortune of Pilchard to remind him of an alcoholic Australian vulcanologist, encountered on Mount Fuji just before the war, in the act of relieving himself, a desecration of both science and culture. Yet the men here, Catchpole, Post and Pilchard were fellow-researchers, bound to him by values and visions that lay beyond narrow nationalism and mere profit. True, they were sloppy, shambling men who, like all Westerners, suffered from an irritating lack of bodily control but their minds were as focused as his own. His anger shamed him. After all, his own side was little better. When he had arrived in Syonanto, he had found the Kempeitei trucks lazily parked all over the lawns of the museum forecourt and the Botanic Gardens, out of town, were criss-crossed with latrine trenches and strewn with discarded military hardware. The overflow from Japanese military headquarters at the Bukit Timah end of the gardens was elbowing arrogantly into horticultural space and the gardeners had already been conscripted as porters of army supplies, while great brass earhorns, acoustic aircraft location devices, 'war tubas', had been parked all over the grounds. Tanakadate had struck back with classical calligraphy, firm, scholarly brushstrokes, more artistic than was strictly necessary for mere communication, and set up signs invoking—quite illegally—the highest Japanese authorities to declare both museum and gardens a specially protected space out of bounds to all ranks. He had visited the commanders of both neighbour organisations, drunk studiedly deferential tea and let drop his close comradeship with General Yamashita in dewy-eyed accounts of sunlit, boyish romps together, sighingly recalling childhood like a secret conspiracy from which they, as outsiders, were excluded. In this way he had sown doubt and—like everything else in the rich tropical soil—it had thrust down roots and flourished, so that he was now seen as a man with special, and possibly limitless, personal connections, a man not to be crossed lightly and a man whose lawns and fenced boundaries were not to be crossed at all.

He motioned reluctant, disdainful Catchpole over and, together, they shouldered Pilchard up, like in a scene from *Aida*, and into the library where generations had demonstrated its suitability as a place for sleep. He felt surprisingly light to himself. Catchpole's dangling hearing aid bashed Pilchard in the face, unheeded, at every step and cut his lip. Pilchard's only half-formed thought was that it was curious that Dr Post was the one who was *not* deaf.

'There, there,' comforted Tanakdate vaguely fatherly, settling him in a most uneasy chair and modestly folding down the legs of his shorts as he wiped away blood with a snowy handkerchief, plucked from back pocket. 'You'll feel better after some food. Give him some tea, Dr, Catchpole.' Catchpole scowled a 'I'm-not-a-servant-you-know' scowl but fetched, poured, then seized the tin of beans, swallowing eager saliva. There was a big, fat fly swimming in the tea, frothing it up with its death throes.

'I'll take these. No need for you to carry the can, as it were. There's not much on the market of course, old man, but thanks to my old fishing contacts we've got loads of crabs. Make fantastic soup. Better than these beans. Crabs, for some reason, seem to be doing very well this year. Just wait till you get a mouthful of my crab soup, old man. Put hair on your ... Oh! ... Oh I say!'

Tanakadate glided gently away to the window, as if defining Pilchard's thin strings of vomit out of existence by not looking. A minor social *faux pas*, he seemed to say, do not speak of it. Instead, he peered down at Pilchard's dirty yellow pass through pince-nez glasses and wrinkled his brow.

'It says here ... Actually, it's not really clear. There is a muddle. It seems to imply ... but then another soldier has written that you were definitely to come here *not* next door ... Surely, they would never have sent you without an escort if they had meant ... A useful ambiguity.' He looked up with sudden decision. 'I think perhaps we had better send you out to our colony, the Botanic Gardens, as soon as possible. Quieter there. Much more peaceful. Safer from our noisy neighbours.' He glanced out of the window. The grey trucks, with their loads of swaying prisoners, were already reversing out and moving away, crashing gears, engines revving, in a cloud of blue smoke and dust. Silence descended like a blackout curtain.

* * *

They were back in the same room again in Hill Street. HK felt for the comforting gap in the chair's pearl inlay with his little finger. The whole chair felt somehow even bigger today, himself even smaller. He was pleasantly astonished that his feet still reached to the floor. Even to himself, his voice bore tones of piping adolescence though he was already treading the outer edge of youth. In a couple of years, when people complained about 'young people', they would not mean him It was something to do with the unfathomable antiquity of Loh Ching and his own ruthless New Year haircut that made his ears stick out, though there were few other signs of the festival. The shops were empty of new clothes, fish and oranges. There were none of the necessary ingredients for the cake his mother made tearfully every year to distribute to relatives. No cheery British Tommies were abroad to shout, 'I fuck. You enjoy!' at respectable Chinese matrons, in emulation of New Year greetings. The Japanese had even banned the explosions and detonations of firecrackers that were so soothing to local ears. Later, he would go to Lily, who would console him, compliment him on his eager manliness, make everything all right again.

'Thank you all for coming. I have been asked to communicate to you a message from the Japanese commander.' He coughed nervously and his throat knotted itself and it seemed for a second that it would never relax and let him speak. 'Please understand that I am simply the channel by which this message is to be communicated by others, a mere conduit.' Loh Ching smiled to himself as if hearing another word. HK paused and picked up a paper from the tabletop so they could actually see he was reading it.

'The Chinese community of Syonanto is hereby presented with the opportunity of performing a gesture of loyalty towards the Emperor and Dai Nippon to dissociate themselves from treasonable acts supporting the Emperor's enemies in Manchukuo, previously known as Manchuria. As an expression of their gratitude towards their liberators, whose benevolent protection they enjoy, they are invited to make a gift of $50,000,000 towards the costs of their liberation from colonial rule of which they are the joyful beneficiaries. This money to be paid in full within six months of the above date.' There was a collective gasp followed by a high-pitched buzz of outraged conversation. He looked at the angry or incredulous expressions around the table and his whole face seemed to collapse. His voice was empty and flat. 'Truly, I do not know what to do. I have been to see the General and explained that this is a fantastic sum, way beyond our means. He declares the order to have come straight from Tokyo and that, if we fail to meet it, he will be forced to take harsh measures against us.'

There was a shocked silence. Then, at the far end of the table, Loh Ching coughed softly. All eyes swivelled towards him. His voice was a dry rustle, like wind through rice stalks.

'This is a serious matter and I am surprised that Mr Fong seems to have learned nothing from the British. What did they do whenever they wished to increase taxation or tighten immigration regulations, or when we asked them to lower import duties? First they would need to consult, appoint a special committee to examine what might be done in the greatest possible detail and draft a report. If the change might be unpopular, it would be necessary to prepare public opinion for the sake of public order, which would take even more time. It might be necessary to implement any such change gradually in stages to prevent hot-headed young men taking to the streets or the undermining of other programmes that were dear to government's heart—let us say—the recruiting of voluntary defence forces. It might well be inevitable that they give some small concession in return, something that cost them very little but meant much to us, the release of our people from jail or some such. With the best will in the world, it might take years to bring such a thing to a satisfactory conclusion without disturbing the smooth administration of our city, for they are asking us to pay for the bullets they shoot us with. The Japanese are a young and hasty people, angry and cruel like immature boys, and therefore much given to shouting and yelling, whereas we are an old civilisation that appreciates peace. They will need our help. We must soothe and calm them, advance when they retreat, retreat only when they advance.' HK flushed to the roots of his hair at such chiding but he smiled and inclined his head, seeing here a chance to spread the blame.

'As always, Loh Ching sees further than any of us. Perhaps he might therefore take personal charge of this matter where his wisdom and experience might bring great benefit?' Loh Ching smiled back sadly but with hard eyes. He was not about to put himself stupidly between a wild beast and its prey as HK had done.

'Alas, this is a job for younger men, those who have been educated abroad and understand the ways of the foreign world as I do not. This advancing and retreating, I believe, is nothing but the technique of ballroom dancing of which Mr Fong is held to be such a proud master at the German Club, is it not?' A hiss of contemptuous laughter ran round the table. Blood thundered in HK's ears and he dug his nails deeper into the armrests of his chair of office. 'Like the Japanese, I am delighted to entrust the resolution of such an important concern entirely to our gifted, young chairman.'

* * *

The land on which the Botanic Gardens stood was given to the Government by the merchant Whampoa in the 19th century. Although he was a lover of plants and owner of a private garden that was itself a major public attraction, the gesture had not been motivated entirely by philanthropy since he had received, in exchange, a narrow, but much more valuable strip of rock and bitter sand—totally barren—but situated right on the Singapore waterfront. Each morning, the garden emerged afresh from the mists so that to walk across its dew-drenched lawns was to leave a track as in virgin snow. Gently undulant, with a lake that had once housed a crocodile and a jungle that still attracted insolent monkeys, it was, like all botanical gardens, a world in miniature, a dream made flesh, a closed green sphere fenced around with living trees that displayed the apparent benevolence of Nature, a claim to paradise. In contrast to the randomness of primary forest, every plant here actually recalled a human decision, being placed not to reproduce but to pout and pose with a self-knowledge normally only borne by mankind. Each one spoke equally of human passion, of the mystical urge to recreate the primordial Garden of Eden—from which Man had been expelled by a lethal coalition of apple and serpent—and of a scientific obsession with taxonomy and completeness.

The war had brought certain changes of which the casually wandering visitor, still permitted, would probably have been unaware, for the gardens carefully maintained their public face of weeded paths and bordering flowers. In the past there had been conflict between pure botanical and commercial research and between both and the public call for loud carnations and bright bandstands. But behind the scenes, the workers now no longer merely tended the land, they embraced it carnally, lived off it, consumed its yield—fired with chillis and ginger pillaged from the Spice Garden—to supplement their scanty diet. It had become a self-supporting, country estate, plucked from the 18th century. The roof of the Director's house had been repaired with palm-leaves stripped straight from the fragment of preserved jungle. The lake that once teemed with cosseted carp was now regularly fished, not by probing ichthyologists, but by hungry undergardeners with nets of grim efficiency. Even the indolent palms found themselves harnessed to factory production, tapped for sugar and soapy palm wine in the Economic Garden, whose aspirational name became truer by the day. Tapioca, it had been discovered, fermented and distilled, yielded a brandy that revived the dead and almost killed the living and a steady trickle was coaxed from an apparatus housed in a lesser potting shed to raise the morale of administrative staff and soothe the semi-alcoholism of expats. Petrol shortages had led to the acquisition of a breeding pair of goats to munch the lawns smooth while yielding periodic feasts of milk and kid meat. Vegetables and fruits had insinuated themselves beneath the canopy of the protected forest and nested discreetly in amongst the undergrowth as it was surreptitiously de-flowered and, on the trellis where rose and woodbine had once artfully twined, now clambered practical rattan and nourishing long beans. In the early morning chill, despised skills of village and forest—once relegated to the ethnographic section of the museum—were softly taken up again and thumbs that had coolly flipped beer tops and flared lighters now again plaited twine held taut by bare big toes grown stiff in fancy shoes. Around the gardens, little local monopolies established themselves, bringing racial division into the world of culture but breeding solidarity through the need for exchange. Indian toddy-makers warred on Chinese fishermen and both were disdained by Malay farmers but coconuts and little leaf packages of tobacco still circulated in silent and peaceful compromise. But Paradise was sapped by other small flaws. For Europeans, it was the lack of potatoes that grew well enough at first but then abruptly burst and rotted in the steamy heat. For Asians, it was the absence of rice whose special needs precluded discreet cultivation. For both, gritty, tasteless tapioca became a substitute and a penance, the resented starch of life. And Catchpole, like a medieval pope, levied an imperial tithe on it all on threat of denunciation to the Professor, who had already silently noted and winked at all this, as long as the academic work and collections were maintained and gross unfairness avoided. Then, to Catchpole's horror, one morning, Professor Tanakadate had had the workmen set up a big banner blessing all these illegal cultivations as a magnificent 'Victory Garden' in which the employees demonstrated their loyalty to the Rising Sun and from which other Singaporeans might learn. And so secret tithe became lawful tribute and stalking Catchpole was rudely stripped of his power and income.

The Herbarium had always drawn Pilchard powerfully and now he returned to it as to a haven of order and tranquillity that worked according to the slow rain-soaked time of plants and the Catholic Church, not the jostling and impertinent time of Man. It was to him what wine cellars are to others. Its very smell, rich with ecclesiastical overtones of the inevitability of decay and growth, carried a metaphor, on the air, of comforting rebirth and tranquil eternity and offered a peace of mind that he thought of as *compost mentis*. The blinds, 'tatties', were lowered over the windows, against the heavy heat, so that colours receded to muted shades of sepia and light itself was thickened and slowed. Ranges of shiny mahogany cabinets with brass fittings stretched along the walls, each opening to disclose confident, racked drawers, each numbered drawer containing stiff folders of dried samples, laced to the page and identified in browning natural ink harvested from squid. Some were a hundred years old, delicately fading to dust, others new, a sheen still upon them, their place determined not by secular chronology but the timeless Linnaean classifications according to which God or evolution had created the world. Yet the Nature that had born them was also their prime enemy. They had to be regularly checked for infestation by chewing mite and boring beetle. In the wet season, fungus bloomed, for in the tropics there were eager spores and eggs everywhere looking for a home.

Pilchard was surprised to find Catchpole there, acid-free folders spread about him at a table. Pilchard peered over his shoulder, looking down into the seam of the gone-to-seed toupée that was visibly moulting. On his neck, a boil was sprouting, coming nicely to the boil in fact, and Catchpole picked at it's snowy peak absent-mindedly. He was playing with his rubber plants. In the Gardens, everyone had to be able to turn his hand to any subject and here, by selective breeding, they had produced generations of freakish, musclebound varieties that pumped out ever more prophylactic latex.

'Where's Dagama?' Dagama was the gaunt and moustachioed Eurasian who ran the Herbarium with a rule of iron but a heart of gold. Catchpole frowned and his forehead moved up freely under his wig, lubricated by sweat. A Herbarium was a sort of library not, therefore, a place of casual conversation.

'Gone,' he said curtly in a church whisper and returned to his folders. Catchpole was northern and had that form of extreme rudeness that Yorkshiremen call, with pride, 'plain-spokenness'.

'Gone? Gone where? Why are you whispering? There's no one else here. You won't wake up the plants.'

'Oh for God's sake, man, who can tell. These days people disappear without leaving so much as a glass slipper behind. Actually ...' he showed smug rodent teeth behind fat lips, '... it's sort of funny. You know those fungi spores he was always so keen on—cryptogams? Well, apparently, the Nips went crazy after those warships of theirs were blown up by the commandos in the harbour and started sniffing around everywhere for spies. *You* wouldn't know about it, of course, tucked away snugly in Changi but they put the fear if god up the rest of us, exposed out here. In fact, we feared for our lives.'

'Really? In Changi, we feared for our deaths.'

' Well ... cryptogams ... cryptograms ...' He see-sawed with his hands and smirked. 'You can see how they'd get muddled up—perfectly understandable—the Nips' Ancient Greek maybe a bit rusty—so it's my belief they hauled him off as some sort of secret codes expert. I repeatedly warned him cryptogam was a classificatorily obsolete term. Actually, I heard on the QT they took him to Outram Road and he didn't exactly get the best room. I shouldn't think he'll be back.' Said with some satisfaction. Pilchard wondered for a second if Catchpole had been at the collection preserved in spirits but he had always hated poor, gentle Dagama, wanted to get his own hands on the Herbarium, the memory of the gardens, the voice of posterity. It occurred to him to ask just who had let on about the cryptogams. Was this the voice of reason or the voice of treason? Catchpole looked at his watch with piggy eyes.

'Lunch!' he cried excitedly and leapt to his feet like a dog hearing its bowl rattled. Now he was all loud chatter. 'The old man's a stickler for timekeeping, a gentleman of the old school. I didn't know Japanese were big on the concept of "gentleman". A few weeks back we had a meeting about how to deal with the army's trespassing on the garden from the north and everybody decided what we needed was more fencing. The anti-aircraft gunners had moved in you see, made themselves at home. But the Prof got hold of the wrong end of the stick and turned up the next day with a rapier and face guard, ready to throw down a gauntlet in challenge and take them all on. He keeps going on about *bullshito*, you know, the *samurai* code.'

'*Bushido*? But *bushido* is a word of Chinese origin. It was invented at the very end of the 19th century by an American-Japanese Quaker who wrote a book for foreigners called—I think—*The Soul of Japan* in English. Only later was it translated into Japanese so they came to believe it about themselves. We have—had—a copy in the Library though I can't claim to have read it.'

Catchpole considered him coolly. 'Now, that's just the sort of remark that gets you into trouble, old boy, disparaging, juvenile. You never learn do you? I'd keep that bit of wisdom to myself it I were you, hide your light under a bushel, or the old man might well send you straight back to Changi. He's quite capable of it. Sometimes, when he looks at you, you can see he's thinking the space you occupy might be better spent on having a volcano put in.'

Meals for senior staff in the garden were nowadays a communal affair and under the jurisdiction of Ong Kam Yeng, a thin, spidery man with sad eyes, once Pilchard's own cook, now promoted to greater eminence and retaining no residual loyalty. His first move had been to install his nephews, identical twins nicknamed Ping and Pong, as assistants in the kitchen but also about the gardens generally. It was not clear whether these were their real names or a mark of European confusion or just contempt for Asian difference. The brothers deliberately perplexed everyone, joyfully swapping identities back and forth at will and confirming the Western prejudice that all Chinese looked alike and were ultimately interchangeable.

Even before the occupation, racial divisions were unspokenly enforced, here, as across the whole island, and senior staff had eaten apart. Everyone knew that 'senior' meant 'white' and now also 'Japanese'. Eurasians and other hybrids had always been difficult to place but the disappearance of Dagama and the others had relieved that anomaly and restored the calm of a more classical taxonomy. Nowadays, meals began, not with prayers but with what was known as the 'presentation of parts'. Catchpole had brought a large bunch of edible fern shoots tied up with twine. Ong Kam Yeng handled them with a grudging acceptance. The Professor offered two duck eggs, the sort of luxury only a Japanese could command. Dr Post unwrapped a newspaper parcel. The headline read 'Japan victorious all over East!'. They must be doing badly then. Ong grunted and probed the bloodied contents. 'Two squirrel—*tupai* . I make one pie from your two *tupai*.' Tiny Dr Hanada dug in his briefcase and bowed as he offered an immaculate unripe tomato and an obscene and hairy yam, both whisked away. And then Ong was there at Pilchard's shoulder with the expression a wife has on her face when she is waiting for you in the hall at two in the morning on payday with her arms crossed and you are drunk and the money is gone.

'I had a can of beans. I will find them and bring them tomorrow. A beanfeast.'

Ong made a lemon-sucking face and reached to repossess fork and spoon. 'You bring tomorrow. You eat tomorrow.'

'Is that Confucius?'

The Professor looked up over half-moon glasses and batted tired eyelids as a father will at children squabbling over the breakfast table. 'Mr Ong. Dr Pilchard has not yet been assigned a speciality. We must be patient. Let us wait until tomorrow for his contribution.' Ong rescinded cutlery, grunted and left, overruled but unmollified. 'Perhaps Pilchard-san you might look into the Orchid House until your strength has returned. The hybridization programme is a mess, the documentation is dreadful.' Pilchard nodded. He detested orchids, the temperamental, leggy showgirls of the plant world, flowers on a stick, denying the reality that all plants ultimately made their living from dirt. 'You know, gentlemen, there is a strange imbalance in all botanic gardens. In cold countries we cultivate tropical plants under glass in artificial heat. But no one in hot countries ever cultivates temperate plants in artificial cold. It is what you might call the asymmetry of colonised places. Like your own, Japan is a country of the West and of the cold North and so not part of the exotic East.' His face lit up briefly as if with the glow of reflecting snow. 'We might think of it in the future but I am afraid the Emperor's birthday ...' He stopped. Etiquette demanded he now stand and bow to that East of which Japan was not a part, at the mention of His Name, but these were not Japanese so ... 'falls in three months' time. It would be ... helpful ... yes that is the word ... helpful, if we were able to name a new orchid after him and send something off to Tokyo or even General Yamashita ...' his eyes shone '... a variant of the Tiger Orchid for him perhaps, a nice container, some elegant calligraphy ... I can do that part. As we say "We must grind up sesame seeds" for we depend on the powerful. Could you see if we have anything far enough along that might do, Dr Pilchard? A nuisance but truly ... helpful.'

Then Ping, or possibly Pong, reappeared with a bowl of cherry-pink soup that he set down also helpfully. Pilchard looked questioning. What soup, after all, is bright pink?

'Not crab I hope.'

'Lizard,' offered Dr Post, spooning with a sigh. 'You know *chichak*. Not so bad really. Clears you out a treat. One splash and all is silent.' He hesitated and reached nonchalantly across for the triumphalist newspaper the squirrels had been wrapped in, folded it carefully and stowed it away in his pocket, a slight glow of embarrassment about the eyes. 'At least it's better than being here in the sago worm season. Terribly binding sago worms.'

* * *

That night, Pilchard slept in one of the old curators' houses in Cluny Road in a ramshackle bed with too many uncoordinated springs. It was an old mock-English, mock-Tudor building with endless tatty rooms, furnished rather like a seaside boarding school with objects that seemed not to have been chosen but rather to have been simply abandoned where they stood by previous generations. Upstairs somewhere was Prof Tanakadate, exiled from the Director's true house by bomb damage, wrapped in the tinkle and twang of arid *koto* music from a wireless set. Dr Post shuffled and groaned next door like an old dog unable to find comfort in its bones. Possibly they had poor, missing Dagama— gone mad—stowed, raving, in the attic. Mosquitoes whined around the bed net like flies around a food safe. Where had that been? Ah yes, the Three Bears' bungalow. How long ago that all seemed. He lay a while listening to the small, hopelessly fragile beating of his heart in the vastness of the night. The garden lay all about, monochrome as in a photograph and stealthily silent, handed back to the animals that also made a living there, sharp-eared and fleet-footed. Out here, far from the centre, they still had the regular music of the hours, the pre-dawn birds, the morning splashing of ducks, the stillness at noon before the evening whirr of crickets and the nighttime screech of owls. Moonlight pressed against the window panes and gleamed in metallic sheen on the leaves as fireflies flashed and dotted the shadows with Morse. He snuffed the oil lamp, a wick floating in coconut oil, and stared up at the darkened ceiling. In his mind, he slowly retreated to another garden, where his father had worked as a gardener at weekends. It was the garden that had sent him East.

It was a special place, a lush oasis in the suburban desert, a model of and for the world and where Dad worked to escape from the joyless wastes of the British Sunday with its interdictions on play, joy, life. It belonged to Sir Robert Vane-Tempest-Stewart, of an ancient house, who had rekindled his fortunes by marrying an heiress of the Landsmann family, owners of a factory that made Landsmann's Famous Foaming Suppositories, advertised by the first poster to greet you as you turned into the High Street. Pilchard had been eagerly instructed by other boys what you did with them but still didn't quite know why. *In an experimental frame of mind, he had added water to one and seen it fizz to destruction in the sink like a slug on which salt has been poured. Whenever he saw Sir Robert giving Dad his orders or paying his wages, he heard the hiss of those suppositories in which the sound of distant oceans lay curled as in a conch shell. On the whole he liked the VTSs. They had no son, only a stringy daughter who disappeared to Australia and reappeared with her own gawky baby girl and* no *husband. Local women looked at her and pursed their lips and said nothing. They had a gift of saying nothing very loud. There were tales told of a marriage, a car accident, not believed, and the baby was minutely examined for signs of racial admixture—alas not found—but there was still plenty of time for that to show up later to complete her disgrace. If not, there might be signs of mental impairment, opening up other lines of attack through that male cousin she had always seemed far too thick with to be healthy. Where Pilchard lived, everyone always thought the worst of everyone else and was invariably proved right to do so.*

Sir Richard would sometimes ruffle Pilchard's stringy red hair in a regretful, son-deprived sort of way. Once he asked, "And what do you want to be when you grow up, young man?" Expecting no doubt the answer, "an engine-driver." Children were always taught that to be winsome, boys should want to be engine-drivers, girls ballet-dancers.

"A doctor, Sir Richard," he replied in a clear voice.

Sir Richard was taken aback, stared down at him as if seeing something he very much did not want to see. Then he exploded in over-hearty laughter. "Setting his sights a bit high," he snorted to Dad and ruffled again, roguishly.

Later, Dad had paused over the bonfire of leaves he was building. He had shown Pilchard how to pick up great piles by pinching them between two boards.

"What you said about being a doctor." He blushed, overcome by the terrible embarrassment of fathers and sons. "Hang on to that, son." He coughed, pretending it was the smoke, but it wasn't the smoke. The blood had roared in Pilchard's ears. He thought he was going to die from shame.

"Right, Dad."

They moved apart fast. They never spoke of it again and Dad quickly changed the mood by giving him a thudding ride in the wheelbarrow on top of all the leaves.

He recognised the VTS house as the real house that he read about in children's books at school, of which his own was an insubstantial abbreviation, a mere child's model. It was a place where they had even the evening paper delivered and magazines came new, not second-hand and with corners torn. It was large and modern, full of great bare surfaces and sharp edges unabridged by time, an uncompromised expression of the individual human will. Inside, one affectation amazed Pilchard more than any other. The china all matched. He had seen the housekeeper throw away a cup just because it was chipped even though it didn't leak. The basic colour of the walls was white, startling in a world where most were painted in 'practical' dark green gloss at the bottom and cream at the top and a waggly line between the two that shifted slightly at each repainting. It had big metal windows, unafraid of the light and prying neighbours, in which fresh curtains danced. Anyway, the neighbours were so far away they were mostly reduced to the well-mannered sounds of their lawnmowers. At the front, a gravel drive, deep as Brighton beach, consumed space extravagantly, a bare place where the gardener's job lay not in coaxing spindly unmatched plants into life as in his own back yard but eradicating *them utterly. The gravel was so deep, Dad's bicycle skidded and swerved as he turned in. At the rear, lawns fell in swags of serial savannah down to a border that was expensively replanted every few months with exotic colour. They bought plants they knew could never survive the winter just to be able to look at them for a few weeks in summer and then throw them away. And beyond it lay a jungle and swamp of graceless rhododendron pierced with dark and frightening tunnels, dotted with narcissus and crocus and shadowed carpets of thick velvet moss. There was a pale walled garden with fruit trees, covered with netting against the birds like some giant tropical bed. And an arch of roses cut through it like the barbed wire fences in the POW camp at Changi. At the very end, behind all the defences, lay a rustic shed of logs with the bark left on, such as John Wayne would use to do what a man's gotta do while suffering the tireless affronts of the Indians who lived in the tangled rhododendrons.*

Inside, was a delicious accretion of past and forgotten things covered in dust that spoke of people who had an assured place in time, who could look both backward and forward with confidence. There was leaf mould and spiders' webs across distorting window panes, grey-handled rakes and brooms of twigs and cupboards full of things that would be useful some day stored in old cigar boxes. These were a special treasure like big, red Oxo tins. Pilchard took delight in the impossible lightness of their balsa wood, their mortised construction, the hinged brass fastening and the rash of gold embossed seals that swarmed on their lids. Some had pictures of dark, moustachioed men, fandangoing women and inscriptions in foreign tongues rich in vowels that seemed to taste of coffee. Occasionally he would find empty aluminium tubes with screw tops that were clearly valuable possessions to be pocketed even if their possibilities could not quite be defined. Best of all were the skins of aromatic cedar wood that lurked in the bottom. Pilchard closed his eyes and inhaled their dark, whorish odour to know places heavy with spice, gold and jewels where people dressed in rustling silk, a fabric he otherwise knew only through an old blouse of his mother's made from a purloined parachute.

Right at the end of the garden was the greenhouse, paradoxically white, a bubble of contentment where time paused like an animal at a waterhole. Here, the very air was special, the musky exhalation of a dinosaur, a fluid medium that smothered noises into accents of silence. The floors were always wet like in the outside lavatory at home but here the water dripped into a pool of irises on whose surface water boatmen—not to be found anywhere else in his world—catamaraned. Roots stretched down into the water in gnarled white fingers and then faded away in green underwater mist. In one corner nested flowerpots and seed-boxes that reeked of creosote, heaped up like the dry bones of an explorer, and echoed to the tick of the wooden windowframes as they heated and cooled. Marrows and tomatoes sent out thick tendrils of tropical exuberance, weighed down bamboo supports and pressed against the streaming glass. Pilchard particularly adored the cool cucumbers that clung to, encumbered, wires pegged into the frames, a sort of vegetable equivalent of the VTS's gas fridge—through heat to the miracle of ice.

He was forbidden to come here alone, Dad, a confirmed non-swimmer, being haunted by some uncharacteristically metaphysical vision of the dangers posed to children by still pools. He seemed to have glimpsed some dire portent that he could never shrug off. If he caught his son alone there, he would shout and hit out, terrified by his own fear and then repent and be ashamed. All this ensured that Pilchard came anyway, secure in the immortality of youth and sat listening to the pond calling to him, running its warm green water through his fingers, looking down into its swirling depths that danced with motes of gold and flirted with the frisson of death in the innocently circling goldfish. It was here that Dad had drummed into his head not just the difference between right and wrong but right and left, the tomatoes and the cucumbers. In later years, wherever he was in the world and wanted to be sure of left and right he would have to think himself back into this greenhouse through which the co-ordinates of the earth ran as in some personal Greenwich. Babies and the sick are the only creatures who truly live in the present since their bodies are the boundaries of their world. The young live in the future, the old in the past. It was only in the greenhouse that Pilchard reverted to an infantile simultaneity. And in his dreams, he would come here almost every night to find himself.

He woke sweaty and trembling, weighed down with heavy, nameless dread and knew he had to go out despite the curfew. He shrugged on an old sarong and stepped outside into quivering humidity, touch-toed across the verandah floorboards into sandals and crept down the edge of the path, avoiding the crunch of gravel. A cloud shifted and the moon shone out like a searchlight, the road gleaming in sudden clarity like an invitation in copperplate. His own former lodgings were not far from here, a flat in a characterless modern block that was otherwise inhabited by pale clerks from the Sanitation Department. He stepped out onto the tarmac. The greatest danger was from a sentry standing in the shadows, guarding one of the larger houses that had been seized for Japanese grandees and he tried not to shuffle which only made the soles of his sandals slap noisily. It did not matter. He had stepped sideways out of time and knew himself to be magically invisible in the starlight. Ten minutes later, he stood in front of the block. It was a redbrick structure with stuccoed communal stairwell and it was in this narrow compass, on the first floor, that he and Margaret had led their married strife. It was odd that you only knew you were happy afterwards, as history, but misery was always keenly felt in the present. The worst rows had always climaxed on landings. Perhaps they carried with them the sense of a threshold being crossed. It was clearly not nostalgia for those days that had brought him back but he still had no idea what unfinished business it was.

The building had suffered a direct hit, ripping out the front wall so that it was seen as in cross-section, pathetic private parts laid bare to public gaze with the shock of bared buttocks. His feet led him, on automatic pilot, up those same stairs to the door, ridiculously still locked while the whole wall to one side was no more, mere moonshine. Stepping round the doorframe, he clinked over rubble to review his past life in moonlit black and white and was surprised to feel merely tired and hollow with no hint of rage or regret. And then he saw that this was no random damage. The furniture was smashed and overturned by human hands. The walls were scrawled with obscenities, written—from the smell— in excrement, as though his wife had secretly returned to have the last word. The last word being 'drongos', however, argued more plausibly that this was the work of rampaging Australian troops, in the period before final surrender, when they were looking for booze and self-expression concerning the qualities of British leadership. With patient malice, one had taken down the photo albums, removed every single photograph and shredded them all, by hand, to tiny confetti. It was unimportant. That part of the past was mere fiction, all lies and false smiles for the camera. From the floor, Pilchard took the pointless cake slice that was his mother-in-law's wedding present and went to the rear garden. Finally, it would be useful. Three inches down, under a rose bush, was a cocktail shaker with the lid screwed down. Inside, his father's silver Benson wristwatch. It seemed absurd to wear it on his wrist while in a sarong and nothing else so he held it in his hand, as a child does his bus fare, and walked back to Cluny Road, as in that dream where you float through the streets naked. As he lay in bed and tried in vain to rewind the Benson, he saw that it had locked solid, with unconscious prophecy, at precisely one minute to midnight.

* * *

Captain Oishi read, with schoolboy excitement, of Alexander Hare and pirates and female slaves and of the spice trade and rampaging armies. The day waned and he switched on his desk lamp and read on, the tea brought by his servant cold and untouched at his elbow, paperwork piling up in a disregarded heap of yellow paper, like unwashed laundry. He read how Hare had finally despaired of the whole Malay archipelago and set sail for South Africa with his 'family' crammed aboard his merchant ship. There, at the Cape, he had bought a house and estate away from the town and all might have been well had he not made a foolish mistake. He tried to turn the male house slaves into field slaves which they were not minded to accept, so that they went into rebellion. It was not the status of slave that they rejected—as you might at first have thought—it was the loss of prestige involved in the shift from house to farm. The authorities, always nervous of a slave revolt, had called out the militia and the whole story had leaked out to the public. They, in turn, were not shocked to find workers shackled in servitude or whipped to death—such things were commonplace at the Cape—but were unprepared for the blatant sexual ménage of frank enjoyment established by Hare with his magnificent ladies, as opposed to the hushed proprietorial fumblings of their own households. He was ordered to leave. Pausing only to buy some Chinese women at advantageous prices and snap up some Mozambiquan ladies who fired his collector's zeal in wholly new directions, Hare loaded up his followers onto his ship and set sail once again.

* * *

The gardens should have reeked of sex, for every part of them boiled with sexuality. The air danced with storms of pollen as stamens yearned lustily and dustily for their corresponding carpels and pimpish made-to-measure anthers frotted suggestively against the bodies of fertilising insects. Bees, wasps, flies, beetles, moths, even birds were pressed into reproductive service. Everywhere spores and seeds spiralled on the sunlit wind while suckers swelled, tunnelled and thrust into darkness underground. Nature—monosexual, bisexual, transsexual—was equally about its business in the high leaf canopy and the low undergrowth and only the raking gardeners seemed asexual, though—in their way— they were as yoked to plant reproduction as guileless insects. Each movement of air waved the blatant sex organs of flowers that men presented to girls by the fistful in token of their erect penes and promiscuously wafted the same smells that humans expensively distilled and used to complement their own musky odours of crotch and armpit. Hundreds of scents crisscrossed, blended and ultimately pooled into a single blousy belch. High up, on the *coco de mer*, swayed luscious twin nuts that grossly caricatured the groins of Seychelles maidens, a provoking tuft of red fibre at the joint. The mathematics of fertility were prodigious and Pilchard could tell you that this was the largest seed in Nature, some 22 billion times greater than the orchid spores that compensated by being 22 billion times more numerous. And yet the Orchid House was a well of monastic tranquillity and peaceful, flitting shadows. In a style of carved curlicues and glass skylights, it seemed to have been inspired by Simla railway station. There had once been elaborate plans for electric fans, blowing across stands of water, to increase the humidity for sensitive and spoiled mountain species but the electricity had not liked the moisture and the moisture had attacked the electricity so that both had been replaced with gardeners intermittently spraying water by hand. Captain Oishi had never seen so many orchids, hanging neatly from the rafters in little grey baskets made of cross-hatched twigs, like the log cabins of Americans, that aged and decayed most poetically. The General was away building tunnels and this was a chance for an extended break from the office just up the road. Orchids were supposed to recall male testicles but Captain Oishi had little interest in male testicles apart from his own. 'Rice balls' were to him just an end-of dinner treat not the painful affliction of the Changi prisoners and his own testicles were smooth and well-nourished from the yeast extract sent regularly by his loving mother.

There was the famous *Vanda Miss Joachim* with its dense pink and purple flowers, an early, rather flouncy, hybrid, perhaps a little like its Armenian discoverer who, unlike most pioneers, had no need to scour jungles for a new plant but found it and instant fame, to hand, in her backyard, over the polite tinkle of spoons, one day when the Botanic Gardens' director was round to tea. And that, surely, growing exuberantly in a raised bed of broken brick, must be the superlative Tiger Orchid, largest in the world, an epiphyte that favoured the crowns of the highest trees. Oishi hissed with pleasure and stretched to examine the massed flowers that ran from greenish-yellow, through orange-yellow, to ochre and dark purple—ink droplets on pale velum. And there, dangled a *Phalaeonopsis*, a Moon Orchid of purest white, discovered in the 17th century by Rumphius himself, then lost until rediscovered in the early 19th by the aptly named German, Prof Blume, each flower the size of a man's hand. He groaned and reached out to gently touch, fingers anticipating ridged silkiness and received, instead, the shock of a blast of cold water.

'Oh my gosh! Terribly sorry!' Captain Oishi straightened, wide-eyed and face-wiping, to see a very red-haired Englishman smiling excessively innocent regret at him through a fringe of beard from the other side of the flower bed. Behind his mask of apology, the man raised an old Flit gun to an ironic 'shoulder arms' position. 'Just misting the orchids. They tend to dry out so in this weather. I didn't realise we were honoured by an eminent visitor. Oh! Sorry, I forgot to bow.'

The Captain smiled shyly, bowed back himself and peered, without comment, at the teeming rain. 'Yes please. I think we have met before with Mrs Erica. You were to show me the museum but … I wonder … Do you please have a *Dendrobium cruminatum*? I should very much like to see one please.'

Pilchard was surprised. The Japanese military was not known for its use of the word 'please' nor for its taste in rare orchids.

'Well, yes, but not at its best. As I am sure you are aware, *cruminatum* likes sudden drops in temperature. A fall of ten degrees, triggered by a storm, leads to flowering in exactly nine days' time. The natural temperature here is too stable for them to ever flower. But I do have one I can show you.'

The young soldier hesitated, then bowed again and extended his hand. 'Perhaps you have forgotten my name. Oishi.' Across the civilian gesture, he attempted a low-pitched, manly military bark that caught in his tender throat and made him cough. He swallowed and spoke again in a clear light tenor. 'Captain Oishi, 25th Imperial Japanese Army.'

'Pilchard,' the other reciprocated gruffly, smiling in unwilling friendliness. 'POW … retired.'

The Captain straightened up abruptly. 'You are the man with the chest!'

Pilchard frowned. Chest? He looked down at his front, seeing nothing particularly distinctive about his own chest.

'No. No. *I* have your chest.' Pilchard looked at him, puzzled, again seeing no resemblance in his pectoral development. 'The chest with your notes on Cocos-Keeling. I have been reading them. The Kempeitei let you go so soon? But that is good. They are men of little education with no interest in history and your notes are incomplete. Alexander Hare. His ladies. Please can you tell me how the story ends? Many of your papers were missing. I think they sold them in the market to wrap toffee.'

'Why to wrap toffee?'

'Toffee is sticky. It is more convenient wrapped.'

'No I meant ... Never mind.' He brightened.. 'You really want to know?' He was, he knew, something of a bore on the subject of Cocos-Keeling. 'That's hunkydory.'

'Hunkydory?'

'An expression meaning "perfect", "fine", derived—I believe—from the Japanese *honchodori*, the name of the main street of Yokohama, and, in the last century, famed among sailors for its attractions.'

'Please?'

They sat outside, on the soft, shaded grass, under an ancient banyan tree, like Buddhist sages, Oishi neatly cross-legged, Pilchard sprawled, and he took up the tale from across the road. He told, illustrating with the boat of a dried leaf, how Hare sailed to the Cocos-Keeling Islands, tricking the crew about their destination, uninhabited outcrops of coral, thousands of miles from anywhere where he could build a closed world to conform to his imagination. He shredded the leaf and told of his rage and dismay on discovering that one of his own sea-captains, a Shetlander called Ross, had pre-empted him and established his own settlement on the atoll.

'Could they not divide the islands between them?' Oishi

proffered a cigarette case stamped with a perfect chrysanthemum. Changi habit made Pilchard seize a cigarette and pocket it 'for later'.

'No. There was ill-feeling so that the two men who lived side by side, a thousand miles from anywhere, barely spoke but feuded via solicitors' letters exchanged slowly and expensively in London.' A curled twig became London. 'Their intentions were incompatible. There are two visions of Nature that dominate the West. One is Paradise. Nature is perfect and you just build a big, high wall to keep bad things out. That was Hare and this garden. The other is the Wilderness. It has to be cleared and improved, redeemed. That was Ross. He wanted to set up a whaling station where ships could be repaired and the needs of rough sailors met even though he was a Bible-thumping fanatic. Hare just wanted a safe place to stow his collection. It culminated in Hare establishing a sort of stockade and a terrible scene where, one morning, he was found screaming over the fence something about a rose being stolen from his flower garden.'

'Why was he so angry about a rose?'

Pilchard smiled, laying a windblown blossom at his feet. 'It wasn't really a rose. It was one of his ladies that he meant.'

The Captain blushed and shook his head wonderingly, took off his cap and placed it between his knees like a modesty garment. 'Ah-so! A lady.'

Pilchard sat back against the tree, spread his legs in the dry shade, closed his eyes.

'Other things happened until, I think, Hare went a little mad. He took his slaves' children hostage and locked them up. His overseer disappeared in odd circumstances. Ross was short of workers, maybe he lured Hare's people away. Anyway, finally, one night, they rose up and drove Hare off the island and Ross made them sign some sort of primal covenant with him, like the

Israelites with Jehovah in the Bible, giving him absolute power over their lives. On that island, he made himself god. Hare tried to come back with his son and they drove him off again.'

'How did they survive in the middle of the ocean?' The young Captain shuddered in sympathetic loneliness.

'The boys all learned simple, godly, trades as carpenters or fishermen or copra-workers. They brought soil from Mauritius and built up their own island. The fertilising *guano* of Christmas Island was only a hundred miles away and the Rosses grew rich on it. They selectively bred and grew coconuts—cocos. And they were tough. There is a story of the Ross boys being made to build a boat and sail it to Scotland when they got old enough for school. If you look at the photos of the St. Andrews University rugby teams, there are these big, strapping, Polynesian-looking lads—the Ross's intermarried with the local ladies. Then, when steam shipping came in and communications got easier, they could import expensive, fancy, white wives and the boys in the photos gradually turn European again—also less good at rugby.'

Oishi laughed and blew smoke, celebrating the age of steam. 'And what did the ordinary islanders do, just marry each other?'

'Ross also imported women from Java—a bit like Hare, I suppose—by the dozen, and you could pay for your wife on tick—credit—via the company store.' Oishi grinned. Pilchard could see him picturing the women, lined up on a shelf with price tags around their necks. 'You might think that—stuck out there in the world's biggest ocean—they would all pool their differences just to survive but no islander would marry the descendants of the Africans anyway because they were dark.'

Oishi nodded. 'Ah! They were *burakumin*, unclean people. In Japan also we have them.' He yawned and stretched, happy to find other peoples so accepting of Japanese ways. 'And how did Cocos-Keeling end up as part of the British Empire?'

'The story is that, in the 19th century, a young naval lieutenant was sent to grab the Cocos Islands, the ones that lie off Thailand, and got his charts muddled up. After that, the navy was too proud to admit its mistake so the claim just stuck. It was less bother that way.'

'And how is all this know?'

Pilchard laughed softly. 'Ah, well … Hare wrote a journal that was abandoned when he fled. It fell into the hands of his enemy, Ross, who had it copied. Of course, he may have changed it a little here and a little there, as it was copied, to improve his own case against Hare. That cannot be known. The only Hare we know is the Hare of those pages—delivered to us by a man who hated him. Then, after I saw it, all this material was put in a chest that was sent to Colombo, for safekeeping, but that chest too has been lost—just as my own chest with its material on Hare has been partly lost. Perhaps both will be found again. Perhaps neither will and the only Hare to survive is my own Hare that will run for a hundred years. There is no evidence that Hare ever came to Singapore but I like to think he did. I like to see him sitting on the Singapore Stone with his old friend Sir Stamford, trying to work out what it said, not realising that his own trace and meaning were being sucked up and obliterated by the world as he did so.'

The Captain rose rapidly to his feet and blushed again as he adjusted his cap. 'Dr Pilchard. Thank you for helpful insights. Now I must go and write to my mother.' As he rose, he glimpsed a notice, pinned to the tree, in the Professor's own careful brushwork. The style was rather old-fashioned and conventional, he thought and he bustled breathily away, improving the calligraphy in his head, leaving Pilchard lying sprawled on the ground like a beached whale or a small, unclaimed, Pacific island.

* * *

From the first, HK had disliked Baba Chinese furniture. It was heavy, overornate and fussy. The hard, black wood spoke of iron duty, obligation, the dead hand of the past. It smelt of incense and embroidered textiles and it was full of gaudy, tasteless colours like a tart's parlour. Come to think of it, he would much rather be in a tart's parlour than sitting here again, trapped in this chair that felt like the execution chair that the Americans used. Matters had gone from bad to worse—from worse to worst. The Japanese, great diplomatic prevaricators and oblique strategists in their own right, had not been fooled by his delays and requested clarifications. HK explained, like a pupil before the headmaster, the many promising and devious routes he had taken only to see them swiftly closed off and sealed against him.

'In short,' he concluded, 'the General insists that the money be paid in full by the end of this month.'

'If it is not,' asked one, 'what will he do?'

'You know what he will do.' They knew. A second Sook Ching massacre. A fly, as if to make the point, gave up circling and ran in on a strafing run the length of the table, pulling up at the far end to circle again.

'Can we not,' another wailed, 'at least pay him in his own worthless Japanese banana money?'

'He has demanded Straits dollars. He will not accept banana money. There is no way to raise this sum. Our people have given their life's blood already.' He himself had been squeezed till his eyes nearly popped out—heirloom jewellery, the gold sovereigns bricked up in the fireplace, the houses in Bukit Timah—all gone at crazily low prices. At breakfast he had found himself staring at the rings on his mother's fingers. At all costs he would hang on to his visits to Lily. That alone made life tolerable. He sighed at the remembrance of the feel of her long hair tickling his shoulder.

'What does the total of contributions stand at, the collections already made?' This from Loh Ching, ringing out like the voice of the Jade Emperor himself.

HK sweated, pulled out a sheet of paper, totted desperately with pencil and bowed head like a child having difficulty with his homework. 'We are $22 million short.'

Loh Ching smiled. '$22 million only?' Despite themselves, they laughed. He took from his pocket a crisp folded letter and pushed it across the table to HK. Not quite *to* HK but far enough so that he could just reach it if he prostrated himself uncomfortably across the table. They stopped laughing.

'What's this?'

'Through my contacts I have arranged for the Yokohama Specie Bank to lend us up to $25 million dollars for one year at 8 per cent.'

'Eight per cent is high.'

'Not given the circumstances. We use Japanese money to pay the Japanese.'

'General Yamashita would never agree to this. Why would he agree to this?'

'Because it allows him to report to Tokyo that he has carried out the order and it takes the problem from his desk and places it on another's desk. That is all that is required in the army.'

'And what happens at the end of the year when we cannot pay?'

'If Heaven is right, the war may be over by then and the Allies will quash the debt.'

'What if Heaven is wrong?'

'Then we extend the loan.'

'What if the bank will not extend the loan?'

Loh Ching chuckled. It was not a sound they heard often and

it made the hair stand up on their necks. 'If, if, if. Then we owe a Japanese bank in distant Yokohama many millions of dollars that we cannot pay, instead of owing a similar sum directly to the Japanese Army who are heavily armed and angry and bored and a mere half a mile down the road.' He stared at HK with bottomless contempt. 'Which would you prefer?'

Part III

The Wilderness in the Garden

'Today,' declared Professor Tanakadate roundly, 'is a verry special day.' He twinkled around the table where plates and glassware winked back the light from the flickering oil lamps. It was, Pilchard thought, all inappropriately romantic. 'Today is day when Greater East Asia Co-prosperity Sphere comes to the Botanic Gardens, the Emperor's Birthday. All races celebrate together happily under Japanese flag and we share a meal as one family.' He bowed his head down slowly towards his magnificently sere, grey *kimono* and then raised his eyes to embrace his somewhat hushed and overheated household, mostly unused to being here at night, this celebratory meal an unwelcome penance. The windows were flung open but not a breath of air stirred the bushes and trees. Inside, the atmosphere weighed on them like a hot, wet, blanket. Lizards chased each other around the dead light-fittings.

In the past, formal dinners had often been served in the house's rather grand, panelled dining room but now fine linen and candlesticks had given way to Robinson Crusoe improvisation. An old damask curtain had been dextrously salvaged from one of the devastated Cluny Road houses and pressed—unpressed—into service as tablecloth. Beneath it, the ancient but rickety table itself had been extended on packing crates and the Indian, Malay and Chinese staff crammed around it, gamely supported the unsure tabletop on their bare legs, the curtain rings digging into their knees. Each place was set with an old jamjar for drinking, polished to crystal perfection, and a wad of newspaper substituted for placemat. Only the Professor gripped an incongruously perfect balloon brandy glass, sole remnant of vanished elegance. In the centre, steamed a heap of chewy manioc bread. As the occupation continued, more and more had to be made of manioc as everything else disappeared even from the black market. Now it made unconvincing loaves, biscuits and brandy but very good glue that served, amongst other things, to anchor the Catchpole wig. Elsewhere in Syonanto had been marches, patriotic songs parroted by schoolchildren, endless waving of flags, the usual tired hypocrisies suffered, without particular rancour, by subject peoples, but nothing so uncomfortable as this forced propinquity of race and class.

The first course, borne in, aloft, by whippet-hipped Ping and Pong, had been a nightmare of mixed crustacean *sashimi* that had appalled all but the Professor. The Indians had been repelled by its rawness and slithery blandness and picked at it with reluctant and disbelieving fingers. Revenge might be a dish best served cold but not shellfish.

'Prawns. Heads full of shit like Malays.'

The Malays had feared, as always, the introduction of unclean species, liminal creatures that moved between sea and land and were therefore forbidden. They sipped water virtuously from their jamjars, fingered unbreakable manioc bread and argued in whispers over the acceptability of sorting one creature from another on their plates or whether all were now hopelessly polluted. Pilchard had sat queasily and recalled his walk on the beach at Changi and watched reluctantly the Professor's busily clicking chopsticks as they probed and plucked at the meat of crab joints and sockets. Post and Catchpole frowned and nibbled innocently and old-maidishly with dabbing forks. Like Brussels sprouts at Christmas, such food must be faced. Only the Chinese fishermen reached forward eagerly.

'Chinese eat everything with legs—except table only,' they laughed indifferently, shrugging down the raw ingredients as welcome fuel.

'Yes! Eat! Eat!' the Professor urged with high crablike waving. 'Syonanto people are always so polite and shy. Not like Japanese. Eat!'

The Indians' palmwine concession had been abrogated for the day to provide drink for all and Tanakadate swigged happily between mouthfuls—the musty, mildewed flavour recalling student bouts of sake-swilling in fair Kyoto—till his eyes grew misty. Around the table, hands of different colours profited from the darkness to stow food away in pouches and banana leaves or simply dropped the loathsome flesh out of sight onto the floor and Ping and Pong had seized the scarcely depleted platter and carried it away rejoicing like Salome bearing off the head of John the Baptist. All the more for them. Their already-smoking *wok* would soon turn these primitive chopped ingredients into a proper human meal. The Professor smiled benignly through his milky glass like an old man through cataracts.

'Yes, yes. Please take for your families, for those you love who are far away and so cruelly missed.' He cleared the catch in his throat and gulped more palmwine.

'I hear,' Catchpole growled authoritatively in Pilchard's ear, 'that the Japs are shifting more of the Changi prisoners to rest and convalescent camps by the sea in Thailand. Lucky sods! Plenty of food, clean water, decent climate—not like us poor buggers penned up here working our backsides off. They'll do nothing but play football on the beach and go fishing. They even took a piano with them to help pass the time.'

'How do you know these things, Catchpole?'

He tapped his nose wisely and winked. 'Be like Dad. Keep Mum'. Sources, old man. Sources. You forget, I have taken over

133

as religious correspondent.'

Like all such institutions, the Raffles Museum received a stream of mail from lunatics of every political, racial and religious stripe—people who found messages from God in every artefact or held themselves to be wronged pretenders to the sacred Riau throne or reincarnations of Queen Nefertiti. It fell to the current 'Religious Correspondent' to reply to all these in tones of evasive politeness, avoiding giving either offence or encouragement. Pilchard had prided himself on earthing all such enthusiasms with a single, devastating page, known within the confines of the institution as a 'Fuck Off You Red-Nosed Bastard Letter', that blended high condescension and sneering world-weariness with the lawyer-proof pedantic scholarship and icy politesse that were a form of rudeness. Should any fellow acadenic write in criticism of the museum or gardens they would receive a letter reading, 'Dear X, In the gretest confidence, I feel I should warn you that someone has been writing absurd and offensive letters to the Director and using your name.' Catchpole clearly operated otherwise.

'Sauces? There are no sauces,' complained Dr Post, sadly mouth-watering 'Gravy. Ketchup! Oh my God, HP sauce.'

'I thought you said, last week, they were to be used to build a canal directly across the Kra peninsula and cut off Singapore's trade for ever.'

Catchpole blushed and bridled. He must be boiling to death under that caked and implausible thatch. '*That*, old man, was something quite different. I do wish you'd try to keep up. Priorities change. The war is in constant flux.'

'Flux?' questioned Post. 'I had a dose of it at Easter.'

'Our next course,' said the Professor, bowing to the idea of it, 'is a gift from General Yamashita from the magnificent herd of deer that eat the grass of the Governor's palace, the same as is eaten today by the General himself. It is to say thank you for the gift of the new Yamashita hybrid of the Tiger orchid that we have developed here and loyally named after him. Thanks to Dr Pilchard, its father.' Applause, laughter.

Ong swept in grandly with plates on which lay two thin slices of crispy-fried venison, arranged to occupy maximum surface area, and completed with bowls of slimy manioc paste. Of late, the plates had seemed to get steadily larger, the portions of food smaller. The whites dribbled and drooled and thought of lost Sunday roasts, pined for gravy and potatoes, missed family rows over the sliced sirloin.

'Mustard,' whimpered Dr Post in a pang of Surbiton nostalgia. 'Do you remember mustard? Does anyone? The English sort, all hot, that brings tears to your eyes.' He cried in demonstration. 'And thick slices of meat with fat. This is so thin it looks like something prepared for a microscope slide.'

The Professor raised his glass again. 'A toast!'

'Toast,' Post snivelled tearfully. 'Proper bread cut into soldiers. Crust! Butter! Butter melting from the heat of the toast. My god, thick-cut marmalade. Now it's always jam tomorrow.'

'I see some of you made to cry by great, grateful feelings. It brings me such joy to see us united in a common endeavour as all the world around us is disturbed by necessary readjustments and we alone still live and work in harmony inside this garden, an example to the whole Greater East Asia Co-prosperity Sphere. To harmony!' Jamjars waved unenthusiastically as he drained his glass and Pilchard—roughly versed in Japanese etiquette—rose and deferentially refilled it from the Winchester bottle on the floor, marked 'Sulphuric Acid'.

Now the Indians were chattering excitedly, peering at their plates in horror, pushing them away in rejection. 'Beef!'

'No.' Pilchard, reseated across the table, hastily mimed

135

soothing but inaccurate moose horns with spread hands. 'Not beef. Deer. You can eat it.'

'*Not* beef but very *like* beef, then,' disdainfully conceded a Tamil barrackroom lawyer who otherwise worked on the drains and now burst into watery, bubbling Tamil to his mates. They shuffled themselves rapidly into sects of greater and lesser tolerance, some eating, others not.

Mustafa—previously the driver of the Gardens' tractor, when there had been such a thing, and now acting head of the Malay staff—prodded his own plate unhappily.

'Islam?' he asked dolefully. Pilchard lay down his fork and sighed.

'Oh Christ! Why does every little thing have to be so complicated?' Then he caught himself in time and smiled. 'Yes,' he encouraged smoothly. 'Islam. You can eat. Islam yes. The butcher was Muslim, too. Completely *halal*.' What the hell was the word for deer?

Mustafa pouted and looked as if he was about to cry through his moustache. 'Islam?' he asked again in a little boy's voice and wriggled on his seat.

'Yes, Islam, Islam.' He was tired, had drunk too much. His body, unused to food and drink, was sending agonising shafts of dyspepsia through his guts and he opened his mouth to snap something back—many a true word is spoken in indigestion—and then, from somewhere plucked a soft answer. 'Well look. I'm not a Muslim myself but I'm sure there's nothing in the Koran against eating deer.' Mustafa reluctantly speared the flesh. Then the word came to him suddenly from somewhere, like a blessing. 'Kijang,' he said. 'It's called *kijang*.' Hang on. Maybe that was Javanese not Malay?

Mustafa's mouth snapped shut then gaped in horror. 'So … is NOT lamb.' His eyes were all betrayed trust, brown pools of shocked innocence. 'Oh Mr Pilchard how could you lie to us about such a thing when you know our ways?' The scandal buzzed through the Malays. 'You say is lamb but is NOT lamb. How could you do that? You have betrayed our trust.' They pushed away their plates, sulkily.

'No, no. Islam ... is lamb ... Don't you see? I thought ... What I meant ...'

Catchpole sniggered. 'Looks like the fasting month has come a little early this year. That's what you get for telling porkies, old man.' A gross feeder, he reached swiftly across to grab the abandoned meat, gripping Mustafa's plate with two hands. Sweat trickled down his forehead from under the wig. 'Waste not, want not,' chewing greasily and tipping. 'It's an ill wind ...'

Mustafa stared down at a picture in the newspaper marking his now-empty place. Freshly revealed, it showed a dumpy Chinese, caught blinking against the flash of the photographer, like a man snapped in adultery—therefore looking drunk— presenting a huge cheque to smirking General Yamashita, himself in the pose of a man who has won the football pools and is keen to display the figures on it. 'See!' he sneered. 'Even when the rest of us are starving the Chinese still have millions.'

'Pickles,' announced the Professor, happily. 'We should now eat delicious pickled plums but owing to inconvenient war developments cannot.' But under Ong's directing finger, Ping and Pong reappeared to deal out rings of pineapple like deck quoits. The *Bromelidae* patch had been stripped.

'Actually, what you were saying about the Kra peninsula, old man, I rather gather that plan has been dropped. All their efforts are going into the capture of your favourite place, Cocos-Keeling, preparatory to the attack on Australia.'

Pilchard was peeved at the gloating voice, chewing through pineapple slush. He turned, irritated. 'You know Catchpole, I sometimes think that it's not the enemy who really get up one's nose but those who are supposed to be on our side. If even half the things you claim to know are accurate, then the Japs ought to shoot you as a spy. On the other hand, you may just be a complete idiot and one day I will shoot you myself.'

'Well really ...'

'Now that we are all stuffed with refreshing food and joyful to delirium, I should like us all to consider an old Japanese poem that teaches us to be happy where we are and not sad for where we cannot be,' said the Professor, seemingly, to the ceiling, as he dribbled juice and sagged in his seat, 'for living is an activity that leaves no survivors. It is from eleven hundred years ago from a work of great wisdom, the *Hinky mond ka*.' He began to croon in a ghostly chanting voice with lightly bouncing hand-gestures— like the ping-pong ball over the subtitles at the cinema—the sound echoing around the room, seeming to dim the lamps by its insistent rhythms, conjuring spirits out of the woodwork and terrifying the staff with memories of village *bomohs*. '*Yononaka wo, Ushi to yasashi to, Omohe domo, Tobitachi kanetsu, Tori ni shi arane ba.*' An unearthly hush fell over the table, as from a magic spell. A quavering hoot and some great insect flapped across the glass of the window as if summoned from Hell, to be beaked away, squirming, by a silhouetted owl. The Professor ran his hands through his long hair and sniffed back tears. In his time at the Gardens he had reverted to civilian hair that now gleamed like snow on wintry Mount Fuji. 'It is a little hard to translate but something like ...' He rose to his feet, 'I feel life is sorrowful and unbearable but I cannot fly away since I am not a bird.' He stiffened and bowed, fluttered tired arms sadly in emulation of absent wings and walked with unsteady dignity out of the room and upstairs to his quarters. They heard the door shut softly. The protesting creak of springs. Snores followed immediately.

'Well,' said Catchpole, self-righteously wig-straightening. 'Now, that's what I call a rum do. I sometimes wonder whether the old man's really quite all there.'

* * *

Pilchard had been aware of the heliotropic cat for several months. It kept mostly to the roofs and other elevated areas as it moved slowly round to bask and purr in the shifting sun but sometimes whorls of pigeon-feathers on the ground marked points where it had come down to strike. The solar timetable made the general sweep of its movements relatively predictable though it seemed to realise the importance of varying its routines and scheduled stops. During the occupation, cats had become as jumpy as nuns in a night club, rightly interpreting all friendly overtures as marks of evil designs. Occasionally its emerald eyes and Pilchard's own would meet and it would briefly pause and stare down at him, jet black and glossy, with a terrible clarity of vision that stripped away all human dissimulation, before sneering and moving on.

Ong was becoming more insistent. Pilchard's duties in the Orchid House offered few opportunities for gleaning edible supplies and Ong had unilaterally cut his rations. Often, when the food reached him there would now be nothing left but fermented manioc that smelt of babies' sick and when fruit was distributed at the end of a meal, there would be none for him. Their previous master–servant relationship counted for nothing and had, if anything, been reversed. He was the child sent home from the party without an orange. All his life, Pilchard had been a pudding-lover in a savoury world and now sugar was rarer than TNT. It had taken a long time to teach Ong the principles of English cooking—that fish only existed as an excuse for eating chips and that a main course was only valid as a precursor of puddings.

And now those bitter lessons had been forgotten. Appeals went unheard. The Professor simply stared away into the distance, defining such practical unpleasantness out of existence, and lit a cigarette. The heliotropic cat would have to pay the price of his admission back into the charmed circle of survivors. It would have to be hunted and killed for the table, flung contemptuously at Ong's feet. But how? The Japanese had announced the confiscation of all means of death at a distance—on threat of death close up—and the ancient shotgun that had enforced the rule of law on the monkeys and squirrels in the gardens had been solemnly surrendered by the Professor. The roofs, over which the cat ranged, quickeared, with such poise and confidence, were fragile and inaccessible so high-level ambush was not an option. He had a fantasy of stealing Catchpole's wig and using it as a lure, a sort of fake rat, to trap the cat. Sometimes, he had seen it climb trees, presumably to catch the rodents that ate the coconuts, and so there must come a stage when it came down again in a series of ill-coordinated, backward-facing, jerky drops. That would be the moment to strike. He set a watch.

It was three hungry days before he caught sight of it through the pink mass of *Cymbidium insignine*. It was working the coconut trees over by the forest reserve and he watched with admiration as it emerged from the shadows, flexed its claws and leapt up at the trunk and then progressed just like a native nut-picker in a series of barbed leaps up into the canopy where it disappeared into silence. In the early afternoon, a brief but violent rustling announced a kill, probably a squirrel, and Pilchard crouched in the cover of a crimson bougainvillea, clutching a pruning knife, to wait until thirst drove it down again. A sleepy hour passed. Another. And then the scraping of claws on bark came from far up in the green shade as the cat slid, braked, slid again, edging ever closer until it stopped some ten feet above the ground and looked around with sharp eyes and pricked ears. Pilchard froze and held his breath. His thumb slid appraisingly over the edge of the pruning knife. The cat slid a little further down the trunk, now on the side away from him. Closer. Ever closer. Softly, softly catchee pussy. He could see its claws flexing and sliding and coiled his body to spring and ... a hand fell on his shoulder.

'Jesus Christ!' In a single moment he felt the knife drop from his dead fingers, his heart sought to burst out of his chest and the cat shot, a spitting, scratching horrent furball, between his astonished legs and skittered off into the undergrowth. He turned, shaking, and found a small Chinese, somewhat older than himself, wearing what seemed to be navy blue knickers and a torn vest, laughing up at him. Over his shoulder was a woven bag like those in the Malay twigware section of the museum.

'Good afternoon, Tuan. I apologise for startling you.' It seemed to Pilchard that he spoke English far too well for someone who thought of navy knickers as an outer garment. 'Cat got your tongue?'

'What?' He leaned on a tree for support, wiped the sweat from his eyes.

'I said "Good afternoon, Tuan". Tuan works here in the garden?'

Pilchard nodded. He badly needed a drink—palm wine, tea, pond water—anything.

'My name is Chen Guang. I have come from the mangrove research station specially to see Tuan.'

Mangroves had been largely cleared from around the shores of Singapore except in the northern backwaters where the gardens had been granted generous rights over several hundred acres of acrid and valueless mud, swamp and sea. As a mere research outstation, in the present situation, it had been left to its own devices, Britain abandoned by the Roman legions.

'The mangroves? I don't understand.'

The old man smiled patiently. On closer examination, he was maybe not as old as he had seemed, maybe only in his forties. It was not the face. The body had stooped, now it straightened, seemed spry, almost youthful.

'I have been protecting the mangroves for Tuan.' He spoke gently as if to a slow-witted child. 'From tomfoolery.' He smiled at the trail of the absent cat. 'There are bad men who come there to steal the mangrove poles. They take them and sell them in the market. Because they do not rot, the Malays use the poles to build their houses over the water.' Pilchard had seen the sellers hauling the great orange aerial roots about in the market, Tamils, big, hairy men, very dark, machete-wielding and muscular but with skinny calves—scary. He wondered how this little man could ever hope to stop them. 'In return for my guardianship I ask only for a place to live with my small family and the right to fish for shrimps and prawns. They are very prolific this year.'

Since when did a simple fisherman ever use a word like 'prolific' or 'guardianship', very schoolbought words?

'You know why they are so "prolific"?' The man smiled. 'Death,' he said simply. 'It is life from death. We do not care to eat them ourselves so we sell them to the Japanese who gobble them down and always want more. There is a sort of justice in it, eating humble pie. One day the prawns will consume Japanese bodies and *then* we will perhaps eat them but I do not think so. That is why I have brought Tuan this.' He stretched out his hand, closed. palm downward, like an invitation to play Stone, Paper, Scissors. Pilchard stared at it curiously and then held out his own upward-cupped hand and the two mated. Something soft was pressed into his palm and, looking down, he saw a roll of banknotes fit to choke a horse. 'It is half the money of the prawns. Since the mangroves are Tuan's, perhaps the prawns are Tuan's too. Is it good?'

Pilchard was astonished. 'Yes,' he said, taken aback. 'Yes. It's good, all right. Very good. Thank you.' He slipped the money rapidly in his pocket. Enough to make a cat laugh.

'One thing more I need from Tuan only, a simple paper for the Japanese, showing I am the official guardian of the mangroves. It is an administrative matter. The Japanese want so many pieces of paper. Otherwise they will trouble me and I am a man who treasures tranquillity.'

Pilchard thought rapidly. The money bounced comfortingly against his thigh, evoking memories of days of more rampant sexuality. There was no chance he would give it back.

'Er ... Let me think ... Wait here. Please sit. I will return with a paper.' It was a matter of some ten minutes to get to the office and bang out a pompous letter on leftover, fancy, headed notepaper, backdated to the previous year, appointing Chen Guang to his non-existent office. He paused, then signed it 'Fernando Dagama' with a great flourish and added a couple of the Professor's talismanic Japanese notices from the perimeter, slipped them all in an envelope. 'If you put these on the gate, they will discourage visitors.'

The man smiled and tucked the envelope carefully away in a cheap wallet and stowed it in the bottom of his bag.

'In three months, if we are spared, I will send another payment but I am getting old, it is far, I may send someone else. Don't worry. You will know them.' He walked slowly away without further ceremony or even a backward glance. Pilchard had the odd feeling that he had just sold his soul to the Devil. A silly fantasy! Reality lay in the roll in his pocket that he fingered lingeringly and translated, in his mind's eye, into a wealth of bully beef and eggs frying in luxurious fat-splatter. This was a real life-saver, incredible good luck. And why not? After all a black cat had just crossed his path.

* * *

'*This is Orphan Annie broadcasting to all my little orphan friends—I mean enemies—in the Pacific. Do you feel hated tonight? Are you worried about your wives and sweethearts back home? Don't be. You can be sure they are being taken real good care of by the non-combatants and those lonely young foreign workers with their big blue eyes. For any boneheads from the American South, well the news is, it's true what they say about Dixie and the big black boys down there are being* real *friendly to all your gals while you're away so they'll hardly be missing you at all ...*' They were in the sitting room of the Cluny Road house, a room too small for social comfort, tuned to 'Tokyo Rose', or rather any one of the dozen women who broadcast in English for the Japanese radio. The sound swelled and throbbed but could barely be heard over the pinging calls of frogs outside, excited by recent rain and eager to share their own southern comfort. Of late, reception had been poor but no one listened anyway until the evening, when radio waves zithered off the ionosphere to give a better signal. Whatever the reception, the Professor would allow no other station to be listened to. Having the wireless ostentatiously tuned to NHK was as necessary as the Emperor's photograph hung on the wall, an obligatory pinch of incense flung on the altar of conformity. To have a radio at all was anomalous, due to this being registered as a Japanese household, and listening to All India Radio was punishable by death. As a precaution, the tuning knob had been removed so that only permitted listening was possible.

'Couldn't we at least have a local station. It's not the childish propaganda I object to so much as that dreadful American music,' whined Catchpole. 'It's all right for you, Pilchard. You are not musical and therefore feel no pain. Do you suppose anyone here could afford to buy some new records? I'm sick to death of 'Begin the Beguine' with the scratch at the end and side four of 'Madam Butterfly'. Even having side three would be a change or waiting for the scratch in a different place. They have plenty in the market. Looted of course.'

The question was directed at Pilchard. It was understood that the Professor was Nelsonically deaf to any remarks made in English in this room. Pilchard's sudden rush of wealth had not passed unnoticed though he was careful to drip-feed it into the general economy of the Director's household. In the world outside the Gardens, after the first year of the occupation, food was only distributed by the official monopolies for the first twenty days of every month and thereafter people had to survive on fresh air and their wits. Only employees of Japanese companies, the *butais*, had access to extra supplies, much of which ended up on the black market, but Pilchard's white face stuck out far too much for him to dare go near it. Inflation raged through the city like a fever and he had to rely on Ping and Pong to buy for him, expensively and at largely theoretical risk of their own lives, so that the money went nowhere near as far as he had hoped. Their regular contact was a member of the police auxiliary, a 'three-star-man', kept honest by the fact that he was also a cousin, who delivered straight to the Gardens. Pilchard had finally become carriage-trade. Catchpole, as ever sharp-eyed for advantage, had picked up on the new state of affairs at once, while the Professor was moved to surprised tears at the sudden appearance of two priceless pickled plums, one evening, on his dinner plate but knew better than to ask any questions.

'I cannot stand records,' interrupted the Professor, looking up from his *Syonan Times*, 'any records. There is too much sadness

145

about sitting in the tropics at night listening to gramophone records of far away. The wireless, for some reason, is quite different. The wireless is in the present tense—as you would say—the gramophone a quotation.'

Catchpole was watching Pilchard. Previously, by mutual consent, their paths had barely crossed. Now, suddenly, moon-faced Catchpole swam into his orbit, by accident, a dozen times a day in the Gardens. A few days ago, Pilchard had even been invited—absurdly—to Catchpole's bachelor room as if they were undergraduates together, about to have an earnest conversation about god or play chess far into the night. He half-wondered whether Catchpole would abandon the wig in his room, as women did the veil, but no. In the centre, stood an ancient iron bedstead whose resentful springs clinked like chain mail. The space around the bed was stuffed with useless loot, grabbed, with greed and no forethought, from the other houses in Cluny Road in the early days when their owners had been marched off and before they were taken over by Japanese. A radiogram with no plug was heaped with assorted dressing gowns on tangled coathangers. A worthless trombone, snapped in the middle as though by an infuriated practiquant of the instrument, leant drunkenly in one corner, while, in another, stood a pile of—surely almost priceless—dry batteries for the electric earhorn. There, Catchpole had perched awkwardly—as though incubating an egg—on a Regency-style striped banquette with lions' paw feet and plied him with Japanese plum brandy that tasted like alcoholic seawater and left a ring round the inside of his mouth rather like a greasy bathtub.

'I can't help noticing, old man, that you're a little more flush these days. As senior curator, I think I should know where it's coming from. When all's said and done, we don't want the Japs getting interested do we? Bringing us into disrepute. After all, when you turned up here, you hadn't got two cents to rub together and we took you in, you know. And it's only thanks to my quick thinking, as senior curator, that the governor authorised this whole arrangement.'

'Senior? You're not senior to me.'

'In terms of years of service, I have seniority and it's my right to know ...'

'Perhaps Captain Oishi is paying me for his botany lessons. He comes to the Orchid House most days as you know.'

'Then that money should come to me as senior curator.'

'Oh. Go boil your senior head, Catchpole.' He bit back on mentioning the wig to be removed before boiling. It was such a bad example of its kind that it was an insult to the intelligence of those about him, not just in the texture but the implausibly youthful colour.

'Well. Really. I'm afraid that's going on your file.'

To all the boys in Burma, they call you "the forgotten army". Well, I haven't forgotten you and nor have your Japanese chums. They think of you all the time and you'll be hearing from them real soon. In the meantime, here's a record that maybe sums up how you all feel in the East, before the big attack that's coming. Are you ready for a devastating assault on your morale?—Hoagy Carmichael sings you all Hong Kong Blues. *Now don't any of you boys go kicking ole' Buddha's gong.'*

There came a knock at the door and there was smiling Captain Oishi, not kicking any gongs today but bowing and *sensei*-ing to the Professor. It was true that he passed through the Gardens on most days, sometimes stopping for a chat or a game of chess with the Professor, sometimes asking about plants, mostly just waving as he strolled lightly through. Evening visits to the house were rare. 'Hi guys,' he called in an American twang. Perhaps he, too, had been listening to Tokyo Rose. Pilchard stood and offered tea made from twice-used leaf, leaving him and the Professor to work their way through the minuet of whatever courtesies and nodding deference were demanded by the ways of the mysterious East. He had been experimenting with teas from the leaves of various plants about the Gardens. *Bougainvillea* tasted better than *hibiscus* but stripped the skin off your tongue. Oishi accepted the tea, sat down on the worn moquette, leaned forward with his hands on his knees and sighed contentedly, his face aglow, more beautiful than merely handsome.

'I have had some good news. It seems I may be going home soon.' He blushed.

Catchpole scowled enviously. 'Lucky sod!'. The Captain smiled wanly. 'To Tokyo?'

'Kyoto. It seems the General has been recalled. It is a political thing of the government. There are many groups within the army and one of them has risen. He has been ordered to return.'

'To Kyoto?'

'To Tokyo. For the moment I am to remain behind with my squad and act as liaison officer with the new commanders but it cannot be long before I can go home too.' Pilchard was suddenly puzzled to realise that he would miss Oishi, his youth and innocence, his ... neoteny. Instructing him in the orchestration of orchids filled some sort of need. The Captain drank without using the handle and set the cup back primly on its saucer, made it look barbarous in such delicate hands. In a time where everything was chipped and broken, he was still shiny and new, fresh and crisp from the box. There was something wonderful about the way Nature just kept wiping the slate clean of all the dirt and scratches and starting again from the original design with each gleaming, unscathed generation. Perhaps age brought paternal longings to us all.

'Maybe they want to make him Minister for War.'

'The telegramme made it clear it was disgrace not honour. Yet it will be so good to return home. It will be—as you say— hunkydory. Before I was chosen to fight for my nation, I had never even left Kyoto and seen the capital. My mother did not wish it. The war, for me, has been a very interesting experience. It is most fortunate. Otherwise I might never have learned to propagate orchids.' They looked at each other blankly, wrong-footed by the innocent understatement. The broadening of Captain Oishi's experience from human to plant nursery scarcely seemed a reasonable justification for all the mess and inconvenience the entire world had been put to. 'My only concern is that the General should not be dishonoured. His was a great victory. The army should be grateful to him.'

The Professor snorted. 'It is always a mistake to think of an institution as a person, Captain. Armies have no feelings. Armies cannot be grateful any more than can universities.' He bit down bitterly on his pipe, as if grinding on an old personal resentment. 'Both are just ill-calibrated machines for crushing people without feeling.' Said fiercely. 'That is why I prefer volcanoes to armies. Volcanoes have souls. I have reached the age where I merely wish to live quietly on the slopes of Mount Fuji and read her changing moods.' The Professor puffed his pipe volcanically, then, as if it followed logically, 'Who is to be the new commander?'

'It is not yet known. The politicians will decide. We must respect their choice.' He lowered his head reverently. Now it was Pilchard that snorted. Oishi looked up, astonished. 'You do not like politicians, Dr Pilchard?' He shrugged. 'Are they not important?'

'Something can be important without being in the least interesting. Politicians are like drains, sadly necessary but unglamorous. They should do their humble job without bothering the rest of us. And every so often, the system breaks down and then you have to take notice because there is a terrible stink of leaking corruption and then you clear the whole lot out and start all over again.'

The Professor chuckled. Captain Oishi looked from one to the other, shocked.

'I think you two are growing too much alike.'

The Professor smiled across at Pilchard. 'Perhaps. When the name is announced, we should hybridise a new rose—something big and floppy with a nice smell that would hide the stink of the drains—a very vulgar tea rose—and call it Tokyo Rose, or some such nonsense, and send it to the new general. These days you cannot have too many friends. Armies may not be grateful but generals can sometimes be.'

'Right Professor.'

'And now ...' Captain Oishi turned in his chair, '... please to explain, Dr Pilchard, what is this place I have heard of called Gracie Fields? Where exactly is it? Is it a green and pleasant place?'

This is your number one enemy saying goodbye to all you little orphans. But don't worry. There will be more of the same on the "Zero Hour" tomorrow night. Now it's time for fighting news for fighting men. Goodbye to you all and be good ...'

* * *

It was the sort of day you dream about in Singapore, where cold brings a similar blessing to sunshine in Europe and bears the same optimism within it. By some miracle, the usual steambath had been abruptly switched off, the windows flung open and the wonder of a cool wind blew through the Gardens, tousling the palms and rattling the blinds on the Orchid House and bringing relief to the whole sprawled and baking city. Only the heliotropic—and clearly endothermic—cat glared down resentfully from the rooftops and shivered in its ruffled fur. In the Orchid House, having worked the miracle of fertilisation with a deft flick of his pollinating paintbrush, Pilchard had collected the spores and was now preparing the medium in which they would grow. In the wild, the mortality of orchids was enormous and millions were produced with evolutionary indifference so that just one might survive—a little like humans these days, for the Greater East Asia Co-Prosperity Sphere had erased the difference between plant and Man. In the Gardens, orchids were spoiled brats, their every demand met with deference since their reaction to any small frustration of environment and schedule was to simply swoon and die. Spores contained very little food to enable them to survive and flourish and normally depended on the presence of a specific fungus to germinate and might even then take up to twelve years to flower. The Gardens had long given up the use of added fungus and now embraced a German technique of starting the embryos in a sterile glass vessel of agar jelly boiled in a pressure cooker. But each kind of orchid required magic additions—banana, coconut milk, pineapple juice, minerals, ammonia, caustic soda—a whole sorcerer's cookbook of recipes that was one of the treasured and evolving resources of the Gardens and locked away in the safe at night. Without it, the calculations never worked, mere mathematical pi in the sky. Some horticulturalists, of course, refused to write the recipes down and took them sullenly to their graves while others gloried in their own intellectual fertility and covered whole chapters with their hocus pocus. Pilchard waved his glass stirring rod like a conjuror's wand over the dog-eared, stained volume, its leather cover shiny with sweat and handling like a *gaucho*'s saddle. Some would call it filthy but he preferred to think of it as the 'rich patina of use' so treasured in the exhibits of the museum, as he grumbled through the book's contents, seeking the right scribbled and blotchy section. Today's unusually low temperature was a nuisance—orchid cultivators made as much deft use of a thermometer as gynaecologists—so he propagated slowly and pedantically in solitary and hushed sterility. And then, perhaps not surprisingly amongst all those fermenting, but unfeeling, uterine flasks, a bleak thought suddenly broke in of his absent wife, martyred by her own barrenness, and he sighed 'Oh bugger, bugger, bugger!' like a magic incantation.

He and Margaret had married as young, freshly qualified doctors setting out into the world as into a great adventure. Their pre-departure honeymoon had been one cold week in blustery Minehead where, on the beach, they had found a mine from the last war. He had quipped that it was just as well they had not gone to Maidenhead. She had been unconventional, uncompromising, free-thinking, -drinking, -smoking, with a heady air of the *bohémienne*, so that he had been shocked to find her maternal instinct so strong. For him, the lack of children was not a problem. He had no urge to reproduce. He had not yet grown up himself and you would have to be crazy or totally selfish to bring a child into a world like this. Colonial life, for a disgruntled and unfulfilled woman, offered few outlets so that her adulteries had seemed less a matter of the betrayal of their love than of her own unconventionality and thus herself. Her partners had been sadly predictable, the tanned tennis champion at the club, then a flashy, white-toothed lawyer with plenty of money and a big car, so that he had felt pity rather than rage and that, of course, had been unforgivable. They had both taken to drinking too much, fighting too much, and their marriage had ended up—like their scotch—on the rocks. She had left on one of the first boats to Australia with no pretence that they would see any armistice or reunification after the end of the larger hostilities that had swamped their own. 'Bugger, bugger, bugger!'

He felt the sudden awareness of another presence and

stiffened, the hair standing up on his neck. The heliotropic cat? No. He looked around and there, in the corner, peered a face, a girl's small face, glimmering though the foliage like a woodnymph. He blushed.

'Do you always talk to yourself like that?'

She stepped out onto the bare, wet concrete. The closeness of the Japanese headquarters ensured that few women normally came near the Gardens. She was slight, elfin-faced, politely wide-eyed. Chinese. Maybe twenty. Maybe a little less. Ivory skin but wearing the sort of hideous, shapeless dress, gathered in ruffles at neck and wrists, that nuns made their charges wear, the tiny, yellow primulas of the material a mockery of prettiness that did nothing to hide her beauty, merely hung a theatrical curtain before it. Her hair was gathered together in a single, sex-defying plait as though she were the member of a no-nonsense hockey team and she exuded warm bunny-rabbit smells of young flesh that effortlessly overwhelmed the plant hormones boiling in the air. He was surprised to find himself so attracted, then told himself sternly that this was not a spontaneous reaction, just an old dog's remembrance of an old trick. Down boy!

'I was not talking to myself. I was thinking aloud.'

She laughed. 'You must be Mr Dagama.' The English was a little stiff, starched, like a governess's frock, imposing grammar that had been learned not felt.

'No. Mr Dagama has gone. He has not been here for ages. My name is Pilchard.'

She frowned. 'But a friend sent me to see him. He described him. I thought it was you.' She had those little, even teeth only Asians can have and now she used them to bite her lower lip, making her back into an adorable, perplexed child.

'How did he describe him?'

She laughed again. 'He said Mr Dagama was tall and skinny

with long red hair and a beard like a demon—just like you.'

'Don't all round-eyes look the same?' he teased. He was almost flirting—one of the forgotten arts of peace. After so long, it felt good—silly but good.

She bit her lip again. '… and a big nose and bad teeth and ugly. But also young, You're not *young*.' She frowned at the flasks. 'What are you doing?'

'I'm making babies—making new plants with beautiful colours and smells that have never been seen before—or smelled.'

'Hmm. Why don't plants make noises?'

'What?'

'Plants make colours for our eyes, smells for noses, tastes for mouths, why they don't make noises for ears?' Pilchard was taken aback.

'Well … I'd never really thought about it. An extraordinary question. I suppose the generation of sound requires rapid vibration, lungs, and plants have no muscles and are therefore only capable of slow motions which …' She scowled. 'What noise would you like them to make? Should they hum, or whistle or perhaps …' He executed a monstrous lipfart and she laughed as would a baby. 'That would be the raspberries making that noise. Of course, the noise would be louder in the case of mass wisteria or perhaps that's just begonia's luck.'

'Why do all men not know they have to make you laugh. They just want to be admired all the time. Men and their ideas and principles. If you tell any man he is irresistible, he will believe you. Plants should make music. They should sing us songs like birds. So do you want to know who is my friend?'

He was confused by the zigzag of her thoughts. 'What?' The penny dropped. 'Chen Guang? From the mangrove research station?'

She shushed, nodded and looked around, the lashes heavy

on her eyes. The plants might not make sounds but perhaps they had ears.

He lowered his voice. 'Let us say, then, that my name is Pilchard but sometimes I am also Mr Dagama. Do you have something for me?' He had expected some crusty peasant. She dug in her prim little school bag and drew out the same envelope he had given her friend and dropped it down on the wooden workbench, eager to be rid of it. It was rude to look inside but he did so anyway and saw a ruff of greasy money. Less of it than last time but welcome enough. He bowed gallantly. 'Please say thank you to your friend. What is your name?'

She looked around wildly. 'Er ... Okid'

'Orchid? What kind of orchid are you? Ground-growing, tree-growing, monopodial, sympodial? I suppose it really doesn't matter as long as you smell nice and you do smell nice, like vanilla. A *Rosa banksiana* by any other name ...'

'Just Okid. Goodbye.' She set her head on one side and looked at him the way a puppy does. 'You're funny.' She spun round and took a step straight into Captain Oishi and dropped her bag, spilling its contents on the ground with a little squeal.

It was as if they were both struck by lightning. Pilchard thought of the French and their *coup de foudre*. Neither looked down at the bag, just at each other. Time froze, together with their young faces, and the world seemed somehow to wobble and warp around the pair and he was sure he heard the glass panels overhead creak and pop in their frames before reality steadied and hardened back into shape and then they both bent to retrieve the bag and cracked their heads together.

'Ayo!'

'Itai!'

'Oh my God!'

Even cries of pain carry their cultural load. Before the war,

155

Pilchard had been treated by a Chinese dentist called Ow, who was blissfully unaware of the associations of his name but laughed endlessly over the joke that dentists were people who attacked your teeth with steel spikes then complained that you had holes in them. He slid the envelope deftly inside the dirty book of orchid recipes and crossed over to where the two sat, rocking on the wet cement floor and clutching their heads. Assuming the pose of the blessing Christ on Sugar Loaf Mountain, he offered each a hand and helped them to their feet so that they all ended up in a sort of paternally approving embrace, two infants with wet bottoms being comforted. 'Miss Orchid. May I present Captain Yoshi Oishi.'

As they touched fingertips, Captain Oishi felt that a great, roaring wind blew in from the sea, sending loose blossom whirling down on their heads and fluttering their black hair. The universe was heaving a cosmic sigh of relief at finally achieving the statistical near-impossibility of bringing two such fated but distant lovers together.

* * *

Sleep came fitfully. School. School clothes. Pilchard drifted back to his primary school, his first traumatic day, painted in primary colours. Across the table, on a long bench sat a little, Chinese girl who would grow up to be called Orchid. She was picking her nose and eating the product. It was all the Prince of Wales's fault. He had gone off on another of his jaunts around the Empire, somewhere hot to avoid the English winter. The children had to bring in newspaper cuttings and follow his progress every day on a big map pinned on the wall that they had surrounded with crowns wastefully cut out of sticky paper. His naval vessel had started in Sierra Leone—"Principal exports timber, minerals and copra. What is copra?"—Pilchard with his hand in the air, the infant expert on copra and its uses in the manufacture of paint and margarine. He had never eaten margarine. His mother didn't believe in it even if it was cheaper. It totally lacked a magical quality called 'goodness'. But then he had never seen a coconut either. It could have been as imaginary as a unicorn.

As the Prince travelled, faces of happy black children in clean clothes waving Union Jacks spread across the wall towards the games cupboard. He had gone on to the Gold Coast—"Principal exports timber, minerals and copra. What is copra?"—where more people with smooth, shiny faces and very white teeth waved flags and shook hands under palm trees with officials in feathery hats and chiefs wearing big frocks. It was all a bit boring really. You could see the Prince was bored too. Pilchard preferred it when he went to America and they put out a big sign "Hi Ed!" In school they had laughed for days over that. Miss Dixon had explained that the Americans probably meant well but weren't too bright.

The map was a big map of the Empire spreadeagled over one wall. The ends looked very far apart but—by some great mystery—actually joined up. The British bits of the world were coloured red. There were lots of them. At the top sat sexless Britannia behind her shield, a coalscuttle helmet on her head, as the different races jostled to pour imperial bounty about her feet.

His best friend at school, Kevin, was bored with Nigeria— soon it would be "Principal exports timber, minerals and copra. What is copra?"—and colouring in the Prince's route in royal blue crayon. The chiefs here wore bandages wrapped round their heads. He nudged Pilchard. "I hear," he said in an offhand, toffee- nosed way that told you this was a joke, "that they've just opened a cannibal restaurant. Say 'is it expensive?'"

"Is it expensive?" asked Pilchard.

"Nah. Five bob a head." He collapsed giggling.

"*All right Kevin. You have something to say. Share it with all of us.*" Miss Dixon.

"No Miss, nothing."

"*But I insist Kevin. If you want to say something in this class, you put up your hand. Now what was it that was so urgent that you couldn't wait to put up your hand. Sit up and cross your arms*"

"Well, Miss. Please, Miss." He opened big, innocent eyes. "Why's the Empire red?" The children looked up sharply from their crayons. The chatter died. He had said it in a certain tone they had grown to listen for. They knew this was one of those big, simple questions, the sort grown-ups could never answer, that tied them up in knots.

"Well, Kevin Matlock." There was a set smile on Miss Dixon's face and a bright, empty, lightness in her voice. "By colouring it red you can see how much of the world we rule compared to the French. Their parts are green, you see, and the Italians' are that nasty grey colour. In our part we bring peace and hope and justice to suffering millions of the subject races. Red is a nice happy colour like pillar boxes and telephone boxes, also Beefeater's uniforms."

Kevin screwed up his face. "But why red Miss?"

The smile began to erode and be replaced by a very great patience. "Red is for the blood that great men in the past have shed for their country so that children like you could all grow up in safety and freedom." *Pilchard stood up now, put anguished puzzlement on his face.*

"Please Miss," *he piped.* "My Dad says red's for communists. Are we communists then?"

The patience had gone by now to be replaced by naked authority. "No, we are *not* communists, thank you very much. Sit down please."

"Does it mean the people there would be communists, then, if our soldiers didn't stop them? Aren't the rioters in Freetown communists?"

"Well ... I don't think that has much to do with it. Sit down please."

"Red's for danger," said Kevin loudly. "That's right isn't it Miss Dixon? It means people who don't do as we say had jolly well better watch out." He bunched his fists across his chest and scowled to screams of laughter.

"That's enough now," snapped Miss Dixon, clapping her hands. "You've all read that little red book we have that tells you all about the heroes of the Empire. Red cover, you see. Let's think about that—who can name them for me?"

A little girl at the front put up her hand and lisped, "Nelthon."

"Good. Any more?"

"General Wolfe"

"That's right. Any more?"

"Grace Darling."

'Well done. Any more?'

Kevin put up his hand. 'Please Miss, Gracie Fields' Miss Dixon looked weary.

'You always have to go too far, Kevin. Now stop being silly.'

"But Miss ... Kevin hitched up his trousers with two hands. "It's not really red. If you look at it properly, it's pink. But pink's for sissies, Miss. It's a girrrls' colour."

Cries of "Errgh!" from the boys.

"The Empire ought to be blue for boys. Pink," he sneered. "Pink's for pansies."

Kevin had said a terrible thing—a wonderful thing. Pilchard had laughed, audibly, visibly. Kevin had somehow brought two things together that created a flash of electricity, of power, of liberation. He had made a new world. And then the old world *came crashing down about their ears with a sound of thunder and they were held to have 'made fun of the Empire'. The two were immediately isolated like an infection and marched off for summary court martial by Miss Deedman, the headmistress, and a beating across the bare legs with an old plimsoll—obscurely called Webster—that she kept in her cupboard.*

"Whoosh!"

Pilchard took his beating first. It stung and he had to blink back the tears. But he was used to beatings at home and, anyway, he was proud, not ashamed. Technically, he knew, he could plead innocence. After all, it was Kevin who had said it, not him. But they had not compromised. They had both stood firm. Really, when it came down to it, for all their blustering, there was little they could do to you as long as you stood firm. And today he had made a second discovery that he would never forget—that there was a difference between that which was really wrong and that which was merely forbidden. Pilchard looked across at Kevin and risked a smile of encouragement that was returned. This could not touch them.

"Wipe that smirk off your face, Kevin Matlock," Miss Deedman spat, raising Webster yet again. When she lifted her arm the flesh hung down from the bone and he could see the white hairs in her nostrils quiver.

"Please Miss," screamed Kevin, cringing, his face like 'Desperation' on the Fry's 5-boys chocolate wrapper and pointing at Pilchard. "He made me do it!"

* * *

Now a time of dry heat came to the city and an unseasonal hot blast blew in from the northwest, dancing in little dust storms along the streets and tugging at the tired red suns that hung, exhausted, from the buildings. Birds dusted themselves in the alluvial sand that accumulated in the gutters where once water had tumbled. In Changi, the civilian prisoners slumped and swore and fought with each other, exploiting every distinction of rank, nationality, religion and age to strengthen division without unity. In the gardens, the grass shrivelled, the tops of the palms bleached and matted and the flow to the lake shrank to a trickle. In the intemperate heat, the heliotropic cat was finally fulfilled and—oblivious to threats—rolled on its back to bathe its belly in sunshine till the fur there smouldered to deepest shades of roasted henna. Catchpole no longer stood at his morning window, encrusted with sleep, and cursed the endless rain. Now he stood and railed against the pitiless heat as the day's first sweat trickled down his chest and groin. The Professor pottered about in a huge straw hat, as if in early retirement, and planted the fat seeds of slow-growing, bitter cucumbers, a vegetable that retained a suitable moral dimension, against the workshop walls. And the lovers met almost every day, at noon, two merging shadows under the high forest canopy, as Pilchard ceased wrestling with his petulant orchids and left his little back room, with its narrow cot, studiedly unlocked and unvisited. Nothing was said. Everyone knew it was simply the way the world wanted things to be.

Captain Yoshi Oishi knew little of love. He had been like one of the high-ranking officers billeted in a vast colonial house of which he fitfully used one or two rooms only, the rest left dusty and shut up in darkness as irrelevant to his life. Now, for the first time, he was unlocking new doors, flinging open shutters, tearing off dustsheets, taking possession of himself in his entirety, surprised and enchanted to find the space within so much larger than he had been led to believe, more elaborately figured. He was still at the stage where he totally identified love and powerful visceral sensations, rather than seeing an area of overlap between them whose dimensions waxed and waned with its own internal logic. And he was fascinated with Orchid and had embarked on a voyage of discovery of her body, removing the thick serge knickers and old aertex vests, still with their school laundry numbers, to reveal the different textures, undulations, exudations of her form, the subtle shadings of her skin at the joints, the places where it stretched and moved, tensed by the strong muscles underneath. He wondered at their nesting concavities and convexities. The smooth, arched curve of her neck delighted him. Her eyes were endless fascination. They were Asian eyes but different from the Asian eyes he had known, flatter, more tilted, smaller and darker with a dramatic, diacritical flick at each corner. He adored kissing them and feeling them squirm under his lips yet, as he stared into them, he was puzzled to see nothing but himself reflected. He loved to close his own eyes and nuzzle blindly at her breast like a puppy to its mother.

'Orchid,' he smiled. They were sprawled in damp, post-coital torpor behind the Orchid House. She was surely younger than him and he felt a guilty tingle of incestuous elder-brotherhood whenever he looked at her. A thought of Erica flashed through his mind and he shuddered. Why did your mind do that—make you think of the one thing you did not want to think of? In answer to his query, it sent him an image of the wind lifting Erica's skirt to show ribbed support hose.

Orchid's voice came from over his head. 'It is not my real name, you know.'

He was appalled and looked up. 'Not your real name? Orchid not your real name? But you are so like an orchid, so slim and fragile and beautiful and ...'

'No. It is a name I chose for myself. Do you know what my real name is? It is "hope for a little brother". There. My father, like all men, only wants sons, so that's what they called me.

Chinese do that. There was no need for him to do so. I already had an older brother who's a pig. And now I've got a little brother as well. He's a pig too.' He laughed and rolled over to reach down into his bag.

'I have something for you, my love—my piglet.' He had never tried the silly endearments of lovers before. The words were fresh and new and made him giddy. He took out a slip of pure white paper, thick and smooth and soft, lay it gently down on the bed beside her naked body and unfolded it with exquisite care. She stared at it blankly.

'What is it?'

'It is a poem. A love poem. You will see that I have written it in *kanji*, Chinese characters, so that you too can read it. Each character I have written on a red rose petal and glued it with manioc paste, in a circle, so that it goes round and round eternally. I did it this morning while I was supposed to be writing a report on the possibilities of balloon warfare. I took the rose petals from the Gardens without permission. I stole a rose from their flower garden! You have already made me a criminal and a bad officer.' He laughed then saw her sorrowful face. 'What is it Orchid?'

'Oh Yoshi. I can't read Chinese. My father does not believe in educating girls and my mother was Christian. It was as much as she could get him to do, to send me to the nuns' school. I only know a few characters. It was all in English, you see— Shakespeare and Wordsworth and so on. I am so ignorant. But I want to learn everything I can about you. You're so clever. So tell me. What exactly is balloon warfare?' She snuggled in closer so that he breathed in her hair, 'I never even heard of it before. I'm sure you're the only person in the world who knows about it.'

He leaned back and swelled with manly pride and sated love. Japanese peppers are hot though small.

'Well ... we know that the Americans are developing new

explosives and the Germans have pilotless aircraft and rocket bombs but we too have something new that our research scientists are perfecting. It is a marvellous weapon—hydrogen bombs.' His eyes shone. 'Balloons, filled with hydrogen, that have already been used with devastating effect against the United States. They can be made in their thousands by our schoolchildren who paste together sheets of tissue paper and varnish them for the nation as they sing patriotic songs. They will be released from the mainland or from submarines and rise to a height of over 30,000 feet to carry fire-bombs or biological agents over enemy territory. A special electrical or clockwork mechanism keeps the balloons at the right altitude by dropping bags of sand if they drift too low and a timer releases their bombs, one by one, over the correct area. Many are killed by the bags of sand alone, dropping from such a height. Then they descend by themselves and finally another bomb blows up and sets fire to the wreckage as they crash in flames. They are such beautiful devices! From Syonanto, using the monsoon winds, they can be used against both India and Australia to bring both to their knees. We are making trials right now. We are very hopeful.'

'Yoshi, darling. You are so clever! How do you ever think of such things?' Her eyes were bright and admiring and her hand was—most excitingly—stroking the hairless muscularity of his inner thigh. 'But I can't think what it would look like. Draw it for me, darling. That's right. Just here on the back of this piece of paper. Lovely!'

* * *

Professor Tanakadate leaned over the breakfast table, gathered his workaday kimono about him and sat back to light a cigarette—a sort of oriental Noel Coward—to take away the taste of the endless manioc paste. They had grown so bored with it that they had just used it to create a model of a volcano, the Professor explaining its inner workings with congealing slime and demonstrating the erosive effect of rainfall with the Flit gun filled with water. Its ruins lay before them—*magma cum laude*—on a chipped non-tectonic plate of blue PWD china. He drew the moral, as in one of his lectures at the university.

'That is why the eruptive as opposed to the sedimentational model of atolls such as Cocos-Keeling has attracted more support. But perhaps one day we shall go there together and do joint research and finally settle the matter.' He sighed and eased stiff thighs. 'But before that, I have received an unusual request from Captain Oishi at the new Shinto temple. It seems they need a botanist you see—like yourself. Not a vulcanologist, like me. I expect it's a matter of trees, plants, grass—what to plant, how to get a satisfactory display at all seasons—you know the sort of thing.' Pilchard made a questioning face. 'Apparently Captain Oishi asked for you specially. You can use the motorbike.'

In a lean-to out front, stood a raddled BSA motorbike combination, painted matt grey and looted from God knew where, that served as the Gardens' only official transport. It too leaned from the fact of the third tyre being the wrong size. Pilchard knew that riding it would be an adventure, a welcome excursion from the confinement of the Gardens, his first real journey since release from Changi, but ...

'But I am not a real botanist. It is just that, out here, we all have to turn our hand to whatever crops up—botany, zoology, anthropology, geology ...'

'Then this is what has cropped up.'

'But we have no petrol.'

The Professor smiled. 'I have two gallons ... tucked away? Is that the expression? Yes, tucked away in my bedroom. Under the bed.' He gestured upstairs with his head.

'You keep petrol under the bed? What about the fire risk?'

The Professor shrugged. 'When there are so many easy ways to die, one more or less seems unimportant.' He rattled the matches roguishly.

'But it's endless trouble what with the roadblocks when they see a *gaijin* riding a bike. I wouldn't get through. They'd take the motorbike. You would have to come with me.'

'This conversation sounds like a British song I learned in school called "There's a hole in the bucket". If you take the goggles and crash helmet and wear an armband that I shall give you, they will not notice what you are.'

And so it was that, the next morning, Pilchard left the Gardens from the northern gate, relishing the sound and the surging vibration of the old engine between his legs and hammered on rattling pistons up towards Bukit Timah, where the stench exhaled by the camp on the old Sime Road golf course wafted foully across from behind screening trees, restoring the animality that humans habitually denied and reducing them to it and nothing else. A sweet compound of woodsmoke, toothrot, farts and despair, it was somehow far worse than that he remembered from Changi, the boiled-down essence of human misery choking in its own filth. Perhaps it was simply that it had had—how long?—eighteen months more to mature and fester. Being mainly for Eurasians rather than whites, camp conditions were much more relaxed in Sime and many proud Brits had suddenly discovered multiracial skeletons in their fitted, pukkah closets and rattled them at the Japanese in their haste to be reclassified. He turned off onto the rutted, dirt track that led to the MacRitchie reservoir, grateful for the cleansing breeze that blew off the water. Each time he hit a bump, the ruined saddle poked sharp metal into his backside. There had been a lot of heavy traffic, army trucks mostly, churning up the soil to the unsightly morass of water and weed that he thought of as 'a French lawn'. Quite a few were parked there, some with the big rubber bladders on the roof they used to run them on coal gas and idle soldiers were just lying around. There is nothing so dangerous as idle soldiers. All the uniforms made him nervous and he retained the helmet and goggles as a mask.

It was around here that he had served most of his short, sharp time in the Volunteer Force during the battle for Singapore. He had seen the craziness of it all—the men having victoriously fought lethal hand-to-hand engagements with the Japs being then ordered to retreat and offering easy targets for their planes as they made their way bunched along the open roads. The insanity of Dalforce—Chinese volunteers without uniforms, just a bandana and an armband, fighting off Nippon Imperial Guards with old shotguns and *parangs* and the odd grenade after a few weeks' limp-wristed training in the woods. Being totally divided between communists and nationalists, they had to fight in separate sections and often preferred shooting each other to killing the designated enemy. British officers, not too sure about their own backs, indulged their private sympathies by issuing the nationalists three times as many bullets as the communists. He had himself seen the famed Madame Cheng, over sixty years old, fighting hand-to-hand alongside her husband, dodging from tree to tree and spitting out invective and bullets against the Japanese as only a very angry grandmother could. There were other things he wanted more clearly to forget. He fought off a flashback, refused to see the tying of survivors to trees to be bayoneted, the hanging of mutilated body parts of Allied conscripts in the branches like Christmas decorations by chortling Japanese troops. It seemed fortunate that the human mind adjusts by being no more capable of recreating, from afar, the true feeling of horror than it is the sensations of ecstasy or gratitude. Then suddenly the fresh, friendly face of Captain Oishi, blushing under long eyelashes, was there and immediately banished the Japanese of his recollection and he pulled the suffocating memory with crash helmet and sticky goggles from his face.

'Dr Pilchard. Thank you for coming to Syonan Jinja. Here, the souls of the dead are transformed into land-protecting spirits.' He bowed, contrary to regulations, though less to Pilchard than to the idea of spirits, then hesitated. 'To be honest, I had not expected to see you so soon. I had thought, perhaps next week ...' The ground behind him had been cleared and finely landscaped and rose towards an arched wooden bridge, painted bright red, that crossed one of the many small inlets of the reservoir. Where it touched the ground at both ends, pink irises had flowered as though its colour had bled, diluted, into the earth and water. Beyond it, stood the Shinto shrine itself, a series of pavilions, some without walls, some hidden behind fences, with thick, thatched roofs and innocent wooden pillars, that explored various shades of muted grey. A snaking path, paved with polished pebbles, led off, under a stone arch like a Chinese character, among bamboo and large rocks. In the midst of it, a man was washing his hands methodically, like a surgeon, at a fountain hewn from a single block of granite. Captain Oishi's eyes followed his gaze.

'The stones were intended for the filtering of the city water but now we have a better use for them.' By the bridge, a bank of *bonsai* trees and tortured flower arrangements displayed the results of a contest among Japanese forces and showed rain-flecked photographs of bashfully grinning winners. So peaceful, so far from war. The Captain posed winsomely before one of them—standing laughing to attention—two intertwined *Cymbidium dayanum* tweaked up into a slim tower of blossom.

'This is mine,' he preened, unconsciously stretching up with his own thin neck. 'In the most modern style.' His hushed voice indicated the daring of it. 'My teacher in Kyoto would say *too* modern. Honourable mention.' The long word attacked him like a foreign enemy.

'Splendid! If cameras were permitted, I would take your picture. My congratulations. Orchids taken from the wild, I presume?' Pilchard bowed again. Now to business. 'Captain Oishi. The Professor sent me here but I don't know how I can help at all. After all, I know nothing of Shinto gardens, Zen gardens, Buddhist gardens—whatever it is that you require.' He arranged goggles in crash helmet, folded in the soaking earflaps and tucked the package neatly under one arm, like a medieval knight waiting to be cast in brass. 'I am sure it involves rather more than the planting of a flower clock or a lush, herbaceous border. But rocks, gravel, trees, the religion of Nature, *ikebana* flower arrangements—I have no idea what is the correct relationship of it all. It is like asking me to cook and serve a Japanese formal banquet.'

Oishi laughed lightly, covering his mouth with one hand. 'Oh Dr Pilchard, I realise that. We have not brought a southern barbarian here to teach us about Shinto.' He would repeat that one back at the mess and make all the other officers laugh too, maybe even Mother back home in Kyoto. 'In the course of our work we have disturbed certain orchids that I should like you to look at. Please to follow.' He led down a path, torn through rampaging bamboo and ferns. After several hundred yards, they came out into a clearing where twenty or more burly Japanese soldiers, stripped to the waist, were working at digging an enormous excavation. It is always ill-advised to dig a hole next to a reservoir and they spent more time bailing out water than digging. As he stepped out into the clearing, they looked up, bathed in perspiration, surprised, assumed expressions of extreme unfriendliness, some stretched out a hand for their rifles, then saw Oishi and grumbled quietly among themselves. A colder sweat trickled down Pilchard's back. To one side, a dozen or more aluminium containers were stacked in a pile, roped together, snarling with ideograms. You never saw Japanese troops doing physical labour. That was for POWs, or—sometimes just out of spite and contempt—for the Indian National Army.

'What is this? Something in case the balloon goes up?'

Lieutenant Oishi spun round aghast. 'Shh! Balloons? What do you know of balloons?'

Pilchard shrugged. 'It is an expression only, meaning "in case of a major event".'

Oishi frowned, unconvinced, and batted the question away. 'Oh, it is a thing...a thing for the General. This is my squad. The orchids are over here.' He led down a path over the other side and soon the vegetation swallowed them up. Since he had met Orchid, he could not bear any thought of unkindness to the plants that bore her name. When he returned to the office, he would try again to perfect the *origami* version of her flower that he had been labouring at, a work of art folded out of drab military circulars. Failed attempts overflowed his wastebasket like tribute. Pilchard peered into the tangled shade. Insects buzzed around them. It was some kind of *Aerides*, a monopodial epiphyte, attached to the bark of a non-shedding tree, long pendulous inflorescences, waxy pink blooms. Hmm. Perfectly standard but, at the Gardens, he had been schooled in sparing the tender feelings of ... amateurs.

'Absolutely fascinating! Highly unusual. But then this is a unique environment. Let me take some samples and I can compare them with our own back at the Herbarium.' He dutifully snicked with the illegal weapon of his penknife. Thus had the great pioneers of his profession whittled and sliced their way to posterity in a dozen hazardous lands. 'It may be that they are unknown to science. Then we can name them after you, can't we? Let me see. That would make them *oishii* wouldn't it? All those i's in a row.' The Captain glowed and purred with-horticultural pride.

'Yes. I should like to live long enough to have an orchid named after me.' A simple statement said quite without affectation, unperfumed. Pilchard tucked the samples away in the crash helmet. Once inside, they looked ridiculously small. Ungratefully small. He took more just for the sake of it, trying to make a sort of gracious bouquet of it.

'I am surprised to see you still here, Captain. I thought you were to go home. Is there some delay?'

Captain Oishi led the way back, taking another, much longer path and avoiding the clearing and his own men. 'The command of the Seventh Army is still unfixed. I have no orders from Tokyo. And there are matters left from the General that I must finish before I can travel.'

'And perhaps you have new interests that make you less eager to leave. Orchids, for example.' The young man blushed and laughed in delight.

'Yes, yes, orchids. I am very interested in orchids. All sorts of orchids.' He looked swiftly sad and snapped off a branch from one of the bushes, shredding the leaves and scattering them miserably. 'Orchids are very different in books and in the flesh. Of course, in Japan, people do not like orchids so much as here. There it is all *bonsai*, twisted, stunted.' He tied his hands in demonstrative knots.

'No. I should imagine transplanting them would be very difficult and perhaps they would not thrive there if you took any home with you.'

'Impossible,' sighed the Captain ruefully. He carried his burden of unwieldy emotions around with him, like a man toting a long plank through a crowded street. They arrived back at the motorbike and Pilchard bowed low to him for the benefit of the other soldiers lounging there and received a smart salute in exchange. He hung the goggles round his neck and braced himself for the clammy humidity of the helmet. Too late, as he placed it on his head, he remembered the samples now falling about his ears. Oishi politely averted his eyes. As he grubbed for them in the mud, a grey, wood-burning truck heaved axle-wrenchingly towards them and stopped. Two Japanese infantrymen jumped down and waved fixed bayonets at the interior, shouting the inevitable, 'Speedo! Speedo!' Guards were always angry. What were they so angry about? And why were they all in such a perpetual hurry? What did they intend to do with the thirty seconds gained by all that shouting? A group of POWs clambered wearily out clutching Asian hoes. At their head was Major Spratt. He and Pilchard looked at each other and hesitated. One of the guards was already striding across, rifle raised for a blow when Spratt went into a deep reverential bow to Captain Oishi, who further wrong-footed the soldier by saluting smartly so that he fell back, perplexed. Pilchard shook hands in a determinedly civilian fashion.

'Major Spratt. I thought all officers were excused labour.' Spratt snorted and cast a wary eye at Oishi. 'Tell that to our Japanese masters. You seem to have done yourself all right. My god, you've got your own motorbike?'

Captain Oishi intervened, 'As a botanist, Dr Pilchard, would you say those coconut palms over there need to be removed for the proper development of the garden?'

Pilchard looked at the grey, worn men and imagined them hacking away in the broiling sun.

'No,' he said. 'I see no need for that. That would be pointless labour.'

'Shut up, you bloody fool,' hissed Spratt. 'They'll make us work anyway and if we cut down the trees the men get to keep the nuts and the trunk will give palm wine for a week.'

'Yes, Captain. I would consider cutting down those trees as essential.'

Oishi smiled and shouted irritated orders at the guards who led the men away, grumbling. They exchanged mute glances of complicity and embarrassment. Pilchard cleared his throat. 'Thank you,' he said softly. Then, 'I'm surprised not to have had more checks from patrols.' He lay the plant samples respectfully on the sidecar seat and, settling back onto the saddle with assumed dignity, kicked the engine into reluctant life. He ignored the renewed sharp poking in his buttocks.

'Your armband,' Oishi pointed. 'It says you're a German, friend of Japanese people.' He stepped back a pace and saluted again.

Embracing his role, Pilchard heelclicked and *Sieg Heil*-ed parodically—Spratt staring at him in horror—let out the clutch and bounced off germanically down the track and back onto the tarmac humming the Ride of the Walkyries. He clattered along Bukit Timah Road with Wagner pounding in his head until he reached the big crossroads, paused for a moment, then, glimpsing the orchids out of the corner of his eye, switched to soaring *Rosenkavalier* and, on sudden impulse, pointed the handlebars away from the Gardens and turned north, threading out through the traffic heading towards military headquarters. It was as if his heart were infected with the lightness of the love that young Oishi leaked from every pore. Lovers, he decided, were like vomiters. They induced involuntary, sympathetic contractions in everyone who witnessed their spasms. As the morning heat grew, the road shrank down and traffic ebbed to the occasional cart and bicycle. Fields were dotted between the trees, becoming rarer as he moved north with small Malay *kampungs* set back from the road. The vegetation changed. Bigger, older trees. The wind tugged at his

173

thin, worn shirt and rain prickled in the air. There was another POW camp here and occasional work parties trudged along with shovels over their shoulders, prodded and harried out of his official way by guards who watched him with more interest than was comfortable. The men seemed to look like Spratt but a Spratt with all the starch and swagger knocked out of him, mostly bare-chested and scrawny, like skinned rabbits, with eyes that were either dead or burned with hatred or fever. What did they see in him? Not a German but someone pinker and better fed certainly, probably just a collaborator. Is that what he was? Possibly. But one foreign occupation of Singapore did not seem, to him, any more inherently outrageous than another. The British, it was true, at least had to justify themselves—as Protestants— with good works. Yet it was more that—as the conflict widened and became more abstract and algebraic with people fighting others just because they were the friends of enemies—his own loyalties shrank and became more hesitant, less easily engaged, more focused on those around him. Spratt detested the Indian guards in the camp for their reluctance to lay down their lives for his country. Pilchard simply disliked them for what they had done to him and his friends and despised them for believing one fairy story rather than another. Ideologies, myths, imperial destinies— all such nonsense. All his life he had been told that selfishness, cowardice, lack of faith and belief would be the world's undoing. School spirit, patriotism, the reputation of the Museum—it was all the same empty words. He suddenly saw that this was the message of his first day at school. It was noble self-sacrifice, blind courage and the willingness to suspend critical judgement in the name of a greater cause that were actually destroying mankind. It was the people with a coherent vision of things that caused all the trouble because certainty was a form of stupidity. The rest of us, who only managed to make the world intelligible for short stretches, were relatively harmless.

The land on either side of the road became more wooded with scrappy, unhappy-looking trees. He turned off onto an unsurfaced track dusted with sandy soil and glided along smoothly, on hushed tyres, for several miles, over leaf mould until the land beneath him turned sudden black and sullen. There was still the foul, sweet smell of human putrefaction that clung to the branches and leaves from the vicious battle fought as the Japanese crossed the strait from the mainland, a lingering stench of gangrenous flesh turned to mulch, tainted with terror, now being rotted down to anonymous plant food. Big, black birds were circling on the horizon. Something had freshly died there. The earth was crosscut with brackish rivulets and trickling inlets that had to be skirted round or splashed through and when he came to a point where two paths met, he hesitated, his engine suddenly very loud in the forest as he coasted to a stop. Some largish animal skittered away into the wild bushes and he had a terrible urge to look behind him for unseen monsters, as when a little boy lost in the rhododendron garden. He had only been here once before, years ago, and memory was sluggish. His foot engaged the gear but the combination had settled into the sodden soil and he let out the clutch too fast and stalled. In the abrupt silence, his own heart throbbed in his chest, then he saw, tacked to a dispirited tree, one of the Japanese signs he had given Chen Guang and he knew he had found the mangrove research station. Dismounting, he pulled off goggles and helmet, stowed them in the sidecar and set off down the track, the soil sucking at his heels.

After a few hundred yards there was a gate, old but freshly repaired with a big sign proclaiming the reserve in three languages, like a translation test, and threatening dire penalties for trespass. An expensive new lock and chain showed it meant business. Climbing over, he walked towards a simple hut built out on poles over the ooze. The tide was coming in on a black and white world, leached into shades of grey, where mudskippers flapped in the shallow encroachment among the bullyboy crabs and clenched roots He strode up to a door of plain planks and knocked. An old towel was drying over the rail by the water.

'You should not have come.' The voice was soft behind him. He turned and saw Chen Guang, very close, with another, bigger man behind him. They both held long, sharp *parangs*.

'What?'

Chen Guang hung a smile on his face. 'You should not have come without letting us know.' He slid the *parang*, rasping, into his belt. The other man did likewise. 'We have nothing to offer an honoured guest.' He pushed open the door and led across the room on bare feet to the platform over the water and indicated an old rattan chair. 'Please sit, Dr Pilchard, or is it Mr Dagama?' The other man hovered uncertainly.

'I think perhaps it had better be Mr Dagama.'

Chen Guang laughed softly and sat. 'My boy will bring tea.' Was that boy 'son' or boy 'servant'? He spoke to him in odd-sounding Chinese. 'So...excuse me if I am blunt. Asians are not supposed to be blunt are they? What is it that brings you to our shores, Mr Dagama?' He gestured magnificently across the mudflats. 'Have you come simply for the view or the rent or to bring me flowers or is it—I wonder—curiosity?' Pilchard smiled. They had checked over the motorbike.

'Well, perhaps curiosity—a little. I rarely have the opportunity to leave the Gardens and I thought ...'

'We all treasure our tranquillity, Mr Dagama. I believe I told you that. I thought you had understood me. My boy and I rarely have visitors. Your very loud motor bicycle risks disturbing our neighbours. We should not wish to attract attention and so be considered bad neighbours.' There were six chairs on the platform, arranged in a circle. Six. On a shelf by the door were ten cups. But they had no visitors. Something gleamed in the middle of the floor. He stared at it idly till it shifted into focus. Jesus! It was a single rifle bullet encased in brass and copper. The Chinaman had seen it too and seen that he had seen it. They lifted their eyes to stare at each other.

'I apologise Chen Guang. I too would not wish to be thought a bad neighbour. People should not concern themselves with the business of their neighbours. I have often thought that the world would be a better place if we all minded our own business.' He stooped, picked up the bullet and handed it back to his host, then calmly sat again. His knees were shaking. He realised how easy it would be for him to disappear in this swamp. No one knew he was here. His life, he sensed, depended on the next few minutes. 'That is the reason I obeyed the Director's personal order, sending me to check on the station today, so that I could confirm that all is well here and spare you visits from others who would be more inquisitive. We have an arrangement, you and I, and, now I think of it, I am a very incurious man.' The tea was brought, allowed to cool in silence, drunk with a polite show of reluctance. Perspiration, fuelled only partly by the tea, flowed down his chest, while outside, over the bleak mud, the rising water swirled in and pooled silently under the platform they sat on. The son—if such he was—ignored the vacant chairs and crouched in a corner in a way that only emphasised his bulk, took the *parang* out of his belt and lay it on the floor declaratively within easy reach. He would be one of the solutions to the problem of Tamil incursors into the mangroves.

'How is your daughter, Chen Guang? She does not live here with you?'

He frowned. 'My daughter?'

'Orchid?'

177

'Orchid? My daughter Orchid?' He furrowed his brow. 'Ah. No, no. She lives with her ... mother.' Pilchard was surprised to feel a stab of disappointment. 'This is not a place to bring a woman. It can be dangerous here—marshes, tides, crocodiles, snakes. And bodies everywhere. It is not good for a young girl to see such things.' Suddenly, there were voices outside, young, male voices, speaking happily in Chinese and laughing. Chen Guang shot a sharp look at the son, flicked his eyes towards the door and he rose and went out. The voices stopped. He came back in, his face a blank. Chen Guang smiled.

'The fishermen who catch the prawns. You work with the Japanese? You collaborate though you are British?' He said it so it sounded like 'brutish' and that hard word 'collaborate' was always carefully avoided at the Gardens. They spoke instead, more kindly, of 'co-operation.' Pilchard shifted uncomfortably and the rickety platform beneath them shuddered.

'It is like the men at the Electricity Plant and the Water Board. The Governor ordered us to co-operate with them for the wellbeing of the public and the preservation of heritage.' Not quite true. They had not been exactly 'ordered'. The small dishonesty itched at the back of his neck. Chen Guang pouted skeptically.

'The Electricity Plant? They say that when the Japanese air raids started, it took the man with the keys half an hour to come to the office, yawning, to turn off the streetlights. So the targets were all nicely illuminated and, when he finally threw the switch, the only people hindered were the emergency services. Is that true?'

Pilchard felt personally challenged. 'That is not my concern. You must understand. I am a trained medical doctor. Doctors are always to some degree neutral, having a higher, humanitarian duty.'

'The Japanese who shot the doctors and nurses at the

Alexandra Hospital did not seem to be thinking of that higher duty. The patients bayoneted on the operating tables there might also not agree.'

'That was a terrible thing.'

'Yet this higher humanitarian duty is only for the benefit of plants.'

Pilchard blushed. 'Occasionally, there is a medical emergency. I do what I can. But Man is not simply a material creature. The mind, science, the wider, cultural world must also be maintained. The inhabitants find relief in the Gardens. Everyone has a need for a little beauty in their lives, especially now.'

Chen Guang chuckled and stared at his mug. It had a hideous red flower painted on it. Contempt flickered in his eyes. 'Then perhaps the Governor should also have allowed the flouncy hat-makers to "co-operate" with the Japanese for the good of the people? A nice hat can be so very lifting.'

Pilchard felt suddenly dog-tired. He was being seduced by the fact of talking a common language, by reference to overlapping worlds of literary reference. He had nothing in common with this man. Language was no bridge across to shared understanding.

'Look. I just don't see how it would make the world a better place if I were stuck in Changi prison for years. That would help no one.'

Chen Guang smiled and bounced the bullet in his hand as if assessing its worth, tossing it up and catching it again confidently. 'The question then is whether the best way to make the world a better place and to "help people" is to sit in your garden and just play with your plants. You inhabit an artificial bubble of niceness and ignore the real world. A young man should engage the world not seek to hide from it.'

Pilchard wasn't standing for that. 'An odd remark from a man skulking in the marshes. And how do you know that the

Gardens aren't the real world and what is out here an artificial bubble of nastiness? Perhaps it is the things in the Gardens that we are really all fighting for.'

Chen Guang grinned. 'A good point.' His teeth ground out words with bitter relish. 'Anyway, you might argue that people are just cockroaches and you are not an entomologist.' He reached out and forensically tweaked a questing ant to death. 'I think you must be a recovering idealist. The only pure thing to serve is an idea and perhaps people are just the accidental hosts that carry the truly important life form, ideas, that may be thousands of years old. Even scepticism is an idea. Perhaps you should consider that Mr … er … Dagama.' He squeezed his voice, making it small and mocking. 'Or perhaps—I think—you are now going to defend notions of bourgeois, romantic love or maybe quote Voltaire at me.'

'Voltaire? You mean that thing about "we should cultivate our garden"? You're no fisherman. Just who the hell are you?'

'Perhaps a fisher of men? It does not matter who I am. At a time like this, we are all forced to compromise, to be someone else, to become men of action—everyone but you perhaps.' He grinned in superior triumph and stood, walked over decisively to a corner and reached up into the roof thatch and peeled off some notes from a bundle there. Returning, he pushed them into Pilchard's top pocket with the tired, worldly air of a man paying off a prostitute, wearily keeping his hot, pre-coital promise, despite disappointing services received. 'It is hard for any man to remain aloof. To refuse to engage life cannot be a form of wisdom. It is a sterile stupidity. It makes all the suffering pointless, even one's own. Don't you know, Mr Dagama, there's a war on?'

* * *

That night he dreamed of snow. Thick, heavy flakes drifted, scything and twirling through the icy night air. They settled on the bare branches of trees and sopped up the pools on the ground. As they touched your face, they feathered gently at your eyelashes, melted and slid down your cheeks and nose. Caught in your mouth, they disappeared into water and the dissolved magic of lost space. Within their spidery crystals, they inhaled all sound and sucked in all colour, leaving a skeleton world created by their own sacrificed mortality.

He awoke, his head trapped in a pool of moonlight, panting for water like a dog lapping at a puddle, his mouth dry, his head heavy. Someone had thrown grit in his eyes. Barechested, Pilchard rose and reknotted his chequered sarong, his normal sleeping garb in a bachelor household. Downstairs was water. He padded down the darkened stairs and was surprised to find light in the sitting room, one of the oil lamps turned down low. In two armchairs, pulled together, perched Post and Catchpole, facing the fireplace, a brickbuilt deliberate irrelevance since the British did not know how to sit in a room without the focus of a fire that could never be lit. Each wore looted silk pyjamas, the daytime uniform of the Armenians from Change Alley, busily whispering to each other, Catchpole with his hearing aid around his neck and the wig atop his head with greater than normal approximation, almost jauntily askew. He had lost weight and swags of loose skin now covered the suspension cord of his earpiece. The two of them whirled round and stared at him as he entered, like guilty schoolboys.

He was irritated to find Catchpole here but then he was always irritated to find him anywhere. Living cheek by jowl like this had made Pilchard realise that it was not the big things in life that really annoyed, it was the small ones. Propinquity yearned to turn into commitment, understanding into trust, awareness into concern. But Catchpole put used matches back in the box so that you picked up a matchbox anywhere in the house and found that the comforting rattle inside was illusory. All the matches were already dead. Catchpole could only stir tea with a teaspoon—dessert spoons, knives, pencils etc. could not be used and, since the house only possessed two teaspoons, he was constantly searching, creating upheaval and complaining about the damned things. This sat curiously with the mess in his bedroom but Pilchard had a nagging fear that the apparent disorder might really be arranged alphabetically and clockwise. Had a telescope not stood between the trombone and a tambourine? True, dressing gowns had been all over the radiogram but perhaps that merely showed that, in Catchpole's world, they were garments on a gramophone. Also, Catchpole washed up in the order in which dishes were served. Soup plates must be washed before pudding bowls. To see ranks of crockery lined up on the draining board in strict chronological order at a time when all food was just fuel, drove Pilchard insane, yet he could not explain why. Such discoveries worried him. They suggested that the rift with Margaret might not be a matter of deep and incompatible feelings. It might be a mere nothing about teaspoons, matches and the petty friction of just living together with clashing classifications.

'It's happened,' croaked Dr Post, stifling a sob. 'It's finally happened, old man.'

'What's happened?'

'The invasion of Europe, D-Day, the Second Front. Dominion and American troops are knocking the Hun for six from one side, while the Russians are pushing down from the East, on the other. It's all over, old man. Just a matter of time now. There's going to be an end to all this.' He snuffled wetly and buried his face in his hands. From outside a frog croaked disbelief. Pilchard, shocked, plonked his behind on the dining table. If he had been French, he might have put his arm round Post to comfort him. Brits couldn't do such things.

'Bloody hell!' He had only been a fake German for one day and already the real Germans were losing the war. 'How do you know?' Then. 'Are you absolutely sure?'

Catchpole sneered back in glossy, grey stripes. 'It's on the wireless. Even Tokyo Rose has admitted it though of course she goes on about "determined resistance" and "imminent counterattacks".' He tapped the bakelite box around his neck. 'Did it never occur to you that there might be more to this than meets the eye, that it might be a crystal set as well as a hearing aid? It's one of the latest models and I can tune the cat's whisker to Radio India and walk down the street listening through the earphone without anyone knowing. Wonders of science. As for the war, it'll all be over by Christmas. The Japs will start behaving a bit better now, you'll see. I think we might celebrate with a cup of tea. Why don't you make us one Post?' Dr Post snuffled and shuffled off to the kitchen. Catchpole settled back imperiously in his chair and arranged the flaps of his pyjama jacket chastely across gaping crotch. Then, breezily, 'There's going to be some changes around here. There's nothing like a war for making a little space on the promotion ladder. I think it's clear which of us will be the new Director when the Brits come back. I should watch my P's and Q's a bit more if I were you, old man. I have always kept a loyal distance from our occupiers and fearlessly sought out information to subvert their propaganda but I can't help noticing you're very thick with your young Japanese friend, Oishi, which I suppose explains where you get your money from, and collaborators will get pretty short shrift round here, once things get back to normal, if I have any say in the matter. Those of us who have worked to resist the invaders from within will deserve some reward for their sufferings and I intend to see they get it. On the whole, I should do rather nicely what with my arrears of pay, interest added, and so on.'

Pilchard goggled in sheer disbelief. He felt his face stiff with choked rage. 'You still expect to get *paid*?'

'Of course. I realise that your position is rather different, old man. You express it in the careless way you dress. Officially, I suppose you're still in the Volunteer Force and therefore a POW and not a proper employee of the museum and gardens at all but I have a contract of employment with fixed annual increments and expect my contribution to be recognised.'

Pilchard gripped the arms of his chair till they creaked, fighting back the urge to suggest that Catchpole should splurge this windfall on a new wig and shoot the old one.

'If I may say so, Catchpole, your only contribution to bringing down the Japanese has been trying to eat them out of house and home and, as for your dress, you look like a junior official from the Ministry of Fat Bastards. I don't believe you have so much as set foot outside the safety of the Gardens throughout the occupation. And I wouldn't race to hang out Union Jacks if I were you. It could take years to finally bring down the Nazis. They could see us all out. And the Seventh Army here are not about to surrender to anyone. When I was in Changi, the commandant always threatened that if the Allies tried to retake Singapore his orders were to massacre all prisoners and then fight to the last man.' He was gratified to see Catchpole blanch. 'The models have already been established for what will happen. You recall those myths of Wendigos among the Algonquin Indians of North America? Monsters that prey on humans, created by acts of human cannibalism. A typical culture-bound myth of inappropriate consumption. Well, we are not short of Japanese Wendigos nowadays. You saw what they did to perfectly innocent Chinese when they arrived. What do you think they would do to someone like yourself who has so fearlessly undermined them from within? And we have the other psychosis, more Asian, *amok*, a sudden, wild outburst of indiscriminate slaughter after brooding on wrongs. There will be no shortage of that when the time comes. Anyway, soon we'll all have bombs raining down on our heads which makes the idea of sides something of a luxury and an irrelevance.'

Post reappeared clutching mugs. 'The third cup is always so difficult but somehow it never seems worthwhile to make a second trip, does it? Since it is a special occasion, I gave us a spoon of fresh tea each and the last of the sugar.' He popped them down with wild abandon on the unprotected tabletop then looked around. 'Oh, such long faces. I thought this was a jolly occasion.'

'I was just saying to Dr Catchpole that we are going to be walking on eggs for some time. In fact, we can't even count on having eggs to walk on. The Japanese could turn very nasty if they feel threatened and ...'

The door was pushed open with a melodramatic creak and a great shadow fell into the room.

'What's this? A staff meeting?' Prof Tanadatake, ruffled and owl-eyed. His hands were thrust down in the pockets of a Chinese dressing gown, supplied from Catchpole's hoard. A large, yellow dragon swarmed over his back and embraced his shoulders. 'Are you all plotting a coup behind my back?' He laughed. 'Is there some tea there?' Dr Post leapt to fetch it. He sat down and sighed. 'You could not sleep perhaps? There is a message carried on the wind, I think. Let me open the *kimono*.'

'What?' They recoiled.

He smiled at their shock. 'A Japanese expression, merely. As you would say, "let me put my cards on the table".'

'Ah.'

'So, you have heard of the invasion of Europe? I will not ask how.' He cast a suspicious look at the radio, its permit tacked

185

to the wall above the apparatus. 'This must be a happy time for you. I do not know if it is a happy time for me. There can be little doubt that the Allies will finally defeat the Germans. I have long expected this and hope it may shorten the war. We cannot know what will happen then in the East. We may have to tolerate another generation of war or perhaps a separate peace may be possible where Japan remains the victor.' He pulled out a pack of cigarettes and lit one wearily. In the course of the conflict, the cardboard mouthpiece had got longer, the tube of tobacco ever shorter. 'These are two wars that have become connected and they can continue separately. So, Russia is at war with Germany but not Japan. Before the war, I was a professor of vulcanology. After the war, I wish to be so again, if the new world still has volcanoes. I think it will. That is my only interest, together with the well-being of my family. But in war we must not jump the gun. We must all accept that things will get much worse before we can hope for improvement for we are small fish, carp on the chopping board, and our one aim must be to survive by not being noticed by bigger fish.' The cigarette was finished already. He clapped his hands on his thighs and rose. 'I should not have talked of food. I have made myself hungry.' He seized his tea from re-entering Post's hands like a bitter resolve. 'Let us go to bed. There is nothing for us to do. We dare not make plans. We must wait. Always just wait until … until …'

'Until the cows come home to roost?' suggested Pilchard.

'Exactly.' The Professor looked around, as if seeing the drab, weary interior for the first time. 'We have a house full of botanists, acres of gardens and there is never one single flower in this house to spread a little beauty and joy. Why is that?'

* * *

The camp tingled with excitement for the inmates knew of D-Day before their guards. It seemed impossible that such a momentous event could leave matters entirely unchanged on the ground but so it was. News was circulated by a roundabout route so that it would be impossible to trace any individual report back to its source and so find the hidden radios that were concealed in beams, water tanks, and, most ingeniously, in a functioning waterbottle that a squaddie carried dangling around his neck at roll call. Being caught with even a spare part for a radio was certain death. The extraordinary news burst upon the world via the wooden sidings of the lavatories in tiny but exuberant latrinogrammes, was pushed through the chink in the wall into the women's section of Changi prison on a scrap of paper from a book lining, whispered, with alleged medical intent, in the ears of patients at the hospital and rapidly translated into a dozen tongues for people who had no clear idea of where Germany even was. Normal routine was enforced as before and was suddenly unbearable.

Then, without warning, the Japanese erupted in abrupt rage without even admitting what they were angry about. The camp concert, an extravagant production involving tinselly sets of the Queen Mary and Busby Berkeley dancing by hairy-legged transvestites, was cancelled on orders of the commandant. Ruthless searches were ordered, among both POWs and civilians. These were always an opportunity to pay off old grudges so it came as no surprise that one of the Japanese women in the bitches' barracks, married to a British mining engineer, a guileless woman who could not have changed the battery in her own torch, was found to be in possession of advanced condensers and capacitors for the maintenance of wireless equipment. To the immense satisfaction of certain co-inmates, she was dragged away screaming. Pilchard's abandoned stash of toilet tissue was discovered but, since it was blank toilet paper down a toilet, nothing was made of it. By now there was little for searchers to loot but still plenty of opportunity for gratuitous damage to property such as the slicing up of clothes and the ripping open of mattresses. Men were knocked about, the rice in the food hall overturned on the floor and walked through, the sick in the hospital driven from their beds and made to answer roll call. Sergeant Fukui's boots played a prominent role in all these activities and his particular spite was reserved for the Javanese whose gardens he trampled underfoot and stomped to death, pausing only—good greengrocer that he was—to pick up a couple of papayas that he carried away laughing.

Sergeant Dewa decided right then that Fukui must die. It was a necessary tidying up of the world for, as he had explained to his several wives and many mistresses, he was a man who valued order above all else. This was the attraction for him of employment in the service of the Dutch, a pernickety, regulation-strapped people, whose way of life created many snug interstices in which a man of private morality could dwell.

Fukui was small and skinny and Dewa could easily have squeezed the life out of him like the pulp from a ripe *marquisa* fruit but that would have terrible consequences not just for himself but for his men. It must be done another way. He must die naturally. An accident seemed the best way, during his rounds perhaps. He speculated on arranging for a heavy tile to fall from the roof of the rickety lean-to but that required exact positioning of Fukui and experimentation that might attract attention—also accomplices. He needed something he could do alone. Two days later, in the early morning, he found the dead monkey tangled in the scorched wreckage of his garden. At first he thought of it as a marvellous windfall of meat then saw the patches of mange and the skin covered in pustules and recognised it at once as the inedible instrument of his vengeance. In the forests around his village, he had seen things like this before, a disease like smallpox that animals caught. Most of the time, it lay dormant, but occasionally, it would burst out of the trees and bushes like a wild thing and men and women would catch it and some would die or be horribly scarred. As a child, he had survived the smallpox that had left its clutching clawmarks on his cheeks. And smallpox gave immunity.

He knew exactly what to do. He would use papayas. The Australian troops did not like the Javanese, called them paw-paws—papayas—'green on the outside, yellow through and through on the inside and makes you throw up'. They had first fallen out over the Javanese refusal to collect and surrender snails to feed the chickens kept by officers—naturally, all white. Since then, the grudge had found more than enough to feed on and grown. Even the Japanese had started calling them 'pawpaw'. It was fitting that the fruit should now be turned to a weapon of offence. Although immune to the disease, Dewa was reluctant to touch the unclean body and, instead, coaxed it cautiously across to the foot of the papaya tree that Fukui had ravaged, using the blade of his home-made hoe. He quickly dug a hole, by the edge of the path where Fukui passed, and tumbled it in, smoothed down the earth and waited, week by week, as the plant recovered, scented out the rotting body and sent down hungry roots to feed on the rich putrescence. Dewa knew that there are male papayas and female papayas and some that are both sexes and, if you prune the top of a papaya in the dry season, it may change its sex like a transvestite. This one was female, one male plant to about fifteen females being about right, just—as he liked to think with a smile—as was the case with himself. Dewa cosseted that plant, brought it water, picked pests from its shoots with his hands, removed damaged leaves and it grew thick and indecently green. Finally it set new fruit, great clusters of shiny pods, and he settled to guard it from those who would eat them or make medicine from its leaves or sap. To his men, he explained that the tree had a special holy purpose, was sacred, that it was protected from thieves by a great curse he had set upon it that invoked the power of the very Walisongo saints who had first brought the gift of Islam to their home town. They recognised the familiar signs of a man who had made a covenant with god and asked no questions but watched in awe as the papaya thickened, flourished and burgeoned like a cosmic *waringin* tree and its ripening fruit swirled with yellow and pink just like the Changi sunset.

And then, one day, as Dewa was attacking the weeds with his hoe, Fukui was there, his ratty eyes fixed on the fruit, as always a Korean guard towering behind him with a rifle slung over his shoulder. He stopped and smiled, looked at Dewa, then back at the fruit. Dewa bowed low. The worst part of bowing was that you couldn't see what they were doing. If a blow came, it was always unexpected—even if half expected.

'You give me that.' Fukui pointed, stretched out a hand and leeringly fondled the bump on the bottom of a fruit. Dewa blushed, feeling his own nipple tingle with sexual violation. Just as well he had not planted a banana tree. With reluctance, he broke off the ripe papaya and handed it, poutingly, to Fukui, cupped deferentially in both hands. Fukui seized it, clicked his fingers, gesturing rudely. 'More!' Dewa broke off another with difficulty, for the stem was strong, and handed it over. Fukui snatched it, threw back his head and gloated, stalking off, deliberately clutching the papayas triumphantly to his chest like looted breasts as Dewa watched with dark eyes of quiet satisfaction.

The last time the monkeypox had come to his village, he had been just a young boy. It could not pass directly from man to man but, when they thought it was all over, it had come back and killed all the goats that grazed in a field where they had buried the dead livestock and they had nearly starved. The forgiving earth could cleanse almost anything but this disease lived on, unabsolved, for years, nested deep in the soil.

It was two weeks before the news came that Fukui was sick. Smallpox, they said, a name of sudden but mixed terror for few of the Japanese troops had been vaccinated while most of the Westerners had. He was whisked away in an ambulance to the Quarantine Camp of the Leper Hospital, with several of his close companions, their faces pale and sweaty through the glass. And Dewa grew in stature, a man—they said—full of divine power, *sakti*, a man very close to God, protected by him and given the power to strike down the ungodly with his curse. Little offerings began to appear at the base of his papaya tree. Its unconsumed fruit began to rot in luxuriant divinity.

* * *

Corporal Higgins had been greatly upset by the cancellation of the concert. He had worked long and hard on his Marlene Dietrich. The wig, he had constructed himself. Not one of those deliberately absurd things of grass the other comically female parts wore but real hair, much of it from a tonsorially blessed Indian trooper who had asked to have his thick locks completely shaved to mark his state of mourning for a brother. Bleached, teased, knotted onto an old bathing cap, it provided sweeping curls and an enigmatic, limp forelock to drape over the pasty makeup and red-lipped pout. It created an effect that would be greeted not with the usual alibi of excessively loud hilarity but with stunned and breathless silence. The fishnet stockings had been a real nightmare. He had contemplated pencilling a mathematically fiendish latticework directly over his legs before running into a commando who had seen service in Norway and retained a, now redundant, string vest. With a rather lower skirt than Lola might have wished and much

191

higher boots, dyed black, it plausibly sheathed the gap in between in the stuff of male dreams. The voice was surprisingly easy to imitate, slack-jawed and breathy. The walk was challenging. The blank expression simply impossible for he had cultivated facial animation all his life and it was this that had fascinated his special friend, Dong-ju, one of the Korean guards, who dropped in for a scrape and a trim.

Dong-ju was not exactly young and was even getting a little thin on top but the short hair on his strong neck formed the most attractive whorls and his ears were a perfection of symmetry and such things count for a hairdresser. Moreover, he was a fan of the musical theatre, bitterly disappointed when the concert was cancelled, since, in the camps, the guards were as imprisoned as the prisoners. The most appalling stage acts were savoured by both guards and guarded, even especially so, for in badness, language counted for very little. Applause was thunderous, audience participation vigorous and vocal, things were thrown so that almost no turn was left unstoned.

It was immediately understood that no one must know of their involvement. Such a relationship could prove lethal to both of them but danger revived youthful excitement. Their cover for such frequent visits was the need for an extended programme of dandruff-control. And then, one day, two commandos with big arms—one the owner of the string vest—elbowed their way into the tent and eyebrowed the other intimidated customers back outside. Higgins was impressed. To control POWs with one's eyebrows showed class.

The camp, like any public institution, was a loose aggregation of more or less criminal subsets, some under army control, much simply private enterprise and monopolies in trade, extortion and violence were ruthlessly enforced. This visit could be anything but trouble was certainly part of it. Unlike most of the prisoners, who wore an eclectic assortment of rags, they sported clean uniforms. Their bulk, and muscularity argued for control of private food supplies which then implied involvement in some rich racket. Probably, that meant the horse races. There were no actual horses in Changi, of course, but some prisoners were designated as such while others were 'jockeys' that rode them round on all fours over a pre-set course with ancillary delights such as gambling, nobbling and odds-fixing and occasional excessive use of the whip—all a useful outlet and sublimation for that unruly male energy still boiling, pantingly unspent, beneath the malnutrition. One sat cross-armed and silent in the doorway, the other perched on the box that was the barber's chair, with landlady gentility, and started to preen his nails with the scissors. The box creaked beneath his weight. Higgins half expected him to pull out a mouth organ at any minute and embark on some sentimental Blighty tune.

'So, Higgins. We've been meaning to pay you a visit for some time. How are things?'

In his eventful life, Corporal Higgins had suffered a good bashing on numerous occasions and knew the smell of it. Escape was impossible. Resistance would be futile. These two could kill him with their bare hands. It would be safer to let them do what they had clearly decided to do so they would stop before he was quite dead.

'I think maybe things just took a turn for the worse.'

They chuckled. 'Oh, don't say that. We hear you have a Korean fan. You've been seeing a lot of each other.' So that was it. It was to be a good manly bashing with particular attention to the goolies and face. Teach him a lesson. Sleeping with the enemy added to the other thing. 'That's nice. We're romantics at heart, him and me.' He leered at the man grinning in the doorway. 'The stars of the botanical drawings class, us two. I done some lovely sketches of petunias just last week. We like it when two people make each other happy. It's heartwarming.' He snipped at a thumbnail then threw down the scissors and stood up. Higgins gasped. Scissors were valuable, irreplaceable. Something black and shiny slipped from inside a sleeve. It looked like a truncheon. Higgins closed his eyes, waiting for the first blow. He hoped they would not break his teeth. Dentistry in the camp was non-existent. 'This is for the two of you.' The voice was very close. He steeled himself, then felt something pushed into his hands. He looked down and saw a bottle of whisky, it could even be the real thing.

'What?'

A huge hand took a pinch of his cheek and shook his face as a dog would a rat.

'We want you to go on seeing your little friend. As they say, "Keep it up". Something else.' He took a key from his top pocket and dangled it in front of his face. 'It's hard to get a little privacy around here, so here's the key to the theatre changing room. No one will bother you there. You can even do him a private version of your act, sing the song about Lola's squeezebox, put on a nice, little show to keep him happy.'

'Why?'

'Oh I don't think you need to know that. Let's just say that, since we are your friends, any friend of yours is a friend of ours. Right? Got it?' They shouldered their way out through the flap. Loiterers outside bent and peered in the hope of catching a glimpse of mayhem and destruction inside then flinched back to avoid being elbowed. 'Let's say this is your last big push in the East, your war effort, seeing action nightly. Get you a medal, like as not. We'll be rooting for you.' They swaggered away laughing and backslapping.

He weighed the key to the theatre backstage in his hand and stared at the bottle in sheer disbelief. So, he was the overripe cheese baiting their trap for poor Dong-ju, of whom he had grown more than a little fond. But since Dong-ju was already trapped, there could be no harm surely in letting him have the odd additional nibble at the cheese before that fact was made clear to him.

* * *

The first explosion came just after midnight when the streets were empty and, since the site was so low-lying, it was actually heard only in the south of the island. One minute the Quarantine Camp was going about its sleepy business in Moulmein Road next to the Leper Asylum and Paupers' Hospital. The next, people were staggering, dazed, from the ruins, some naked, some in ripped nightshirts, wondering where the roof and water tank had gone to, while the only fatalities were a group of guards from Changi, freshly cleared of smallpox infection, and about to return to their duties. The effect on the Japanese was out of all proportion, with troops running around in all directions, waving weapons, seeking someone to be aggressive to, like ants when some great animal blunders into their nest and lumbers off into the dark. Indian street-traders on their way home were beaten up and their barrows overturned in pools of pungent curry, the transvestites of Bugis Street were searched and harassed, revealing several surprises but none explosive, and Erica was apprehended, driving back from a night club in the uniform of an able-bodied French sailor, more than a trifle drunk and very angry.

The soldiers, surrounding her car and teasing her out at bayonet point, were nonplussed and exalted by their prize. This was clearly a foreign agent but why was he wearing a uniform? Could he be the spearhead of some attempted landing? And why did his mannerisms recall those of Bugis Street? This unexpected detention did not prevent Erica deploying her mouth to good effect but, since her Japanese was of a very male form, acquired in military company, it only added to the confusion. In her bag, they found a card, bearing an officer's name and radioed headquarters. Some problems you could beat up or simply shoot but this was clearly a problem of officer quality, so they tied Erica up, confiscated her pom-pom, adopted poses of acute military preparedness on either side of the prisoner and waited for an officer to come.

It was over an hour before Captain Oishi appeared, lightly unshaven and rumpled but very cross. What was all this? Sabotage by communist guerrillas, they said. Why had they tied up this woman of deep diplomatic connections? Diplomatic connections? Not a communist then? The soldiers saw, with dismay, their hoped-for promotions and congratulations turned to rebuke and sulked. And from Erica, of course, no thanks for Oishi but pouts and loud reproach.

'So,' she said, 'the Japanese only have spies, not eyes for me any more?' Then, to the horror of the gaping soldiers, she began to sing that horrible, little song in a cracked voice while performing some sort of gruesome little girl's skirt-lifting dance. 'Are the stars out tonight? I don't know if it's cloudy or bright, Cos I only have eyes for yooooou dear.' Why had he not been in touch? Had he forgotten her? Had he found someone younger and prettier? Drink turned her lachrymose. He found it hard to understand why, in his heart, he should feel such guilt that the answer to both was emphatically 'yes'? He wondered idly what she had done with the French sailor whose clothes she wore. Eaten him alive, perhaps, or just stripped him and turned him out to wander the streets naked. Finally, after much soothing and coaxing, she was enticed back behind the wheel and gone in an irritated crashing of gears and with hot promises from Captain Oishi, easy lies that he had no intention of keeping, so that he felt a kind of sad sophistication dawning upon him. 'Easy-peasy-Japanesey', as Tokyo Rose put it. As he turned to walk away, his foot struck something soft and heavy, a melodramatic metaphor for his heart perhaps. Bending down in the flickering light of the burning building, he saw it was a sandbag—the sort you found on military balloons, the kind of balloons he had just released on test flights and that sometimes blew back in shifting winds, the balloons that gave him an excuse for staying in Singapore and not rejoining his unit. He saw the soldiers looking at him with curiosity, reduced to blank silhouettes by the blaze behind them, and kicked the evidence swiftly into the roadside ditch.

'Dead rats!' he said with a grimace. It did not sound military enough. 'You find them everywhere in this damned place—just like communists.' He was shaking.

* * *

HK looked noticeably less crumpled. He had even regained a little of his bounce and sucked air in through his teeth with something like gusto. Uniquely, he had visited Lily *before* the meeting and was calm and in control. Shriven. Tea had been served. There was something of celebration in the atmosphere. In a rare moment of electricity supply, the ceiling fan was turning.

'I have spoken to the Yokohama Bank people down at the old Chartered Bank of India building. The loan has been extended for another year, at a slightly higher rate. But perhaps we should not concern ourselves too much with the rate.'

They all knew why but no one wanted to say it. Heads turned automatically towards Loh Ching, sitting up the far end as immobile as an ivory statue. He frowned with a sound like rustling papyrus and asked the forbidden question. 'Why should we not concern ourselves too much with the rate? The interest is already ruinous.'

HK grinned. 'I believe we have all heard the news—the ... er ... latest developments in Europe and the American invasion... I mean ... the activity reported in the Philippines. There is every reason to think that the loan may be ... lost sight of in the larger issue.'

Loh Ching snorted. 'Perhaps the Chairman does not agree that it is darkest at the foot of the lighthouse and that conversely too much light may be dangerous to moths?' They laughed. HK blushed. 'Let us be frank. I have sought information on the situation. Manila has not simply been liberated. The Japanese navy have turned it into a battlefield, inhabitants massacred, respectable women violated, shops looted. The entire city is blood and flames. We saw it when the Japanese arrived. We shall see it again if they leave. Do you not think Yamashita has left his orders? And this time it will be much, much worse. All civilians will become hostages in house-to-house fighting and the whole city will be reduced to rubble.' Fear tingled around the table.

'Perhaps,' said HK nervously, 'this is not the time or the place ...' A murmur of horrified dissent broke out. 'Let Loh Ching speak!'

'It is the time for us to prepare. We cannot wait any longer. We have seen that we cannot rely on the regular British army for they will always save themselves first. But in the jungle, I have heard, there are men in another uniform, Chinese and British together. They are not fools and they grow daily stronger. You all saw their bold attack on the Changi guards a few nights ago in the very middle of our city. That was a warning from the British to the Japanese not to harm their prisoners. We must contact these men.'

'But are they not communists who wish us ill?'

Loh Ching sighed and looked round the room, gathering the threads together. 'Some are communists but their enemies are our enemies, so they are our friends. They must be told that clearly before the bad time comes. We must send them an ambassador.' His gaze wandered around the room and came to rest on HK. He puckered his lips sourly. 'Sometimes people can be very stupid.'

* * *

'Yoshi? What is it?' Orchid joined the ghostly figure on the balcony of the block of flats, looking out over the dawning city. They had abandoned all pretence of caring what people thought and nowadays she walked boldly past the sentry and up the front steps, the little room behind the Orchid House left forlorn and empty. The sentry, too, simply ignored her and no longer even bothered to try to look up her skirt as she highheeled up the stairs. Nobody seemed to think much about anything any more. In the brooding, sullen silence, everyone was waiting intensely for something to happen. The whole city was liked the wispy husk of an insect once a spider has sucked it dry. Oishi had no idea where his squad were or what they were doing. He had not been to headquarters for several days. A series of dull thuds shuddered from the north.

'The naval base.' He said it with relief. The navy was nothing to do with him. He could not be blamed. 'At Sembawang.' They would be bombing the oil depot, spreading blazing oil on troubled waters. At least that could not be his balloons running amok yet again. He had a momentary vision of one of them, soaring away into the sky, like a lark, free and untrammelled, with the sun glinting on its varnished top and felt envy. No. Not balloons. This must be something else, something far bigger, possibly something worse. The city had been drawing breath for another hot day. Now it held that breath.

'Could it be the British?'

He shrugged. 'Perhaps.'

'When are you expecting them to come? Next month? Another year?' She scanned his face with sharp eyes. And then, suddenly, a huge silver shape flashed, in a great curve, across their field of vision, so clean, so beautiful, like a great dolphin but trailing smoke—wounded. He span round.

'American B-29 Superfortress!" It would be coming all the way from India or Cocos-Keeling. He had never seen one before but had learned to recognise the intelligence silhouettes and felt a train-spotter's excitement as he picked out the neat rows of rivets, the stars on the wings, the diagnostic remote-controlled machine gun turrets of the latest model. Above it, in the high heavens, now glided wave after wave of identical creatures, hardly more than sparkling dots, droning by in perfect, invulnerable formation as this one struggled vainly to rejoin the herd, coughed and finally collapsed behind the trees, where the war-tubas had once stood, in a groaning crumpdetonation that shook the ground and broke windows on the upper floors. They threw themselves down behind the brick balustrade and coughed mortar dust and hot kerosene stink.

He peered over the edge, then, cautiously, drew her up, hugged her, parted, began awkwardly pulling on clothes. 'I must go. *You* must go.'

She looked at him with exasperated affection. 'Be careful, Yoshi'

'Of course. There is no danger.' He gripped her bare elbows. Warmth flowed between their bodies displacing all else. He had felt terror, hatred and triumph before but never this kind of melting, all-accepting love. It sapped him of energy and he slumped against her in something less akin to joy than despair.

'Oh Yoshi. I *do* love you but you are like all men. Well, there is one way that is different. Most men just see women as more territory to raise their flag over. I never felt that with you. But you can be so stupid, especially when you are being clever. Please remember that, whatever may happen in the future.'

'What?' He laughed. 'What does a little girl like you know about all men?'

'That's just it. Like all men, you think innocence is like ice-cream for you to just gobble up but that when this war is over I will just go back to being a little girl, clothes, babies, smiling all the time. But I know that something terrible is going to happen here.' She shook her head in misery. 'I know you will not just give in. I know you will not run away. I see what other people do not. You are a true warrior at heart and that before anything else. Perhaps I'm the only one that sees that.' His face softened.

'Where could we run to? We have no Cocos-Keeling. Even there, the world would come between us. There is no danger, here. I am only going to run about and shout at everyone as they expect me to. They will mostly be just hitting local people who look happy. That organises itself. But you must try not to look happy. Yes, that's perfect. Have you got the pass I gave you? Good.' They would also be beating to death anyone denounced by their spies as brave enough to cheer at the bombing but that, perhaps, should not be mentioned.

She stopped and took his head between her hands. 'What is a ... what was it? Cocos-Kling?'

He laughed. 'Cocos-Keeling. It is a place some people dream of. Sit here on my lap and I will tell you all about it.' They settled the way a father would tell his child a fairy story, his arms around her closing off the outside world, his mouth close to her ear. 'You are so innocent that you may be a little shocked.' He looked in her eyes and stroked back her hair and told her of Hare and his ladies, at which she laughed and pinched his ears as the representative of his whole foolish sex. He told her of the haven on the extinct volcanic rim in the vast blue emptiness and the still, silver lagoon that it sheltered at its heart. He spoke of a simple life of fish and coconuts and of palms, swaying in cooling breezes and of the furthest horizons on earth where the loudest sounds were the distant thunder of the surf and the cries of wheeling birds. He embroidered his dreams and fantasies, in bold colours, onto the bare canvas, evoking a paradise immune to change or strife, a place of warm hearts and honest ways, full of the laughter of children, adding—as a final afterthought—groves of benodorous peach trees, for no paradise is thinkable, for a Japanese, unless framed by flowering trees. Soon they had sunk down onto the island of the bed and were the only people left in the world.

* * *

Lady Pendleberry had never found the Japanese easy to understand. They were, if possible, even worse than the Irish. Inscrutable, was the word one used, an odd, unpronounceable, very awkward word, that was itself suitably hard to grasp. Sometimes they smiled at you and it was then they were most dangerous. She had never seen one cry—not even the twittering Japanese women in the bitches' barracks. But now there was something about them that made them even harder to get along with. It was the constant indecision and prevarication that she recognised in the daily changes of policy that unnerved and displeased her. In any of the large houses that she had run, it would have been a sign that the butler and housekeeper were at loggerheads and marked the moment when the mistress intervened to push through the green baize door, sit them down and bang their silly heads together. First, rations had been cut as punishment for the Allied air raids on the harbour area, as if the prisoners had had a hand in them. This was announced by Colonel Saito with visible pleasure. He really was a horrid little man. The knowledge that his true place in life was that of a greengrocer only made his oppression worse. Then, his assistant had smarmily increased the rations again to be at the same level as those issued to serving Japanese soldiers. Then they had been cut once more to a level that varied according to the whim of the man who had the key to the supplies shed. Then, out of the blue, came an issue of Red Cross parcels that the Japanese had always denied receiving in the first place. Having lurched across war-ravaged Europe, trundled through frozen Russian nights on the trans-Siberian railroad, rattled through deserts, trailed across the islands of Japan and tossed on steamy shipboard to Synonan-to, they were simply dumped in the yard, in the streaming rain, names written on them in blue wax crayon, cardboard boxes of that weird pinkish brown favoured by continental postal services and tied with string. It was immediately clear that the boxes themselves were a valuable resource, that the string must be unknotted and not cut. It could be unpicked and used to suture wounds, or made into wicks for oil lamps or traps for birds and the busybody administrators of the prison bustled into unnecessary action, confiscating the parcels, so that they could redistribute them again with proper lists but no string. The Jews, under a hirsute Armenian with wild hair, immediately came and shouted at Dr Voss, demanding its restoration.

'What for you take our string? It is contrary to the Geneva Convention to take the string. It is not British string but the string of colonial peoples. Even the Japanese do not steal the string of the oppressed.' Wearily, she handed it back.

The boxes weighed more than ten pounds so the prisoners were too weak to carry or even drag them very far. Lady Pendleberry sat on the floor, legs splayed, looking out on the yard and lifted the lid from her own box. Someone had cut two little half moons at the bottom of the lid so that your fingers could slide conveniently underneath without lifting the whole thing. At such a mark of consideration, she started to cry. The pictures and colours of the labels, the disproportionate size of things, transported her back to childhood, Christmas in the nursery, nanny telling her not to eat all her sweets at once. She handled the rusty tins with awkward wonder—cocoa, treacle pudding, greasy meat roll, processed cheese—items from another world, lower class, gross and queasy but undeniably British, part of that distant dream of the time before. Tears refilled her eyes, overwhelmed them and trickled down her thin, crêpey cheeks and her whole body was racked with sobs. She cried for a lost past of certainty and confidence, for houses with white pillars and pattering servants where cups came with matching saucers and tinkling teaspoons, for tea with cake and the fact of idle, smiling conversation taken for granted at meals that were more than just fuel. She cried for her stiff, arthritic hands and her cloudy, unfocussing eyes. She cried most of all to see her name written on the official lid by someone out there who assumed that she still existed while she knew that her old self had gone for ever, like a woman who comes across an old, forgotten photograph from her youth and realises—now that it is too late—that she was once briefly beautiful. And then the sobs were crosscut by shocking titters, the two combining to make a rhythmic sound rather like an old, squeaky bicycle at the realisation that nowhere, in the whole women's section, was there a single tin-opener.

* * *

Professor Tanakadate sketched the cross-section of a perfect volcano in the margins of his annual report. It was a mere doodle that indicated his mood and his distraction—a moodle perhaps. The final draft would be sent to the administrative office. He had no idea who read it, if indeed anyone did but, if he failed to submit a document, some sort of automatic and unstillable cry for food was generated within the hungry bureaucratic machine. Ignoring it was futile and this was no time to attract attention. His pencil gathered a large pool of magma at the side of 'Visitor Numbers' and disgorged it dramatically through the cone of the introductory section. Last year he had asked Pilchard to write the report and have it translated but the young man had regarded it as a work entirely of fiction and felt challenged to supply as implausible an account of the Museum and Gardens' doings as possible. Under 'Staff Changes' he had noted that Mr Dagama had been devoured by a carnivorous plant, leaving behind only his hat and a shoe, and that one of the under-gardeners had been dismissed for public self-pollination. He had then illustrated 'Current Research' with a botanically impeccable image of the Gardens' *Amorphophallus titanum* that had indeed produced its towering, carrion-reeking and steaming phallic flower during the year. But he had added and fluently detailed an entirely imaginary programme leading to the cultivation of vast acreages of beef-, pork- and chicken-flavoured varieties of the plant, with the hope of an as yet undeveloped, cheese-flavoured version, as a contribution to the city's food supply. The Professor had unwisely signed it, unread, and now lived in fear of its being taken up by some higher authority. He sighed and picked up a letter from the desktop, hastily written on thin, translucent paper. It was from his wife in distant Nagasaki, full, he could tell, of deliberately distracting cheery tittle-tattle—equally a work of fiction. The baker just round the corner, had retired, though he was still young, and gone off to a hot-water spa. They had eaten lovely, fresh duck meat on Saturday while the sounds of construction at the Mitsubishi shipyard showed that our glorious Imperial Navy was ever-growing. In other words, food shortages were hitting them hard, there was no bread to be had, the bankrupt baker had been conscripted despite his crippled leg and the ducks had all died. Meanwhile, the shipyard was being bombed, now within range of American forces. The whole world floated and bobbed on a sea of lies. There was no mention of his little daughter, which was a relief. If there had been good news about her, he would really have worried.

There was a knock at the door. Young Captain Oishi entered, bowed.

'Tanakadate-*sensei*.' He accepted the offered chair.

The Professor shouted for tea, accepted a vestigial cigarette in exchange. 'There is so little tobacco in these now that it seems like the waste of a match. What brings you to the Gardens, Captain?' One of the undergardeners bustled in with overstewed, guava leaf tea, plonked it down, left. 'I am afraid it comes with condensed milk and sugar. They save it specially for me, denying themselves, so I cannot complain.'

The Captain smiled. 'Thank you, *sensei*. I have learned to take it this way. In answer to your question, I am here to film the American plane that crashed near the northern end of the Gardens and exhibit the charred corpses of the crew. I am relieved that no damage was done to your Orchid House, just a few native homes destroyed. The film will be shown in the cinemas We have to prove that the enemy aircraft are not invulnerable. In fact, of course, being pressurised, they fly faster and higher than our fighters and we have no modern anti-aircraft guns on the island, so we can only hope to catch one occasionally by sheer good fortune. They have devastated the offshore islands with firebombs and mined the channel. Already, supply ships have been lost and food will become scarcer. I am afraid we are now in the situation the British were in at the start of the war. It is much easier to attack than to defend and we cannot be everywhere at once.'

The Professor tapped the letter on his desk. 'It seems to me that there is something very childish about warfare. It is like two little boys in boots, taking turns to kick each other on the shins. They are raiding Nagasaki. Thank God my family are in a little valley away from the Mitsubishi shipyards and so are safe.' Oishi nodded.

The Professor sighed again. 'It is a lovely spot amongst the ricefields, with a little river and a big meadow where the schoolgirls can do their spear practice after school.'

'Spear practice?'

'Yes, they practise killing American invaders.'

'With *spears*?'

'Well, sharpened bamboo poles really. The good thing is that my daughter learns something about bamboo and its habitats.'

The Captain shook his head wonderingly. 'Is that what we have come to? I am sorry. Spears sound so primitive. The future surely lies in the air. Balloons are the future. Which reminds me, Professor. I wonder if I might use the gardens to launch some test flights of my balloons where no one can see. Teething troubles. I need a place of peace and privacy. For research purposes only.'

Professor Tanadatake did not really want to think about his little daughter, with her flying pigtails, facing a huge, heavily-armed, gum-chewing, American GI in single combat. Perhaps they would even be black GIs who—they were told—ate their rice raw and slept in rudimentary nests in trees. Surely such a confrontation could never really happen? Spear practice must be seen as a military form of exercise only. A poor man's *akido*.

'Of course. Ask Dr, Pilchard to help you. He has some experience of using weather balloons to study wind-pollination in the upper atmosphere. But why do your duties include film-making? Do you not plan to rejoin General Yamashita in the Philippines? I understood you were very close.'

The Captain blushed. He had not liked Yamashita and the

world of green and khaki that he represented. 'Indeed, the General is like a father to me, always slapping me and shouting at me for my own good.' He laughed gratefully. 'The new commander, General Itagaki, is a very different man. Since I am not attached to his staff, he does not know I exist. I sit in my office and the telephone never rings. So I do little jobs for the intelligence section and, in return, I see all the latest intelligence. But, between us, the news is not good. My General has withdrawn his forces to the north of the Philippines. He has no air cover, no fleet support against the invaders. The Americans call their progress a 'meatgrinder advance' since they are paying in blood for every inch of ground and no survivors are left after their passage. General Yamashita will soon have the honour to die for the nation. I must remain here and carry out his final orders.' He sipped tea and grimaced at the mix of sour tannin and sugar. 'And look after his baggage.'

'His baggage?'

Oishi rolled his eyes, sighed and laid down the clumsy, barbarian cup with its gross, ugly handle. 'The General always has so much heavy baggage. He collects things, you see.'

The Professor's mind flashed to the gold he had taken from the Museum. 'Yes. That I have seen.'

After the Captain had left, Professor Tanakadate turned to more immediate concerns. His shoes were worn through and he set one on the table top and examined it. Carefully, he drew around it in a last inch of pencil stub and cut out an insert in old lino—filched from the Cluny Road house and representing genteel parquet flooring—to patch the hole, slipped it on and tapped his foot experimentally. It would do. Then, heavy-hearted, he returned—slipshod and pernickety—to his report. It was too short, too undramatic but the 'Research' section could now be padded out. 'Staff, under the direction of Dr Pilchard, participated successfully in a joint research project with the aim of transforming the Gardens into a state-of-the-art weather balloon-launching facility and valuable on-going links with eminent collectors in Dai-Nippon were established and consolidated.'

* * *

HK hoped to God no one would see him. He had been totally taken aback when Lily had said to him, quite casually, as she brushed her hair, 'If you want to contact the Malayan Peoples' Anti-Japanese Army I can fix it.' First, he had not realised that he had been so open, that she knew so much. And then, it had been as if his mother had suddenly offered to turn his banana money into American War Bonds with full loss indemnity overnight. He had avoided all further mention of it until the news of VE Day. The Japanese newspapers shrugged off the German surrender as the removal of an encumbrance, an act that brought new focus and efficiency to the war but no one was fooled. The British, Americans, Australians, Dutch, French were coming back as landlords and would not be pleased at what their tenants had been up to with the fixtures and fittings. There were rumours of coups and assassinations in Tokyo and some said the Americans had repeated their success with Yamamoto and shot down a plane full of high-ranking commanders. Everywhere was prevarication and faction, a sense of people waiting for the proper moment to switch loyalties. And, for the first time, he had been reading things, books, the naked power of ideas. They were intoxicating, like someone used to well-watered wine who encounters neat brandy for the first time. Abstract nouns did not just name things out there in the world. They actually had the power to conjure them into existence, to carve reality into different joints of meat so that, for the first time, it trembled on the edge of intelligibility. It had started as a necessary preparation for dealing with the MPAJA.

He would master their arguments, refute them, convert them. But as he worked his way through the pamphlets and magazines supplied by a discontented cousin in the Penang motor trade, he began to relish the pungent phrases, the deliberately inverted view of all he had previously known and felt himself grow. Revolution was a revelation. Loh Ching was not his intellectual superior after all, but merely a stupid victim of false consciousness. He was not even a free man, simply a running-dog of imperialist capitalists, a lackey. It was deeply comforting.

They had set out in the constant, needling rain that stitched the days together as soon as the morning rush started up. Lily was very smart today, modern hairstyle, black and white print dress with puff sleeves, ivory makeup and red lipstick. As a lover of American movies, HK had known to cunningly splash his numberplates, divorcee-fashion, with mud to conceal them but now the same rain that made his windscreen dirty washed them clean again. There were patrols everywhere and, on the bridges, they did not just look at the number plates, they jotted the numbers down in notebooks, shielding them under their sodden raincapes. Overhead, thunder grumbled melodramatically in a sky that swirled like a bad oyster and, once they were clear of the city and heading northwest, they met battle-stained heavy artillery pieces rolling southward with hair-triggered, frightened troops astride them and had to show HK's special pass to get through. The wet road hissed suspicion under the worn tyres and in the grim military traffic, HK's flashy American saloon stuck out like a tutu on an elephant. He wanted to give up but Lilly soothed.

'It's not far now, darling, but we shall have to walk from here. We daren't take the car. Pull in behind that bamboo.' She kicked off her elegant shoes into the well under the dashboard and was out of the door, even before he had put on the handbrake, barefoot, the mud squeezing up between her toes and laughing in the rain that tasted like stale sweat. HK had no choice but to follow, grabbing his hat and ditching jacket and tie onto the back seat and crackling clumsily through the scabby stems as Lily splashed, still giggling, up the track, like a child playing in a storm drain, oblivious to her wet hair. He panted after her, slipping and sliding on his smooth, leather soles and they went for some twenty minutes before she paused and grinned round at him, her soaked dress offering an X-ray of stylish underwear and he teetered up to her laughing and then realised the green bushes on either side were suddenly melting into men in olive uniforms with young, hard faces and that horrible, arrogant chink of loose metal that betokens armed force. Their eyes held a hunger that he thought, at first, might be lust inspired by Lily. Then he saw that it was just that. They were simply hungry. More men appeared behind and drove them, like silent sheepdogs, up the path, where finally an older man in civilian dress stepped out from the trees. Despite his shabby dress, he bore an unmistakable air of authority, like a senior consultant in a hospital who sloughs off the sad vanity of white coat, stethoscope and title to become plain 'Mr' in a worn tweed suit. He held out his arms to Lily. She ran to him and they kissed with disconcerting passion on the lips. HK froze and watched, feeling the stale, fishy breath of the man behind him on his neck, making his hair stand on end, half in expectation of a blow.

'Lily!' The man held her at arm's length and looked at her an enchanted smile on his face. HK moved up to them anxiously and the man eyed him, with a curl of the lip, over Lily's shoulder as HK held out his hand.

'Introduce me, Lily. Is this your uncle? Your father? How do you do.'

She half-turned to look at him and laughed with a squeeze of bitterness in the sound.

'Would I kiss my father like that? What are you thinking? That would be most improper.' She blushed. 'HK this is my husband.'

HK gulped. His mouth gaped. On this journey, he had been taken for a ride. But wait. He considered himself a modern man. After all, had he not seen the plays of Noel Coward, at the Victoria Theatre, in the company of Erica and with gin and tonics served at the interval? And the embarrassment, surely, was entirely for the husband in a situation like this. Yet there was the man smiling at him with every appearance of triumphant friendliness. He set his shoulders and smiled back.

'How do you do?' he repeated, suavely. 'I should like to talk to you about workers' control of factories.'

* * *

Above the clouds over the city of Kokura two silver B-29 aircraft circled peacefully. From 32,000 feet below they were silent and all but invisible in the thick cloud. Small groups of planes were usually for reconnaissance only and ignored by the ill-supplied Japanese air force to save fuel. Kokura did not know how lucky a city it was. Three days earlier, it had been designated an alternative target for the first atomic bomb, 'Little Boy', should Hiroshima be overcast. But it was August and Horoshima's citizens were blessed with a bright and sunny day. At the central tram terminus, at the moment of detonation, a female employee was wrestling with the difficult electrical contacts as she turned the tram around. You were not supposed to do that on your own in case the power cables got snagged. As the entire city was vaporised about her, she emerged miraculously unscathed and assumed that this was something she had done through her disregard of tram regulations. When she learned that it was in fact a terrible secret weapon unleashed by the enemy, she felt nothing but the greatest possible relief. After all, she might have been disgraced and dismissed.

Now, three days later, the residents of Kokura were still not feeling particularly lucky. Part of the cloud cover was the result of a huge pall of smoke from a recent incendiary raid by American bombers that had raged through the ancient wooden houses and torn the heart out of their city. But it saved them from receiving 'Fat Man', a bomb of much improved design, on their heads, for the flight-commander, running short of fuel, diverted to nearby Nagasaki where his bombardier applied the aiming skills he had recently acquired over Singapore. It seemed, at first, that Nagasaki too was cloudy, preventing visual targeting of the bomb and various other packages of instruments, as well as a letter to a noted Japanese physicist who was urged to convince the authorities of the threat posed by the present weapon. This ensured that he would be promptly arrested and held incommunicado as a collaborator. A radar-guided attack was one alternative, or they might just ditch the weapon in the sea on the way back to their base on the Marianas Islands where it would make a fine splash. And then there came a sudden break in the cloud cover and the bomb was released, twirling, into a shaft of redemptive Old Testament sunlight. 43 seconds later, at a height of some 1500 feet, it exploded some two miles off target, above the Urakami Valley, destroying the cathedral and many of the Christians who lived around it, traditionally the people who acted as mediators between Japan and the dangerous outside. One man had survived the Hiroshima bomb and been evacuated to the hospital in Nagasaki, arriving just in time to meet the second atomic bomb. Owing to the unusual topography of the city, he survived that too, making him either the luckiest or unluckiest man on the face of the planet, while a small, residential valley, running north east, was shielded by high hills except where the blast waves, five in *number, ricocheted off the slopes in walls of volcanic heat that melted rock back to lava. Worst hit was a little settlement with a river running through it and a large meadow in which little girls had practised to receive their invaders with bamboo spears.*

* * *

'It's time.' The string vest commando cracked his knuckles and worked his jaw. Other dark forms lurked at the back of the shelter, shouldering up bags, eyes gleaming out of blackened faces. Electricity crackled in the air. 'The Nips are being kicked out of Burma. Our lads'll be back here any day. It's time even if it means missing the life-drawing classes just as I was getting interested.' Corporal Higgins knew he needed to be brave. He sat up straight and fought to keep the trembling out of his voice. He reached out and gripped Dong-ju's hand.

'We've talked about it. You know he's Korean, not Japanese. He didn't volunteer. They conscripted him by force. He just wants to go home like us.' He was sweating too much. Dong-ju tried to smile but his face couldn't quite manage it and the mouth fell apart. String vest splayed a huge, gnarled hand over the top of his head and applied just enough pressure to be threatening, as if it were a melon he might choose to crush at any moment. The trio looked like some sort of old-fashioned mind-reading act in a music hall.

'We're all agreed then. The Japs are getting jumpy. They could wipe the lot of us out at any time. We're not sitting here waiting to made into roadfill. We'll at least die for a worthwhile cause. Our best hope is to get across the strait to the mainland and join the MPAJA before the massacre starts. Your mate's job here is to cover our tracks for 24 hours to give us time to get clear and across the water. Like I say, all he has to do is not notice our absence when he does roll-call in our hut. After that, he can do whatever he has to do to save his own arse. Make sure he understands that.'

'He understands.' Higgins worried at the end of a loose thought. 'Why should you trust him—after you're gone? What's to stop him sounding the alarm anyway just to take no chances?' String vest smirked and grasped Dong-ju's head again, squeezed rhythmically as if appraising the skull for ripeness.

'Oh. That's easy. Didn't I mention, Higgins? You're coming with us under the wire. If anything goes wrong, we make sure you're the first one to get it, sunshine, so you'd better hope he really likes you. No, I mean, *really* likes you. Right?' They all laughed. 'You tell him that.' He bent and addressed the Korean with exaggerated mouthing as you would a dog, looking into the worried and confused eyes. 'You comprendo?' and waggled his head in a forced doggy nod.

* * *

Captain Oishi was dazed and baffled. Respectfully prostrate on the floor of his quarters, as was proper in the presence of divinity, he began to wonder how much longer the Emperor's broadcast would last. The odd, poetic palace language was difficult to understand, even for a graduate such as himself, and it was made worse by the hiss, showing it to be not the true Emperor but a phonograph recording that might be the Emperor, except that no one had ever heard his voice before, so how could you tell? It could all be some terrible trick by the enemy. He felt the air go out of him, like one of his wounded balloons, at the thought of such infamy. This must surely be some new exhortation to greater effort, stauncher resistance, acceptance of deeper suffering. His back was aching. He humbly accepted the pain for the nation.

'... *Moreover, the enemy has begun to employ a new and most cruel bomb, the power of which to do damage is, indeed, incalculable, taking the toll of many innocent lives. Should we continue to fight, it would not only result in an ultimate collapse and obliteration of the Japanese nation, but it would also lead to the total extinction of human civilisation.*'

With horror, he realized that this was something far worse. It must be an invitation to the Allies to negotiate a ceasefire. He had heard rumours of this new weapon, even more terrible than his own balloons. His friend in the radio room at headquarters had whispered that major cities had just gone off the air, suddenly, one by one, and no word could be got from them. Perhaps paratroops had already landed? Now his neck hurt.

'... *Such being the case, how are we to save the millions of our subjects, or to atone ourselves before the hallowed spirits of our Imperial Ancestors? This is the reason why we have ordered the acceptance of the conditions of the joint declaration of the powers ...*'

This was no mere ceasefire. This was surrender. He had no idea what these conditions might be but such a thing was unthinkable, unimaginable ...

'... *We are keenly aware of the inmost feelings of you all, our subjects. However, it is according to the dictates of time and fate and we have resolved to pave the way to a grand peace for all the generations to come by enduring the unendurable and suffering what is unsufferable ...*'

He sat up. The world was at an end. Kneeling here like a fool, in deliberate pain, made no sense any more.

'*Beware most strictly of any outbursts of emotion that may engender needless complications, and of any fraternal contention and strife that may create confusion, lead you astray and cause you to lose the confidence of the world ...*'

The rest became a blur and then, through it, he was aware of the announcer coming on and explaining, in a strangulated voice, that what the Emperor had been saying, what he was trying to express, what he really meant, was that Japan had surrendered, then there was gloomy, martial music thudding through the speaker. He groped for some deep, focussing thought that was worthy of this experience of the end of the world but was aware only of the hardness of the floor against his buttocks and his own deep puzzlement, for it seemed that it was only moderate, brooding trouble that ate away at a man and not sudden, total catastrophe such as this, which somehow carried its own calmness within it. It was eleven o'clock in the morning, far too prosaic an hour for the end of the world. The idea could not be grasped. He felt like a man trying to manoeuvre a tank up a spiral staircase. He could only think a word he had learned from Dr Pilchard.

'Bugger!' he said.

He needed to walk to headquarters. In the street, soldiers were on guard as normal. Locals bowed deeply to him as he passed. Nothing had changed yet. None of this was real. The sun still shone and his shadow was attached to his feet, as always. At headquarters, he found part of his squad in a shed at the back of the motoring pool, looking lost and abandoned like some piece of outdated military hardware. He felt a pang of guilt. As he approached, one of them was saying, 'I know all about it. The record was smuggled out of the palace to the radio station in a basket of dirty knickers to fool the army coup-leaders. But I don't see the problem. They say if you wear white clothes these new bombs have absolutely no effect on you.'

'What are you saying?' Namura, a royalist maker of boxwood combs from Nara was aghast. 'The Emperor doesn't wear knickers and certainly never makes them dirty. At most a white, silk *fundoshi* cloth, forever honoured by contact ...'

Captain Oishi snapped. 'Sergeant Eno, assemble the men.' They shuffled to their feet and formed two short lines. They were all older and bigger than him, some unshaven, and he found them intimidating. He put on his barking, gravelly army voice. 'You may have heard rumours ...' He faltered. '... rumours about ... adjustments in the war. I can tell you nothing about this. It remains for us all to follow our orders. The orders I have for you are directly from General Yamashita, whom we have the honour to serve. The General, as you will remember from your own efforts at the shrine, was devoted to the cause of the construction of the glorious Syonan Jinja to our former comrades.' They dutifully bowed their heads. 'General Yamashita was a far-seeing man and left orders with me concerning our duties in the event of ... of ... the unbearable.' That made about as much sense as the Emperor's broadcast. 'We are to return to the shrine to construct a new garden. This time it is to be a Devil's Garden.'

They looked at each other. What the fuck ...?

Sergeant Eno had been a fishmonger in the world before the war, a cool, bone-picking man. 'Begging your pardon, Sir. Perhaps you can clarify. What exactly is meant by a *Devil's* Garden? What kind of devil are we speaking of here?'

Oishi smiled, crossed his arms, got into the swing of it, walked up and down as he spoke, delicately excised the skeleton of the idea for them.

'I have learned that a Devil's Garden has two meanings. First it is a term used by botanists at the Botanic Gardens. In the forests of South America, there lives a certain ant that depends for shelter on a particular plant that has hollow stems. These provide it with a secure home in which to live and raise its young. The ant is very clever and systematically poisons all other plants by injecting them with formic acid so that only this species of tree flourishes and spreads, taking over great areas of the jungle until it becomes so large that the ants can no longer defend it. The Greater East Asia Co-prosperity Sphere is a Devil's Garden of this kind and *we* are its ants.' Only Sergeant Eno laughed. He turned the idea over and flensed the remaining flesh from the bone, forming the second fillet. 'The other sense comes from our German allies. The Devil's Gardens are defensive structures that were built by General Rommel in the African desert, consisting of a maze of hidden mines, barbed wire and ditches that took the lives of thousands of British soldiers when they attacked them. It is this that we shall build at Syonan Jinja to wait for the British who will surely come.'

The men hesitated and looked hopefully at Sergeant Eno as he weighed the information. Captain Oishi smiled to himself resignedly. They respected Eno more than him.

'What about the fresh news, Sir, the Emperor's broadcast? The men have all heard about it.'

Oishi looked at them, uncertain, uneducated. They needed faith. As an officer, he must give it to them.

'The broadcast? I find it impossible to believe it was genuine. Have you all heard the story of the Forty-Seven Samurai?' They made sour faces. 'Then let me tell it to you now.

'It began over two hundred years ago. The lord, Asano, was instructed to receive the envoys of the Emperor with proper ceremony and was taught the proper forms by Kira Kozuke-no-Suke Yoshinaka of the Tokugawa Shogunate. But Asano refused to give him the presents he desired and he insulted him so badly that finally Asano attacked Kira and wounded him within the shogun's castle. This was a grave offence and he was ordered to kill himself. His lands and goods were confiscated and his followers were made outcasts. Under their leader, a man with the fine name of Oishi, they swore a secret oath to avenge their lord and concealed themselves by becoming humble tradesmen or monks. Oishi divorced his wife, though he loved her dearly, to make sure that she would not suffer for what he intended to do. Then Oishi took to drinking, sleeping with prostitutes, keeping bad company and Kira's spies were all deceived and believed he had no thought of vengeance. A Satsuma man even came and spat on Oishi as he lay drunk in the gutter as a disgrace to all samurai and he bore that dishonour in silence.' The Captain blushed at his namesake's shame, thought of Orchid, his mother, his loyalty to General Yamashita. 'Slowly, so as not to arouse suspicion, the rest of the outcasts gathered around Oishi in Tokyo and gained admission to Kira's house, working on it in his absence, as the simple workmen they now were. Then, two years later, in a heavy snowstorm, they learned that he was at home and attacked the house, that they now knew well, announcing to the neighbours that they need not fear for they were not robbers but men engaged in an act of honour. Many of Kira's family and army were killed but, when he burst into his bedroom, Oishi found the bed still warm but empty. In a secret room, they finally found a man hidden but he refused to confirm who he was and they were only able to identify him by the scar on his neck. Oishi kneeled respectfully before Kira in recognition of his rank and invited him to kill himself but he only trembled and cried. So, finally, brave Oishi cut off his head and carried it to the grave of their lord in Sengaku-ji. Then they gave all the money they had to the abbot of the temple, washed and waited. The people begged the Shogun to spare the outcasts who had only avenged their lord but they had also disobeyed the order of the Shogun and so all forty-six must die but were allowed to kill themselves. Their tombs are still there and a great place of pilgrimage for people who would honour them. The Satsuma man who spat on Oishi came and asked forgiveness at his tomb and killed himself there and was buried nearby.' He waved his arm aloft and punched the air. 'Banzai! Banzai!'

The men looked at him blankly, arms half raised in

prevarication, nor sure what they were supposed to be cheering for. What were they to make of all that fancy killing and dying?

'Now I remember,' said one, letting his arm drop. 'I saw the film in Kakura but it was dead boring, so I left and went to a baseball game.'

Sergeant Eno frowned. Baseball had been popular before the war but was now perceived as American and therefore bad. He changed the subject.

'"All forty-six must die" but I thought there were forty-*seven* samurai.'

'Er ... well ... I missed out unnecessary detail. There was another man but the story is confused.'

'What happened to him then, Sir?'

Oishi sighed. 'There is a lack of agreement. Some say he was frightened and ran away and lived the rest of his life in regret. Others that he was sent as a messenger to announce the death of Kira. Then he was pardoned by the Shogun on account of his youth and lived until the great age of seventy-eight and was then buried honourably with his comrades.' They nodded enthusiastically and broke out in conversation.

'We, too, are all still young and would be pardoned.'

'They were samurai, bold warriors, pretending to be workmen. We are workmen pretending to be samurai, fish out of water.'

'The case is not the same. Perhaps the lesson is that they were wrong to disobey the shogun's order just as we would be wrong to disobey our Emperor. Perhaps they should have laid down their swords and lived—perhaps even happily.'

'They were fighting Japanese. When you are fighting *gaijin*, the rules, surely, are different.'

'It is one thing to die at home, another so far away. I too would be happy to die honourably at their tomb in Sengaku-ji at the age of seventy-eight.'

Sergeant Eno swivelled on the spot and turned to the Captain, looked at him with deadpan face and saluted crisply. In such a Devil's Garden, they would all die like fish being shot in a barrel.

'The men enthusiastically embrace your orders, Sir, but there is a problem with the equipment. Our ordinance has been quartermastered by General Itagaki's men and fully incorporated into their own stores. We would need a signed order from the General, himself, before they would agree to release it to us. I think, Sir, this problem might not be resolvable.'

* * *

Corporal Higgins dug into the bottom of the pan for a few lingering fragments of burned meat and licked the spoon. He had no idea what kind of meat it was. Frankly, he was beyond caring. After finding the shoreline too heavily guarded, they had walked vaguely westward for two nights and laid up during the stinking hot daylight hours. There had been nothing much to eat and precious little water and then they had come on this Japanese patrol, hiding out and cooking something for supper they had stolen from a village in a great iron pot. String vest and his mates had made short work of them with knives and bare hands and were sitting about crooning over their captured guns and grenades, cradling them in their sweaty laps, stroking them, happy as sandboys. It was like being back at school with the playground bullies. Matter-of-fact brutality of this kind was scary and Higgins had thought about trying to slip away from them but the truth was that he was afraid of setting them against him and, in this terrible place, he felt safer with all these big boys about him than he would alone in the dark. The Japanese bodies were dragged off the track and dumped like sacks of flour—rice really—and they came back grinning horribly and wiping knives, wearing their victims' hats and smoking their cigarettes. Higgins was half-surprised not to see them chomping on human arms and legs.

'Right,' said string vest. 'We'll head north-west. They won't be expecting that, not in the mangroves. Once we get to the shore, we can find a boat. There may be fishermen we can persuade to take us across to the mainland.' He flexed the big, blood-flecked hands to show how very persuasive he might prove to fishermen. They shouldered the weapons and set off up the track, Higgins following in their wake like a dog, sipping from a Japanese water bottle.

The moon was very bright and cast dark, black shadows across the track, making it hard to tell which were mere phantoms and which solid roots to trip you up as surely as iron bars. Nameless things skittered off into the undergrowth and the air was rank and heavy with the smell of decomposition and loud with the whine of mosquitoes. As they moved across country, his nagging mind filled in the blanks in his vision so that it somehow kept trying to be a prosaic, English countryside. In the middle distance, hardly-seen tropical trees became staunch oaks. Undergrowth reverted to dogrose and blackthorn. The venom of Asian beasts was transmuted into the Cotswold honey and, out there, in the outer darkness, the patches that gleamed with silver phosphorescence and the flash of dancing glowworms became lost lamplight glimpsed through the leaded windows of thatched cottages. It was like the way you recognised, in the faces of strangers, traits of long-lost loves. The thought enchained another and he wondered how poor Dong-ju was managing. After an hour or so, they came to a stream and stumbled across the rocks, water splashing like fire about their feet. He stooped to refill the water bottle. Something big with wings glided silently between them and the moon and threw a passing silhouette over them like a net and then, as they looked up, a bark of gunfire raked the ground.

Higgins stumbled, half recovered, then fell, full length, into the water. Bullets flew in all directions, pinged off rocks. Screams. He raised his head and saw a terrified Asian face hovering over him. An explosion and the face was gone. He lay trembling in the water, waiting for the inevitable shot to the back of the head or slice of the sword from an unseen enemy. He no longer cared. He was too tired, had lived too long. He closed his eyes and embraced his fate with perfect peace. When strong arms grabbed him and lifted him up, he was almost disappointed, annoyed even.

They were not Japanese faces. He had finally learned, thanks to Dong-ju's giggling instruction, to tell a Korean face from a Japanese face but this was different again, Chinese faces. They wore smart new uniforms that he did not recognise and carried new automatic weapons of a kind he had never seen. Torches clicked on and blinded like limelight.

'Oops!' Two trim, grey men emerged from the glare and advanced, with the flat gait of middle age, smiling at him, into the clearing. One was European, one Chinese. Tweedledum and Tweedledee. 'I rather think we owe you an apology. We assumed you were Japanese, you see. The hats, the dark. I'm afraid all your friends are dead. Bit of a balls-up, really. Bad show but can't be helped. Cover up and carry on, as we say in the military. By rights, you shouldn't have been in this sector at all, you know. Now, I'm Major Frobisher, Force 136, Malayan Section and this is my colleague, Chen Guang of the MPAJA. I'm afraid the state of your uniform doesn't permit me to know who you are.'

'I'm Corporal Higgins, Sir.'

Major Frobisher considered him with distaste. 'In that case, I think we'd better have a proper salute.'

Subaltern habits kicked in over the fatigue and sheer incredulity. Corporal Higgins shuffled his feet together and saluted through tears. '578962, Higgins, Corporal suh!'

Frobisher smiled. 'That's much better, Corporal. At ease. And now I think we'll all have a nice dish of tea and a little chat and find out just what's going on around here.'

The Chinese soldiers were already briskly dragging the bodies away into the bush like more sacks of flour—potatoes really—whistling as they worked.

* * *

'If you want to contact the Malayan Peoples' Anti-Japanese Army I can fix it.' Orchid smiled at him then looked down as she buttoned her blouse. Captain Oishi was surprised. First, he had not realised that he had been so open, that she knew so much. And then it had been as if his mother had suddenly offered to arrange a commission for him in the Kempeitei or an audience with the Emperor. How could someone who was little more than a schoolgirl fix something like that? A lizard ran across the wall on suckered feet, pumped its body obscenely and laughed at him. The scene should have been post-coital but was not. The pangs of the flesh had no bite and his appetite for sex had shrivelled, while his untasted banana leaf of cold, congealed, fried rice showed that his stomach had joined in the boycott. It was as if he could not even feel his own body.

The smell of burning was blowing across from the west, columns of thick, black, sugary smoke towering up into the sky. The world made no sense any more. The Japanese supreme command had surrendered in Tokyo harbour. It was signed and sealed. He had been ordered to march his men to the cinema and watch the pictures with them—the images of frail, but immensely powerful, little old men in top hats limping like crabs onto the battleship, the strutting, beef- and creampie-fed American sailors

225

and their accomplices in various Allied uniforms that looked like a photo from one of Erica's fancy dress parties. McArthur and that extraordinary corncob pipe, blowing aw-shucks, hillbilly smoke into everyone's faces. At least the Emperor had been spared that final indignity. There had been shouts and screams in the flickering, cinematic darkness, fights had broken out, grown men had collapsed in tears, fisting their own eyes and been trampled underfoot as the audience rushed out. A brisk civilian, shaming the military, had shot himself right there and then in the jostling crowd, his brains blown all over the people around him. Captain Oishi still heard the shot ringing out across the voice of the jolly American commentator who was talking about Commander Perry's flag, fluttering from his ship when he forced the opening up of Japan to the world just ninety-two years before, having been flown out from an American museum to be displayed during the signing ceremony. What sort of a mind had thought of such a thing? What sort of tattered meaning was it supposed to impose on everything that had happened? Craziness.

The Japanese forces still roamed the streets in tanks and trucks in the token name of social order but they were now supposed to be under the command of the British, who were not even there, and were anyway the same British who had already surrendered to them. It felt as if they had been defeated, not in battle, but by an offstage act of administration. The soldiers' faces were white and strained so that, as they peered from the steel hatches of their tanks, they looked like ghosts being sucked down into the jaws of their own growling and chomping machines. And the first thought of the Chinese at the news had been to kill their Malay neighbours and the Malays had killed Chinese and were burning their shops. Meanwhile, the Chinese were killing each other. He wondered who the Indians killed and whose ancient right and duty it was to kill them. Over there, beneath that pall of smoke, people were running mad in the street, mouths drooling and blood dripping from their hands as the soldiers just stood and watched or turned indifferently away. It was no longer anything to do with them. Their minds were thousands of miles from here. He would ask Orchid no questions.

'Yes. Please arrange it. Thank you Orchid.'

* * *

'Where's the old man?' Catchpole had taken to wearing seedy pyjamas around the clock, had given up shaving in victory, listened openly to a Radio India that throbbed and undulated with strange wave phenomena that Pilchard found extremely irritating. The pyjamas were tied with a great bow at the front, making him look like an unlikely Christmas present. Outside in the wider Singapore, civilians had long worn the oddest combinations of clothing remnants, pullovers with shorts, women's blouses and cut-down jodhpurs, great boots, as if on the way to a fancy dress party in a depressed coalmining village.

'The Professor? I haven't seen him for days. He just went off early one morning.' Tiny Dr Hanada had disappeared too, though that was unsurprising, since he always looked as if he might be about to pop down a rabbit hole.

'Well, he might have given us back the tuning knob for the wireless before he went. Very selfish of him. He can be very high-handed, you know.' He fiddled at the residual prong with thick pliers. There was a flash and he dropped them and licked his finger. 'Damn and blast! I got a shock.' The loudspeaker coughed and cleared its throat and resumed more intelligibly. 'I say. That's fixed it!'

'... *And I want you to be quite clear. This is no negotiated surrender based on the dropping of the atom bombs, it is a*

Japanese military defeat, the first time they have ever been defeated in their history. You have chased their soldiers out of Burma and I have instructed all Japanese commanders to make their way to Singapore where I shall receive their formal surrender from Count Terauchi or his representative ...'

'Isn't that Noel Coward's voice?' It drooped with tropical languor and patrician disdain.

Catchpole looked pained. 'For God's sake. It's Dickie—Lord Mountbatten—the Supreme Commander.' Catchpole spoke as if he were a close acquaintance who dropped by for a noggin on a regular basis. 'Really old man. I've said it before. You must try to keep up.'

'... I assure you I shall put up with no nonsense or impertinence from any of these people, no matter how important they think they are ...'

'Do you suppose, Catchpole, that anyone had given a moment's thought to what happens now? It's a bit like being at school. Your whole world is there. All your achievements are measured by its standards. Your actions are judged by its values. You work your way up to a position of privilege. But when it ends and you get your exam results...what then? You're cast adrift. You have to find a whole new world to move about in, a bigger, nastier one, and go back to the bottom of the pecking order again. It took me years to find out who I was and what I did and now we have to go through all that again. While the Nips were here, we didn't have a whole lot of choice but now we will and I don't really know if I've got it in me to make those decisions any more.'

Catchpole examined the pliers for damage and snapped their jaws in rebuke. 'If you don't mind my saying so, old man, you worry too much. Everything will go back just as it was before, except that this time we'll not be so damn soft. We'll have learnt our lesson and not let ourselves be pushed around so much.' He arranged his waning multiplicity of chins into a failed thrusting jaw of defiance.

'But don't you imagine that's exactly what everyone else is saying? I just had a card from my wife. It took ages to get here but I suppose the postal service is nothing to write home about. Anyway, it seems she's not my wife any more. We're divorced. You see, it's already starting. And all this was just a rehearsal that showed governments how far they could go, how much they could get away with. This is the worst century the world has ever known and we're only halfway through it.'

'Sorry, old man. These things happen even in the best marriages, let alone … Think of the big picture. You're a scientist, a doctor. This is a turning point. Don't you want to see the final triumph of Western reason over all this Eastern nonsense?'

Pilchard groaned. 'Oh for god's sake. If the West was governed by reason, it's men who would ride horses sidesaddle and bath taps would be designed to be worked by toes not fingers.'

'At Port Swettenham, our men are coming ashore in an endless stream and restoring order as they advance. These are difficult times and will call for difficult measures but I know I can count on every man and woman among you in this command.'

Catchpole worried irritably at a broken fingernail with his teeth. 'Your trouble, old man … gnnnn … is that you think not being involved, standing aloof, makes you better than us patriots, superior … gnnn. It's not the case, you know. The truth is, it's just another form of your damned laziness.' He spat the nail onto the floor and they both sat and looked at it with distaste. The house was a tip, with unchronological crockery lying about unwashed, reeking heaps of sour fag ends. No one was cleaning up any more. All the workers had disappeared. Catchpole was just as annoying amidst chaos as prissy order.

'Actually, Catchpole, he left a note.'

He sat up and glared. 'Who?'

'The Professor.'

'The Professor? A note?' He frowned. 'Was it after the nature of being ... a er ...?'

'A Fuck-Off-You-Red-Nosed-Bastard letter? No.'

'I see.' Then. 'What was in it? Really, Pilchard, as senior curator, you know damned well it should have come straight to me.' He had himself turned red in the nose. The supplementary chins wobbled in a face that had the poxed and overripe complexion of a shrivelled succulent—a cardiac event just waiting to happen. Pilchard retained his calm, knowing that to be far more galling.

Pilchard retained his calm, knowing that to be far more irritating. 'It was addressed to me. Perhaps you should have the card from my wife as well.'

'Well, I demand you hand it over at once—the note, I mean.'

Pilchard drew a folded piece of paper from his top pocket, written in meticulous script, each individual letter separately formed as in a demonstration of penmanship. A careful red seal gleamed at the bottom. 'Or what? Perhaps you will give me a good wigging?' Catchpole blanched at the threat barely concealed in the word. Pilchard felt an obscure inner rage grip him. 'Keep your hair on, old man. Perhaps I should read it to you? It starts, "Dear Dr Pilchard, Over the past few years we have worked together in circumstances that were difficult for both of us. My own work, of course, has been fatally hindered by the absence of volcanoes in Singapore and I know that you also are not where you might have wished to be. But birds fly up from under one's feet. I have received news that makes it impossible for me to continue, also pointless. I fear we shall not meet again which is a matter of deep regret to me. Please inform Dr Catchpole that I have arranged the outstanding matter of the paper allegedly signed by the Governor and authorising your co-operation ..."'

Catchpole exploded. 'What does he mean "allegedly". Damn and blast the man!' He was shaking. 'I assure you I had that chit from the Governor personally and gave it to the old man with my own hands. I had to fight my way down to the Fullerton building under mortar fire to get it. If he was stupid enough to lose it, you can hardly ...'

'There is more. "Since no one knows where the original of that mysterious paper is now to be found, I have written to the Minister in Tokyo confirming its existence and listing it as an enclosure. A copy of that letter is in the records here. Naturally, the envelope I sent is actually empty but this may spare you all some inconvenience if things develop as I expect them to. It will be just another thing sadly lost in the war, in which we have all lost so much. I would suggest that you retain this letter for your own, personal records, Dr Pilchard, for your own personal protection. It is the moment for us all to seek shelter under a big tree." It's signed with his seal as you see. I think I'll do as he says and hang on to it.'

Catchpole was thoughtful. 'I see. And where do you suppose he has gone? Where is this big tree?'

'I suspect we shall never know. He clearly had no intention of leaving a forwarding address.'

Catchpole sulked briefly, then ... 'Do you suppose he took the tuning knob with him?'

* * *

'I am quite unarmed,' Captain Oishi assured them. It was a puzzling scene. In the middle of the mangroves. Across the water, a small hut was built out on stilts over the ooze, on whose platform stood a chair where a white man snipped away happily at the hair of a young Chinese, with flashing clippers, holding up the strands and clearly discussing the desired length and style of cut with great energy. A mound of black locks lay already at their feet and a whole line of other men, carrying enormous guns, waited patiently for their turn.

Orchid had made him park a good mile away and walk the rest of the way and then asked him to wait ten minutes before he followed her in. It was like some children's game of hide and seek and he had somehow feared she would just abandon him here and run away. After all, she had been very sad and serious, held both his hands in hers and looked into his eyes.

'Always remember, Yoshi, whatever happens, I do really care for you.' Hadn't she said much the same the other day? 'It's this war. Things could have been so different. Be careful. It makes everyone act like someone else. None of us are ever free to be ourselves. I have lived my life backwards. Your love is the curl-up-and-die innocent love that eats you up like a flame on paper, the sort every schoolgirl should have before the other, more reasonable kinds that are always a compromise. There must be a better place, a better way even if it cannot be together. You will always be my special, my first *real* love.' She pressed her lips to his with soft sadness then kissed him with sudden fierce adhesion. He had protested his bewilderment, tried to hug her, but she was already moving away down the track, sobbing.

'So Captain. My name is Chen Guang. I am in charge here.' Oishi was distracted. The man was perched on a fallen tree trunk and Orchid was sitting on his lap, stroking his face with every sign of devotion, looking completely composed apart from the risk of falling between his parted legs. She had introduced the man as her husband. Chen Guang nodded over his shoulder at the barberous scene. 'You are intrigued? You would be surprised that personal vanity is the last thing men give up. Have you come just for a proper haircut or is there something else?' He, himself, was quite immaculately shaved and trimmed. 'Ah, I see.' He gripped Orchid's thigh through the thin stuff. 'Lily and I have no secrets. She is a loyal servant of The Party. Sometimes she brings me people—a bit like a cat that brings you its catch once it has finished playing with it.' Captain Oishi blinked back tears. Orchid looked at him with big, sad eyes and shook her head. He coughed through a choking throat.

'No. No. It is not for a haircut that I have come.' He took a deep breath and spoke quickly, looking at his own feet, like a man afraid he would change his mind. 'I should like to join the Malayan Peoples' Anti-Japanese Army please.' A silence. Then Chen Guang threw back his head and roared with laughter so that Orchid bounced up and down on his lap. It rang out over the mud. A flock of startled birds took flight. The men, standing around across the water, smiled sympathetically as the platform rocked under their feet from the wave they made.

'You are Japanese and you want to join the anti-Japanese army?' He looked around for support in his incredulity but the men were too far away to hear so he laughed in Orchid's taut, unhappy face. His arm curled tightly around her waist. 'I don't know whether you are a Simple Simon or a Smart Alec. Why would you want to do that?' Orchid climbed to the ground and walked away towards the hut with downcast, unfocused eyes.

'Because, now that the war has ended, I think that quite soon the Malayan Peoples' Anti-Japanese Army will become the Malayan Peoples' Anti-British Army. This war has been ended by the Americans, not the British. Your fight with them, I believe, is not over. Neither is mine. To surrender is shameful, to kill myself is stupid since we are not truly beaten and our cause remains, even if I have even less to live for than I thought. Therefore I have no alternative. I must fight on, like my honourable, ancient namesake. It is not a matter of professional pride. We must be what we are.'

Chen Guang looked at him hard—the soft, downy cheeks, the gentle, chestnut eyes. 'I think you should go home, Captain. Your mother would not like it if you stayed.'

Oishi set his lips in a firm line. Orchid had gone round the other side of the hut and now she was walking alone down the path on that bank, her features made invisible by the light behind her—become a mere shadow—and slowly fading away into the glare of bright sunlight that bleached her out of existence like a stain on fine linen.

'That is correct. She would not like it but women are ... they ...'

'You mean perhaps that the way of the world is that "men must fight and women must weep"?'

'Possibly ... Exactly! Women are a distraction. They are a dream that disappears in daylight. Then perhaps men weep too but then they must fight again.' He looked dreamily after Orchid but she was nowhere to be seen. The sun, his own mythical ancestor, had eaten her up like that fireball at Nagasaki, turning the tears in his eyes into rainbows.

'Captain. It is true that the Brutish once put me in jail but now they are our friends—for the moment at least. Recently some of their POWs were shot up not far from here. It was some misguided nationalists, of course. But we have since taken care of that with our Brutish comrades. We work very hard to stay friends with them. Governments don't really mind their subjects getting killed, it's just that they feel they should have the monopoly rights on that—a matter of deference, then. You have to ask yourself what one Japanese captain could do for us that would be worth all the bother and difficulty he might bring. He might upset the Brutish. He would certainly upset certain Chinese. What have you got to offer that could possibly counterbalance all that?' He shrugged and raised his brows in question.

Captain Oishi showed neither surprise nor disappointment but Chen Guang froze on the spot as he said very quietly, 'I have one thing I can bring you, one thing that might make you let me stay. I have General Yamashita's gold.'

* * *

Admiral Lord Louis Francis Albert Victor Nicholas George Mountbatten admired his distinguishedly greying temples in the cheval glass and smoothed them appreciatively. The Windsors generally did not age well—big Saxe-Coburg noses and premature balding. Alone amongst them, he found himself turning most satisfactorily from blank matinee idol to devilishly handsome silver fox. He knew he was exactly what was required at this stage of the war, a tall, haughty figure with a gritty jaw that could stride up and down lines of much shorter colonial troops, barking encouragement and being photographed saluting outside pillared, gubernatorial buildings. The decorations on his chest looked very well, a multi-hued tickertape of achievement. It was lucky they had picked up on the surrendering Japanese wearing the British Distinguished Service and the Allied Victory medals left over from their role in the last WW, and plucked them off in time. That would not have done at all, clouded the issue— also incongruous, like a man taking a shit while wearing a hat. He pondered picturesquely. Shifting fate, ebb and flow of the tide of fortune. He, himself, had had the odd bit of bad luck, the suicidal sacrifice of Canadian troops on that senseless raid he had organised on Dieppe. Failure was deeply unglamorous. Then project Habakkuk, the exciting plan to build a huge mid-Atlantic aircraft carrier of the revolutionary material, pykrete, a boffin's mixture of ice and woodpulp. Now *that* had turned out very badly with a ghastly year of secret experiments in some frozen meat depot underneath Smithfield market before it had all been torpedoed with a single irritable stroke of Churchill's pen. It had not helped that he had attempted to save the project by a dramatic, last-minute demonstration of the qualities of this material, as opposed to pure ice, by firing a bullet into a block of each before the reluctantly-assembled members of the general staff. The ice had shattered gratifyingly while the resistant pykrete had sent the bullet ricocheting amongst the leaping senior officers and ripped through the trousers of one of them. In vain, he had protested that that was exactly his point. 'Indubitably suitable for the crust of NAAFI pies,' Churchill had quipped in the lethal report's margin. It would have been enough to sink the career of anyone who did not happen to be so closely related to the king. As it was, he was punished by promotion, a technique whose benefits for a commander he, himself, fully appreciated. God knows, there would be enough of it in the giant cock-up that was Singapore. Churchill, it was said, had cried hot tears of shame and rage at the news of the yielding up of his eastern fortress.

The new and improved surrender ceremony had gone as well as could be expected. The real treaties had been signed in Rangoon and Tokyo. The Singapore chapter was pure theatre, an appendix to the Mikado, a public act of military masturbation. The Japanese delegates had turned up right on time but he had made them cool their heels for an hour to make the point that Singapore time had now been shifted back from Synonanto time which had been set to the same clock as Tokyo. The whole takeover was a great bluff, all 'fur coat, no knickers,' since the British warships in the harbour would have been sitting ducks and his troops were heavily outnumbered and outgunned by the Japs had they decided to make a fight of it. The fact that it was armed Japanese soldiers, 'surrendered personnel' *not* POWs therefore not subject to the

Geneva Convention—important legal distinction—that held back the cheering crowds outside, showed how matters stood all too clearly, as did the absence of that absolute shower, Percival, who had surrendered Singapore in the first place. Couldn't run a bath, that johnnie, let alone a war. The very same Union Jack of that surrender, worn and faded from secret deployment on each coffin in Changi, had been hoisted back over the Municipal Building to cleanse it of the dishonour. That story had brought a tear to the eye. The bugles had been good. Bugles were always good though they, too, tugged at the heartstrings. There had come that breath-stopping moment when General Itagaki had hesitated, pen in mid-air for a full thirty seconds—will he, won't he?—milking the moment—before signing the surrender document and then having the nerve to quibble over the placing of the other signatures. Mountbatten snorted and fluffed up his gold epaulettes. Then the victory parade. Trooping down the front steps to the podium amidst a firestorm of popping flashbulbs, with the crowds cheering and some angry Eurasians shouting at the Japs, 'Baka, baka. Bloody fool!' He groaned. But at least that had been better than the moment when the crowd got the Chinese Nationalist and the Japanese uniforms confused and booed the wrong side. Ranks of jolly tars and stout Indian chaps, all well turned out. No one falling down the hastily filled trenches on the Padang. Intimidation by white linen, whiter than the flag the Japs were carrying, and enough white faces rounded up to show whose victory this was. And the mighty noise of the Sunderland seaplanes thundering low over the Padang, like the wrath of god, shaking the ground under their feet. Oh, and those terribly smart young men of the MPAJA who had turned all heads, kitted out with shiny new uniforms, three red stars on their caps, and the very latest automatic rifles, crashing down the road in unaccustomed boots and slightly wobbly ranks that alone betrayed the fact that they had come, not from Sandhurst, but straight out of the stinking jungle. This place could never do without the British to keep everyone in line, facing in the same direction. They'd simply tear themselves apart. There was a perfunctory knock and Wells, his ADC, slid his head round the door, sidling in with a sheaf of loose papers and a school exercise book.

'Come in Rupert.'

'Sorry to bother you, Sir.' He was careful not to come between Mountbatten and his mirror image. 'Just a few things for your signature and sayso.' Poor Rupert Wells had spent time at the mission in Washington and carried the stigmata in his speech. He would be spying on him, of course, and reporting directly back to Churchill. When they had first met, he had asked, 'Wells? Are you one of the Somerset Wells?' 'No Sir. I rather think I'm one of the Ne'er Do Wells.' He had taken to him at once. Rupert understood the need for chumminess in an organisation dedicated to the killing of complete strangers. But now it was time for a little mature reflection, for drawing the conclusions of the past. It always came as a shock, the way the tangled mess of the present became the neat, little blocks of history. Rupert would be writing his memoirs soon, completing that packaging process, and Mountbatten threw a pinch of dreamy, visionary quality into his voice that would look well there.

'Do you suppose, Rupert, that the natives will ever be able look us in the eye again, without blaming us for all this?'

'I don't know, Sir. Will *we*?' Mountbatten laughed and saw Rupert's cynical reflection smile back, then look briskly down. 'Right, Sir. A few gongs for natives and such to be handed out, subject to your and London's approval, of course.' He placed the papers on the desk. 'Would you like me to run you through them quickly or would you like to have more time to go over them later, yourself?' Mountbatten threw up his hands, staggered under the burdens of office and rolled his eyes eloquently. 'Right, well, won't take a jiffy then, Sir. First thing is the Jap currency, banana money. Word is we should declare it illegal tender, except for the largest denomination notes, and release Straits dollars through the banks right away. There are a couple of crates of fresh cash standing ready on the *Sussex*.'

Mountbatten pouted. 'Surely that's a civilian matter that can wait. And won't that mean all the little people will lose everything while the black marketeers and collaborators will make a fortune?'

Rupert grinned. 'Just so, Sir. Very perceptive of you. We have to be careful not to make powerful enemies at the moment. That can come later. Until the civilian admin's up and running it seems we're the only channel of lawful authority, so we have to do it. A note from London. We should avoid loose usage of words like "citizens". Malays kick up a stink if the Chinese get official recognition as even existing, so they're all undifferentiated "loyal subjects of the King Emperor". A few awards and sweeteners. The big show is over and it's time for some applause—a bit of confetti to throw in people's eyes. General theme is last time it was the lads who swam to Australia, gripping knives between their teeth, to carry on the fight, were the heroes. This time, it's the loyal locals who stayed behind to face the foe.'

'You know. When you talk like that, Rupert, I wonder whether you quite believe in our civilising mission East of Suez.'

'I believe in *your* civilising mission, of course, Sir.'

'Right answer, dear boy, bang on. Now, who else have we got that needs my thumbs up?'

Wells held up the exercise book list and stabbed at it with finger, not thumb. 'Mrs Anna Kwok, local Chinese woman working with Force 136, beaten, tortured and starved for two years by the Kempeitei. I thought an MBE would do, after all she did survive—even if it is without fingernails.'

Mountbatten spread fingers to consider his own nails. They needed a manicure. 'Right.'

'Dr Voss, Head of the Women's Section in Changi. OBE. Posthumous, I'm afraid.'

'She died there?'

'No. I'm afraid the old girl was knocked down and killed by the film unit's jeep. After years in jail, the Changi prisoners aren't very good at traffic. Next. Head of local Chinese merchants, HK Fong. Turned up on the Padang in an MPAJA uniform. Now, that rather surprised everyone. We had him down to be charged with collaboration and financial shenanigans. Now, suddenly, he's come good and is a suitable model for His Majesty's Loyal Chinese. An OBE?'

'Fine.' He hesitated. 'M or O? Oh make it an O, since devaluation of currency is in our minds at the moment. By the way, how do we feel about the MPAJA?'

'Official line is they're respected as our worthy allies in victory, though Frobisher, over at Political Affairs, points out they're mostly commies, rotten to the core. They talk a lot of hot air but they'll settle down again soon enough once we disarm them and find them all jobs where they can get their hand in the till. Which brings me to Chen Guang, their local commander. Of course nowadays he's red as a baboon's ...er... backside but—would you believe it?—they say he used to be a priest once. Frobisher insists he's one of nature's gentlemen and has high hopes of him. Political feel a CBE is in order as part of the grooming process. Make sure he knows where his best interests lie and separate him from the hotheads. Apart from that, there's just some small fry up for military gongs and a quick shake of the grateful supremo's hand. The officers who organised the surrender ceremony, arranged the flowers, flags and so on, some corporal who broke out of Changi, sole survivor of a suicide mission, and joined the resistance.'

'A corporal? I like the sound of him, tough, gritty, real man, people's war and so on?'

'Quite, Sir. Top notch PR.' He turned a crisp page of his exercise book. 'Then there's the other side of it. The footage from the concentration camps doesn't go down as satisfactorily over here as at home. There seems to be some confusion of the mind between it and the scenes shot in Hiroshima and Nagasaki after the bombs, so, as far as the A-bombs are concerned, we should stick to distant mushroom clouds, nice, clean and impersonal. New shape. Great image. Political say the people in the streets are baying for blood. If we are going to stop them spilling each others', we need a few war-criminals and collaborators strung up for the cameras to show the locals they live in a just world again thanks to HMG. A few trials that could run for a couple of months with lots of harrowing detail should do the trick—as long as they're found guilty of course.'

'Oh I think we can be sure of that. Who have we got?' Mountbatten admired his left profile and checked his teeth for remains of lunch. Rupert drew his breath over his own teeth like a wine-taster savouring a rare vintage.

'Quite a choice, actually, Sir. We'd need a couple of good-quality Japanese generals. Itagaki would get us started and, if we get in quick, before anyone else, we can probably commandeer Yamashita back from the Philippines and ship him over without leaving the Americans short. We can hang quite a lot round their necks before we hang them *by* the neck. We need a few local supporting acts, of course, some INA traitors, Chinese and Malay police spies. The Japs have been very helpful in giving us lists. I wonder if we shouldn't have a sniff around the Brits at the Raffles Museum and Botanic Gardens. Something very fishy going on there, Sir.'

Mountbatten practised his steely glare absently in the mirror.

'A museum? A garden? I hardly think there can be much for us there, Rupert. Anyway, they've been jolly decent to me and named a new rambling rose "Edwina" after my wife. She'll be pleased as punch.'

'Normally, I'd agree with you, Sir. But it seems it's been a hotbed of collaboration. The Nip director was clearly some sort of a fascist fanatic. He went off and shot himself right after the news of the A-bombs arrived—in the garden of the Shinto temple—that place where the three hundred-odd other hard nuts blew themselves up with grenades.'

Mountbatten raised a carefully calibrated eyebrow of distaste. 'Messy.'

'Yes, Sir. Luckily, there was a great empty pit already dug round the back so we just had to shovel the bits in, or rather the Jap prisoners did. Anyway, out of the Brits, one fellow called Catchpole, seems sound enough. Established some sort of a clandestine news network during the occupation. The portrait of the King we used at the ceremony was one he'd kept pluckily tucked away in his room. Brave man. But this other one, Pilchard, seems a thoroughly bad lot. He cultivated strong Japanese contacts, had a free run all round the island doing no one quite knows what. Alleged involvement in some secret weapons research for them. We know for a fact he blackmailed the MPAJA. Got payoffs on a regular basis and seems to have been involved in the disappearance of a mysterious Mr Dagama who had been protecting them.'

Mountbatten screwed up his face on one side in sceptical appraisal, didn't like it, screwed up the other side. Better. Now how could that possibly be? Something to do with the line of the eyebrows. He *must* get them plucked. 'Mmm? Was he by Jove? I don't like the sound of that. Better get some of our chaps to have a quick shuftie at him on the QT.' He flashed moral outrage into the glass. Now that was really good. He did it again and treated himself to a little smile of approval.

'I should mention that we have been asked to drop in at Colombo on the way home, Sir. A few parades and some soft words to calm the hard feelings about Cocos-Keeling.'

'What's that?' He fingered away an out-of-place eyelash.

'Cocos-Keeling, Sir. A while back now. The mutiny amongst the Ceylonese troops, shot up their officers and tried to contact the Japs by radio to hand over the strategic installations to them. A couple of them were sent home to be put on trial and hanged to encourage the others. It caused a bit of bad blood locally.'

'What the devil did they do that for?'

Rupert smiled. 'Well ... boredom must have been part of it. Once they'd bulldozed the palms, chased the locals away and closed down the copra industry, there can't have been much for them to do on the island, bit of a hellhole.'

'What *is* copra?'

'To tell you the truth, I've never been entirely sure, Sir. I had an uncle once who suffered from coprophilia and that wasn't very nice at all. But, as for Cocos-Keeling, there were two versions of events offered by the defence at the trial. One said that the mutineers were poor, deluded hotheads inflamed by nationalist, political rhetoric. Young sprogs more to be pitied than condemned. The usual stuff. The other was that it was all about some kind of sex ring organised by the senior officers among young recruits. There's always been a desperate lack of available women on Cocos-Keeling, apparently.'

'Really? Maybe I should send Edwina.' He looked round, saw the knowing smile, feigned annoyance. 'That's just a joke, Rupert.'

* * *

Peace had returned to the Botanic Gardens. Elsewhere on the island the earth had been pulverised and punished till its bones showed bare. Here, greening vegetation had scabbed over the light wounds and soon all scars of purely personal horticulture would fade and vanish. Through morning rain, the lawns already rolled once more in unbroken undulations like models of slow time. In the midday lake, the carp swished their coy fins and gulped in sudden surprised immunity from predation. Visitors once more had eyes and noses, not just mouths, so leaves and flowers were stroked and sniffed, not rudely plucked and boiled, while birds now swooped and soared, fearless of nets and snares, as in a Disney cartoon of natural innocence. Orchids put forth delicate tendrils, trees set fruit, buds popped and unfurled, the foul *Amorphophallus* collapsed in on itself and gently deliquesced into oblivion, while the heliotropic cat alone retained a sharp-eared wariness and saw through the world of appearances with acid-green eyes of the deepest cynicism. The workers drafted onto the Burma railway did not return, bringing new skills, as had been promised by the Japanese but every thirty minutes a gaunt white man chuffed round the outer perimeter, entirely under his own steam, with an expression of such ultimate beatitude on his face that he became one of the attractions of the park through the sheer, locomotive bliss that he radiated. The remaining employees proved to have numerous vigorous cousins and fruitful nephews to fill the vacancies and repeople and restock the garden as it slowly healed and rejuvenated itself. Even Ping and Pong were discovered to have each just fathered twins, as if in demonstration of a Malthusian progression.

The choice of Major Spratt as temporary Director of both Museum and Gardens had come as something of a shock to the sensitive and as a disappointment to Dr Catchpole but, as the Major explained with frequent terseness, 'What is a museum but a fancy depot of out-of-date supplies? Just a matter of turning over the stock, bit of spit and polish, checking for bugs and keeping your records straight.' As for academic pretension, behind the wire, had he not run a whole university? As a man aware of his priorities, immediately after his appointment, he embarked on a lengthy campaign of nitpicking complaint with the authorities about the wholly illegal removal of his museum's library to Changi during the war, demanding full restitution and compensation. Under his supervision, the museum whirred and clicked like a well-oiled machine. The staff no longer wandered about as fancy took them, they clocked in and out even between different buildings and his favourite joke was that his only regret was that the exhibits had not yet learned to stand to attention and salute as he entered the building. Bits of old stone, carvings, twiggery-pokery, none of it as neat as his perfect pyramids of tinned butter. The problem of disgraced and treacherous Pilchard had been elegantly solved by obliging Catchpole, who urged seconding him to another unit and shipping him off to do some sort of extended survey on far Cocos-Keeling. Just as well, considering his last act had been to take up with some Chinese woman young enough to be his daughter who had, herself, shamelessly fraternised with the enemy during the occupation. Disgusting. More likely than not, the paperwork would get lost and the two of them would disappear forever into some rustling and bottomless inter-departmental sink. Most satisfactory. He looked up from his desk. There was some sort of shemozzle going on outside in the forecourt. He lay his pipe aside, in the ashtray—the ornate, carved inkstone of his Japanese predecessor—with distaste. Now that proper tobacco was available again, it no longer seemed to have the same flavour that he remembered. There was no satisfaction in it. Perhaps they were monkeying about with the quality. He rose and peered out through the net curtain that smelt of mothballs, then tucked his swagger stick under his arm and strode out of his office, enjoying the tight military clicking of his heels on the stone flags. There were six men standing about, watching two others actually working—about par for the course out here—the idlers contributing by arguing and interfering.

'Catchpole! What's all this fuss about? Sounds like an Irish Parliament out here.' Now even the two who had been working stopped and looked up. His deputy produced a slouching gesture, half salute, half retainer's touching of the forelock. He did not actually touch his forelock, for fear of disturbing his wig. Did the man really think he was fooling anyone with that damn thing sitting on his head like a duck's nest?

'It's Raffles, Sir. They've come to take him back.'

Spratt pouted. The statue was being moved from the Museum and restored to relevance and the loss of Raffles might be considered a diminution of his own power, like the loss of a valuable hostage. But he preferred to see it as the extension of his reach to wherever the statue was now to stand. It had been agreed that only his staff could clean it of pigeon droppings, an important stipulation that he would not let slip. By degrees, slow increments of excrement, all the scattered public monuments of Singapore could be gathered under his skirts to form a gleaming, new empire of antiquities.

'Where did they finally decide to put him?'

'He's going back outside the theatre with a nice new flower bed and some tasteful urns. There is talk of a fountain. He got rather too many footballs in the neck on the Padang. It seems some people used to aim at him deliberately.' Catchpole shrugged. 'Politics. Quite literal loss of face.' His own multiplicity of chins was growing back nicely.

'Jolly good. Carry on. What about our new acquisitions—the Japanese memorials? All shipshape and Bristol fashion?'

Catchpole looked shifty. 'Sorry, Sir. I'm afraid events rather overtook us there. The sappers blew them all up yesterday, including the Shinto temple. No sense of history, I'm afraid, and it seems they had to use up those out of date explosives from the stores before the new inventory could be made. We might be able to get a few fragments ...?'

'Let it go, I think.' Spratt stifled a smile. Perhaps it was all for the best. History itself was never wrong about what to keep and what to do away with. 'You've organised the fund-raising bash for this evening? Everything tickety-boo?'

'Yes, Major. The chairwoman, Mrs Rosenkranz, was just on the blower from the Austrian embassy, said she's turning up at four to lay on the catering and selection of Austrian wines. She's bringing along two stray Austrian admirals—both Rear and Vice—so we'll be well covered at both ends. It seems they have a few left over. Do they even have a navy now? As you can imagine, they're rather keen to impress our military.' His voice dropped. 'She was quite firm no Russians were to be invited under any circumstances.'

Spratt smacked his own leg with the swagger stick as though punishing an impure thought. 'Damned fine woman, Mrs Rosenkranz—you know the Japs always suspected her of being involved in that brave attack on those swine from Changi, Fukui and the others. She should get a medal but I don't think we need any instruction from her as far as Russians are concerned. As it is, Catchpole, Russians have no money and are not welcome. They sometimes come as uninvited guests, as the Austrians should be the first to understand. Don't they know the war's over? But make sure those admirals are on the guest list. Lists, man! Lists! We can't have people just wandering about. There's been far too much of it. Too much slackness all round.'

Major Spratt quick-marched over to the portico and looked

out testily. The untidy riff-raff that had been camping out there had been removed and the grass was growing back encouragingly, if a trifle unevenly, and, next door, the gingerbread YMCA had been closed up, boards nailed over the windows, until some final decision could be made about it. Such was the power of recent history that the locals had it that it was haunted and avoided it like the plague. Sounds had been heard by those passing late at night, screams, howls, hellish laughter. Predawn lights had been glimpsed dancing will-o'-the-wispishly behind the glass as in some witches' coven. Babies had allegedly disappeared from nearby houses and nursing mothers felt ghostly suckling at their breasts at night as strange sweet smells hovered in the air, to be suddenly replaced by foul miasmas of decay so that the Malays spoke knowingly of lurking *pontianaks*. All the usual stuff. He knew there was no point in talking to them about drains and subsidence and bat infestation. The building's reputation had made it easier to clear away the squatters but might now be affecting the museum's own visitor numbers by contagion, so it would need to be looked into sensibly. Perhaps another job for those sappers who so liked to make a nice bang in public every now and then. The important thing was that the museum's dome had been repaired and the front gate repainted—even if the strategic shortage of volatile hydrocarbons meant that it was still wet two weeks later. Although the British had scattered great cities across the globe, they were all comfortingly provincial and could be read in much the same way. Everything in its place. Above the dome, a Union Jack. Beneath the dome, the Singapore Stone glowed in the early evening sun, giving back the heat it had soaked up during the day, and he paused and looked down on the writing and felt brief irritation flare at its incomprehensibility, what seemed like its deliberate and smug obfuscation. Catchpole had enthusiastically shown him a letter from a clearly deranged

Malacca man claiming to have decoded it acrostically into statements prophetic of football scores in the Malay League, according to clues taken from the *Times of India* crossword. Talk English damn you. Too many confounded empires. All the mess and fuss of change, all these monuments cancelling each other out, not to mention the expense. At least that was all over now. A time for rest and relaxation, consolidation and conservation. Back to basics and back to business as usual. He took a deep breath of the soothing, aromatic air and about-turned smartly back into the museum.

Also by Nigel Barley,

published by Monsoon Books

ROGUE RAIDER
The tale of Captain Lauterbach
and the Singapore Mutiny

Nigel Barley

It is the First World War and Julius
Lauterbach is a German prisoner of war
in the old Tanglin barracks of Singapore.
He is also a braggart, a womaniser and
a heavy drinker and through his bored fantasies he unwittingly
triggers a mutiny by Muslim troops of the British garrison and
so throws the whole course of the war in doubt. The British lose
control of the city, its European inhabitants flee to the ships in the
harbour and it is only with the help of Japanese marines that the
Empire is saved.

Rogue Raider is the adventure story of how one ship, the Emden,
tied up the navies of four nations and how one man eluded their
agents in a desperate yet hilarious attempt to regain his native land.
It is fictionalised history but a true history that was deliberately
suppressed by the authorities of the time as too embarrassing and
dangerous to be known. Revealed here, it brings vividly to life the
Southeast Asia of the period, its sights, its sounds and its rich mix
of peoples. And through it an unwilling participant in the war
becomes an accidental hero.

ISLAND OF DEMONS

NIGEL BARLEY

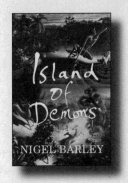

Many men dream of running away to a tropical island and living surrounded by beauty and exotic exuberance. Walter Spies did more than dream. He actually did it.

In the 1920s and 30s, Walter Spies — ethnographer, choreographer, film maker, natural historian and painter — transformed the perception of Bali from that of a remote island to become the site for Western fantasies about Paradise and it underwent an influx of foreign visitors. The rich and famous flocked to Spies' house in Ubud and his life and work forged a link between serious academics and the visionaries from the Golden Age of Hollywood. Charlie Chaplin, Noel Coward, Miguel Covarrubias, Vicki Baum, Barbara Hutton and many others sought to experience the vision Spies offered while Margaret Mead and Gregory Bateson, the foremost anthropologists of their day, attempted to capture the secret of this tantalizing and enigmatic culture.

Island of Demons is a fascinating historical novel, mixing anthropology, the history of ideas and humour. It offers a unique insight into that complex and multi-hued world that was so soon to be swept away, exploring both its ideas and the larger than life characters that inhabited it.

IN THE FOOTSTEPS OF STAMFORD RAFFLES

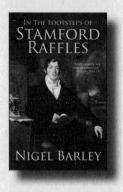

Nigel Barley

Stamford Raffles is that rarest of things — a colonial figure who is forgotten at home but still remembered with affection abroad. Born into genteel poverty in 1781, he joined the East India Company at the age of fourteen and worked his way up to become Lieutenant Governor of Java when the British seized that island for some five years in 1811. There he fell in love with all things Javanese and vaunted it as a place of civilization as he discovered himself as a man of science as well as commerce. A humane and ever-curious figure, his administration was a period of energetic reform and boisterous research that culminated in his History of Java in 1817 and it remains the starting-point of all subsequent studies of Indonesian culture.

Personal tragedy and ill-health stalked his final years in the East. Yet, though dying at the early age of 44 and dogged by the hostility of lesser men, he would still find time to found the city-state of Singapore and guide it through its first dangerous years. Here, mythologised by the British and demonised by the Dutch, he is more than a remote founding father and remains a charter for its independence and its enduring values.

In this intriguing book, part history, part travelogue, Nigel Barley re-visits the places that were important in the life of Stamford Raffles and evaluates his heritage in an account that is both humorous and insightful.

The following books by Nigel Barley are also available as speech-enabled ebooks:

In The Footsteps of Stamford Raffles
Rogue Raider
Island of Demons
The Devil's Garden

Available from leading ebook retailers worldwide.